The H-Bo

Stephen Bax ned author of over thirty s oks for adults and children. His work ha ards including the Philip K. Dick Award and the British Science Fiction Association Award.

Stephen Baxter has written scripts for TV and film, and columns for all the major broadsheet newspapers. He has ked as a maths and physics teacher and in 1991 applied ecome a cosmonaut. He was born in Liverpool and lives in Northumberland with his wife.

nplex plot that is delivered with the deftness and n of a master.' James Lovegrove, *Financial Times*

ting with lots of action and drama.' *Independent ay*

adult novel that never talks down for a moment, as the self-serving schemes of the military-industrial in a very contemporary way, while throwing in ments of real old school subterranean Sci-Fi ' *Starburst magazine*

'Baxter handles a multi-layered narrative well, with imagination and credibility . . . A variety of thought-provoking issues are raised and readers are encouraged to both immerse themselves in the past and consider how the human race could avoid the annihilation of nations which currently seems inescapable.' *Books for Keeps*

'[An] imaginative novel . . . involving and thought provoking.' *Carousel*

'An intelligent novel.' *SFX Magazine*

'A substantial novel drawing on autobiographical elements, Baxter's longstanding fascination with history, and his growing confidence in his ability to drive a novel primarily through character development . . . a pretty exhilarating apocalypse.' *Locus Magazine*

Stephen Baxter

faber and faber

First published in 2007
by Faber and Faber Limited
3 Queen Square, London WC1N 3AU
This paperback edition first published in 2008

Typeset by Faber and Faber Limited
Printed in England by CPI Bookmarque, Croydon

A CIP record for this book
is available from the British Library

ISBN 978-0-571-23280-2

Disclaimer
Historical figures are depicted in this novel. The incidents in which they appear are fictitious, as are speech and actions attributed to them. The resemblance of any other characters to persons living or dead is coincidental.

2 4 6 8 10 9 7 5 3 1

Note on Currency

Modern 'decimalised' money, pounds and pence, wasn't introduced in Britain until 1971. In 1962 the money system was pounds, shillings and pence. You got 240 'old' pennies to the pound, so an old penny, a 'copper', was worth a bit less than half a new penny. You had 12 pennies to the 'shilling', called a 'bob', worth 5p in new money. There were 20 shillings to the pound.

In your change you had halfpenny coins and farthings (a quarter of a penny), threepenny bits and sixpences ('tanners') and half-crowns (two shillings and sixpence, or 12.5p).

A pound was a pound, but it would buy you a lot more in those days than it would now. The average wage was around twelve pounds a week. A Saturday job might earn you thirty bob (£1.50). A pound would buy you a good night out.

The H-Bomb Girl

Chapter 1

Laura's first day in a new school, in a new city, at the wrong end of the country, was always going to be tough.

Even though she didn't know, yet, that the world was due to end in two weeks.

And a bad day got off to a worse start. She wrote in her diary:

Friday 12th October 1962, 8 a.m.

Got out of bed.

Found an eight-foot-tall American soldier on the landing.

She had been woken up by her father calling from downstairs. 'Laura. Get a move on. We leave for school in fifteen minutes.'

Dad was an officer in the Royal Air Force, and when he said fifteen minutes he meant it. She got up, pulled on her shapeless old dressing gown, a hand-me-down from Mum, and opened her bedroom door.

And there was the stranger staring back at her.

He was a pillar of muscle in brown slacks and a crisp white shirt. He was in his socks, no shoes. He might have been forty, about Dad's age. He was standing outside the bathroom's closed door with a towel around his neck, so he couldn't have washed yet, but somehow he smelled of after-shave.

'Well, hi, little missy.'

Laura was horribly aware of every stray strand of hair that hadn't been brushed yet, and of the crust of sleep-time dribble she probably had around her mouth. 'Who the hell are you?'

The American gave her a mock-salute. 'Giuseppe Mortinelli the Third, Lieutenant-Colonel, US Air Force, at your service, missy. Just call me "Mort", like everybody else.'

Little missy. She'd never met an American in the flesh before. He sounded a bit like the colonel from *Sergeant Bilko* on the telly. His head was square, his jaw a slab of bone, his hair shaved to a frosty stubble. His nose was so flat it looked as if his face had been worn away with sand-paper. And his eyes were so deep she could hardly see them.

'Mort,' she said reluctantly. 'I'm sorry I said "hell".'

He just laughed. 'I hear worse in the barracks.' There was something cold about him.

She turned to go back into her room. 'I'll let you go first, once Mum's out.'

'Oh, no. I heard your fifteen-minute warning. I'll go get breakfast.' He headed for the stairs. 'You know, at home we have two bathrooms. I kind of thought you English folks wouldn't have inside bathrooms at all . . .'

Mum came bustling out of the bathroom, a towel around her wet hair. Freshly washed, free of make-up, her oval face looked younger than her years. Laura looked a bit like her, but Mum had always been prettier than Laura would ever be.

Now, though, Mum's pale-blue eyes were sharp with

fury. 'Mort is a colleague of your father's, and an old friend of mine from the war. Don't you *ever* speak to him like that again.'

Laura knew the tone. She was supposed to be a good little piece of furniture, just fitting her own life around whatever scheme her parents came up with next, like the Separation, and selling their home in High Wycombe, and coming to Liverpool, and now letting some American loser stay in this rubbish little house.

'So can I use the bathroom now? Or have you got another lodger in there?'

Mum got angrier.

Dad called up the stairs, his voice flat, controlling. 'Twelve minutes.'

Laura pushed into the bathroom. It was steamed up, and all the towels were wet.

Her new school uniform was black tights and skirt, a blouse that was too big, and a blazer too small. The blazer was a hideous purple colour.

On the way out of the house she glimpsed the American, Mort, in the parlour. The little room was full of bedding. The house only had two bedrooms, one for Mum and one for Laura. Presumably both Mort and Dad had slept on the chairs down here.

Mort was sitting in front of the telly, chewing his way through a mound of toast. The telly was a polished wooden box with a small screen of thick glass. It had come with the house, which had belonged to an old lady who had died. Mort was turning the channel-selector knob, a heavy dial that turned with a clunk. All he got was test cards. Neither of the two channels, BBC or ITV, put out programmes at this time of the day. You would think he'd know that, Laura thought. But maybe they did things differently in America.

Mort didn't look round as Laura left.

Outside, the morning was sunny, warm for October. Dad was standing beside the car, his new Ford Cortina. Mum was already in the passenger seat.

Dad usually kept his cars spotless, but the Cortina was still grimy from the long, unhappy journey from High Wycombe they had made on Wednesday. He was supposed to drive back at the weekend, and today was Friday. Maybe he didn't think it was worth cleaning it in the meantime.

Holding her new satchel, Laura hung back.

'Get in the car, Laura.'

'Why don't I get the bus? I know the way.' Dad had driven her to the school yesterday, to show her around. She had met the headmistress, and her form teacher, a cold woman called Miss Wells. The school was only a mile away. It was early. She could even walk.

But Dad said, 'Get in the car.' Even in shirt and slacks, what he called 'civvies', Dad was just as military as Mort, just as upright, his hair cropped just as close, although he was shorter, thinner, more refined looking.

Laura felt like a fight. 'If you drive me in they'll all think I'm some stupid kid.'

'Get in the car.'

'I'm fourteen years old.'

'I know how old you are. Get in the car.'

Mum looked around. 'Oh, for heaven's sake, Harry, you can't talk to her as if she's one of the soldiers you order about.'

'Airmen,' he said without emotion. 'I order airmen

about, not soldiers. Laura, get in the car.'

Laura knew he could keep up this repeating game all day. She got in the car.

Dad slammed the door behind her and got in the driver's seat. But he didn't start the car. 'Laura. Are you wearing your Key?'

'What Key?'

'You know what Key. Don't be childish. Are you wearing it?'

'I didn't feel like it.'

Mum shouted, '*Oogh!* Will you two stop this? You'll drive me into a home, I swear you will.'

'Laura, are you wearing your Key?'

'Yes!' Dad had given it to her. The Key was a heavy piece of cold metal, like a door key but with a more complicated shape, that Laura was supposed to wear around her neck on a chain. She pulled it out of her blouse and held it up. 'See? Are you happy?'

Dad didn't rise to that. 'Just wear it. And don't tell anybody about it at school.'

'Why not? What if I do?'

But Dad just started the car and pulled away.

Dad turned the wireless on. A news programme on the BBC Home Service droned on about the Russians and the Americans, President Kennedy and Premier Khrushchev, and tension in a place called Cuba.

They were in a suburb of Liverpool called West Derby, a few miles east of the city centre. Laura's school was nearby. But Dad surprised her by driving south a little way, to the main West Derby Road, and then west towards the city. She didn't know why Dad was coming this way, and she knew better than to ask.

The car quickly filled up with the sweet, stale smell of their cigarettes. Laura looked at the back of their heads, Dad's stiff shaven neck, Mum's soft, slightly old-fashioned hairstyle with the loose bob at the back. She could almost imagine she was little again, that they were driving off into the Chilterns on a family day out.

But those days were gone for good. This was the Separation, the fag-end of her parents' marriage. Sitting here all she saw was their differences. They didn't even speak the same way, Mum with her soft, slightly Liverpudlian brogue, Dad with his clipped RAF lingo.

West Derby was quite leafy, with some good houses, a lot of them bigger and smarter than Laura's new home. But as they headed towards the city centre the houses got smaller, packed into rows of grimy terraces, where washing flapped in back gardens and smoke curled up from chimneys. Everything looked mucky to Laura, black from soot. And here and there she saw gaps, like missing teeth, holes made by Hitler's bombs and not yet fixed.

Liverpool was Mum's home town. That was why she had brought Laura back here. Now she pointed out a few sights. 'I used to go swimming in those baths. I used to play in that park. Before the war you could buy an ice cream for a penny.' But neither Dad nor Laura responded, and she soon shut up.

They drove around the centre of the city. There was a lot of traffic, Morris Minors and Austin Sevens, a few Minis. They passed some big stores, their windows stocked with washing machines and posh frocks. Right at the centre, near the main train station at Lime Street, they drove past some grand old buildings like Greek temples, jet-black from the soot. Laura stared. High Wycombe was only a small town in Buckinghamshire, with nothing on this scale.

They got through the centre in minutes, and, still heading west, drove through an area crowded with grubby warehouses. Soon they were going to reach the river, Laura realised.

She spoke up at last. 'Dad, where are we going? This isn't the way to school.'

'We've got a bit of time. I wanted to show you Liverpool.'

'Why?'

'Because this is where you're going to live now.' He drove the car steadily, not looking around. 'I spoke to your headmistress yesterday, and that form teacher.'

'Miss Wells.'

'She said you looked sullen. That very word.'

'I only just met her!'

Mum said, 'Oh, for God's sake, Harry.'

'The only jobs here are on the docks, and they're running down.' He slowed and pointed at a Woolworths. 'If you don't buckle down p.d.q. you'll end up working in Woolies for a few quid a week, and don't expect me to bail you out.'

Mum said bitterly, 'Oh, listen to yourself, Harry. "Bail you out"? "P.d.q."? And I'm a Liverpool girl. You're saying you don't want her to end up like me, aren't you?'

He shrugged, the smallest movement. 'Not you. Some of your family, maybe. Doreen. Marjorie.'

'I'm not going to listen to you any more.'

'Eileen, with her four kids by three fathers, and still living over the brush.'

'You never did like my sisters.'

They bickered on. Laura stared out of the window.

As they neared the river the roads funnelled towards a place called the Pier Head. Big blocky buildings lined the waterfront. On one of them, two exotic metal birds perched on twin clock towers. That was the Liver Building.

Beyond the shoulders of the buildings Laura glimpsed the water, and huge ships passing like clouds. She knew that Liverpool, on the west coast of England facing America and Ireland, had once been a great port of the British Empire. Its docks were seven miles long. And millions of people had drained through here, heading for new lives overseas.

The Pier Head itself, where all the buses started and finished, was a major meeting place for Liverpudlians. It was just a big, empty, windy square. But people swarmed here, white, black, Asian, Chinese, all busy, all on their way somewhere. An awful lot of them were young.

All the way up the motorway Laura had been determined to hate Liverpool. But, surrounded by all this bustle, she felt excited. There was a jammed-together, mixed-up energy here that you would never find in a little town like Wycombe.

At last Dad turned the car back the way they had come, and drove her out to school.

Once there he got out of the car and hugged her. It was an old wartime pilot's habit, he'd once told her. You said goodbye every morning, because you never knew if you would come home that night.

They left her at the gate and drove off.

Chapter 2

Saint Agnes's Roman Catholic Secondary Modern School was a blocky brick pile, murky and old. It looked more like a hospital than a school. Laura heard the kids calling the school 'Aggie's'.

It was a quarter to nine. All the kids were outside. The older kids hung around by the gate or on the pavement. The younger ones messed about in the playground.

There were workmen here, unloading vans and carrying ladders and planks and boxes of tools into the school. Laura's school in Wycombe was always being rebuilt too, classrooms shuffled around or extensions added, to cope with an ever larger population of kids. The workmen eyed up the older girls, and some of the girls played up to their whistles.

Laura waited by the gate. Nobody spoke to her. Anyhow their accents were so thick she couldn't understand a word anybody said.

Miss Wells, Laura's form teacher, came walking through the crowd. She was carrying a handbell. The kids got out of her way. Evidently she wasn't somebody you messed with.

Miss Wells peered closely at Laura. 'Miss Mann. Welcome to Saint Agnes's.'

Miss Wells was about Laura's height, and she was bundled up in a thick overcoat and scarf, even though the morning was warm. She might have been sixty. Her steel-grey hair was pulled back from her forehead, and her face was a leathery mask of wrinkles. But it was an oval face, her mouth small, her nose regular, her blue eyes bright blue.

Laura suddenly saw that this teacher, who Laura had only met briefly yesterday, looked like her own mother, or one of her aunties. That threw Laura, and she couldn't think of anything to say.

'Cat got your tongue?'

'No, Miss.'

'"No, Miss."' Miss Wells laughed. She stared at Laura, as if deeply interested in her. 'A big day for you to write about in your diary, Miss Mann.'

Laura frowned. 'How do you know about my diary?'

'Oh, just a hunch. Lots of people keep diaries.' Miss Wells leaned closer. 'Here's a date to make a note of. Saturday the 27th of October.'

That was two weeks tomorrow. 'Why? What's happening then?'

Miss Wells winked. 'Fireworks. One day they'll call it "Black Saturday". You'll see. Nice talking to you, Miss Mann. Time to round up the flock.'

She strode off through the playground, ringing her bell.

Something was very odd about that woman, Laura thought. But she couldn't work out what.

The kids funnelled into the school like sheep to be sheared.

The classrooms were grim boxes with floors of worn wooden blocks. The radiators were lumps of iron. The whole place was gloomy and cold, with high, grimy windows.

There was an assembly, eight hundred pupils singing a hymn in a hall like a cave, with gym equipment folded against the walls. The school seemed packed to the brim with kids.

Then came registration, with Miss Wells in her form room. Thirty-five fourteen-year-olds crammed into desks that were too small and covered with ink stains. There was one black kid in the class, a skinny boy called Joel. He sat down at the front. As the others filed in some of them made soft jungle noises at Joel, but he ignored them.

Miss Wells stuck Laura in an empty desk right at the back, next to an older-looking girl called Bernadette. Laura heard whispering, a bit of scandal. The desk was empty because the previous girl was 'in the pudding club'.

Bernadette didn't say a word to Laura. She didn't even look at her.

Miss Wells handed Laura a timetable. There was going to be a *lot* of religion, a couple of periods a day, and Mass on Wednesday morning. Laura had been brought up in the Church by Mum, but her old school in Wycombe hadn't been Catholic. Well, she would be getting to know God a lot better.

The first lesson was French. The teacher was a small elderly lady they had to call Madame Minet. Surrounded by a cloud of perfume and make-up, 'Minnie Mouse' seemed kind, and told Laura not to worry.

Laura had been doing all right at school. But her old school in Wycombe had been smaller than Aggie's, and a lot less like a huge zoo. And Laura was stuck right at the back, where everybody smelled of cigarette smoke.

The back-of-the-class crew weren't interested in French

or maths. They were interested in Laura. In the second lesson, the maths teacher picked her out for an answer: 'Forty-two.' Bernadette and the others took the mick: 'Oh, foor-ty-tooo, ee-oh, ain't I prop-ah, Lai-dee Muck of Muck Hall. Who was at your last school, Prince Charles?'

Laura was relieved when the morning break came.

All the kids spilled out into the yard again. A teacher walked around sternly, bell in hand. There was no equipment in the yard. The kids organised themselves into huge games: football with fifty boys on each side, complicated chase games like alley-oh fought out between whole armies. In their purple blazers, the kids looked like flocking animals on the bare concrete.

Laura didn't know anybody here. She didn't want to *be* here. She drifted towards the gate. But the gate was padlocked shut, like a prison door.

Some of the older kids gathered by the gate. Ciggie smoke hung around their heads like helmets. Laura saw a girl from her class snogging a boy, or a young man, through the railings. He wore a scruffy parka with an immense hood and a Union Jack sewn to the back.

'Look at them.' *Lu-chh at th'm.* 'Like monkeys in a zoo. Pathetic.'

Laura turned. It was Bernadette, hanging around by the railings with the rest. She had her uniform skirt rucked up in her belt so you could see her knees – laddered tights – and her blouse was open low enough to show a bit of cleavage. She was taller than Laura, tall for her age, and she might have passed for eighteen or twenty. But her fingers were stained by Quink ink, like every other schoolkid's.

And she had a friend on the other side of the railing, a tall, pale boy in a frock coat, with his black hair piled on his head in a vast quiff. Teddy Boy, Laura thought straight away, though she had never seen a Ted in her life.

He pranced around, showing Laura his drainpipe trousers. 'Hello, gorgeous. Do you like me kecks?'

He made Laura laugh.

Bernadette prodded her arm. 'What you looking at?' This was in Bernadette's thick Scouse, that Laura had had trouble understanding all morning. *Wot chew luckin' atts*?

'I'm sorry.'

That set them off. '*Oh, Ai'm saw-rry, Ai'm saw-rry, look et mee, Ai'm the Quee-een . . .* '

Laura just put up with this until they ran down.

Bernadette said, 'You can never miss Nick. Always done up like a pox-doctor's clerk. Nick, this is the Posh Judy I told you about.'

'I'm not posh. And my name's not Judy.'

That set them off laughing again.

The boy, Nick, looked her up and down. She didn't like it when boys, or men, did that, but there was something cool about Nick's inspection. 'So what is your name?'

'Laura.'

He shrugged. 'That'll do.' It was hard to tell his age: twenty, maybe. He wasn't that bad-looking if you got past the quiff. 'So where you from, Posh Laura? London?'

'No. High Wycombe. About thirty miles west of London.'

'That's where Strike Command is. The air force control centre.' The black boy from class, Joel, came up to them. He was limping. He wore a huge floppy hat knitted in bright scarlet and white stripes. 'Americans too.'

'My dad's in the air force,' Laura admitted.

But she was staring at Joel, and he stared back. She looked away, embarrassed.

Joel snapped, 'If you want to know I had polio. The epidemic in 1956. I wasn't vaccinated in time. That's where the limp comes from. The hard cases here call me the Hunchback of Knotty Ash. Ha ha.' He ran a finger down his face. 'And no, the black doesn't wash off.'

Laura said, 'Actually I was looking at your hat.'

Joel stared back at her for a tense second. Then he laughed. 'My grandmother knitted it for me to wear on the Kop. Liverpool Football Club. My name's Joel.'

'I know. I heard at registration.'

'Isn't this nice,' Bernadette snapped. 'All the class outcasts together. Per-heps we should h-eve a naice cup of tee-ee, Posh Laura.'

Beyond the railings, Nick blew cigarette smoke out of his nose. 'Ignore Bern. She's just got a cob-on because we're not all looking at her.'

Bernadette jabbed him through the railings with her elbow. 'Shut your gob, skiver.'

'I'm no skiver. I'm working for Her Majesty.'

'On the dole,' translated Bernadette.

'Resting between career opportunities, while I develop my music.' He said to Laura, 'Maybe you've heard of my group.'

'Group?'

'You know, beat group.'

'One of only about four hundred and eight in Liverpool,' said Joel dryly.

'Nick O'Teen and the Woodbines. We're playing Sunday. You should come.'

'His real name's Ciaran,' Bernadette told Laura. 'He went to this school. They let him out a couple of years ago, didn't they, *Ciaran*? He's got two A-levels.'

'Aside from Joel, here, I can't say I'm impressed by the company you're keeping, Miss Mann.' Miss Wells had come up behind them, cold and severe in her overcoat.

Even though he was beyond the railings, Nick threw down his ciggie and stubbed it out quickly.

'Hello, Miss Wells,' Bernadette said innocently.

'Don't push it, O'Brien,' Miss Wells said. Her accent was neutral Home Counties.

Laura didn't like what she had said about the company she kept. She had hardly made a friend of tall, too-adult Bernadette, but at least she'd made contact. She said, 'It was you who put me with Bernadette, Miss.'

'Hmm. Maybe I'll have to sort that out.' Miss Wells glanced around the playground. 'Look at all those kids, swarming like rats. So many of them – of *you*. Every school in the country is as crowded as this. There's been nothing but more and more babies, ever since the war. One day they'll call you "baby boomers".' Ignoring the others, Miss Wells stepped close to Laura and stared into her face. Laura looked into those eyes so like Mum's, and she had a strange swimming feeling.

Then Miss Wells turned away, breaking the moment. 'I hope you remembered your plimsolls for PE, Miss Mann. And you, O'Brien, button yourself up. Marilyn Monroe has sadly departed this mortal coil, but we don't want any tributes from you.' She walked back towards the school.

Once she had gone Nick sneered. 'Yes, auntie, no, auntie.'

Laura was confused. 'What do you mean, *auntie*?'

Bernadette said, 'Come on, Posh Judy. You've got to admit that weird old witch looks like you. Or the way you'll look in thirty or forty years.'

Nick laughed. 'In the year 2000, when we'll all be living on the Moon and wearing silver suits.'

'I'm not related to Miss Wells. I never met her before yesterday.'

'Then why's she so interested in you?' Bernadette asked. 'Maybe she fancies you.'

That shocked Laura. 'I'm a girl!'

Bernadette and Nick both laughed. Nick said, 'You really haven't lived much, Posh Judy, have you?' *'Ave yer?'*

Bernadette said, 'Nothing but mysteries about you, is there? The teacher's your evil sister, your dad's in the air force. And what's this you're wearing?' She reached forward.

The Key had worked its way out of her blouse. Laura tucked it back in. 'It's nothing.'

Joel had been standing quietly. 'I think I know what it is.'

Laura was supposed to keep the Key secret. That was what Dad always said. 'No, you don't. How can you know?'

'I read a lot.'

'He's not kidding.'

Nick shut Bernadette up. 'Go on, Joel. What was that thing?'

'I don't know exactly.' Joel's Scouse was as strong as anybody else's, but he spoke thoughtfully. 'I think it's something to do with Vulcan bombers.'

'You what, soft lad? What's a Vulcan bomber? An upper or a downer?' Bernadette laughed, trying to get the attention back on herself.

'It's an air force plane,' Joel said, 'that will drop hydrogen bombs on Moscow, if we ever go to war with the Russians. A British V-bomber armed with American Thor missiles.'

Nick turned his gaze on Laura, lively, fascinated. 'Well, well. You are an exotic specimen. The H-Bomb Girl!'

They all stood there, three pairs of eyes locked on Laura.

Laura's panic deepened. She had no idea what to say. If Dad found out about this, he'd chew her up.

Then, to her relief, the teacher rang her bell, and break was over.

Nick pushed a grubby newspaper through the railings at Laura. 'Come and see us on Sunday. The Woodbines. It's all in there.'

Bernadette stomped off, fixing her skirt.

Joel walked beside Laura. 'Don't worry about Bernadette. She just doesn't like anybody to be more interesting than she is.'

Laura remembered what Miss Wells had said about 'Black Saturday'. 'Joel. If you know all this stuff about bombers, what's going to happen on Saturday? Not this Saturday. The twenty-seventh.'

He frowned. 'Liverpool are away at West Brom. Why?'

'It doesn't matter.'

As they went into the school, he pulled off his Liverpool FC hat and stuffed it into a blazer pocket.

Chapter 3

Friday 12th October. 5 p.m.

Back from school. Good.

Stuck at home for two days. Bad.

Mum in living room chatting away with our American lodger. A fug of ciggie smoke, bottles of beer on the occasional table (Dad will love that), and Glenn Miller 78s playing on the Dansette (Dad will love that too). It's always Glenn Miller with Mum. Always the war. I think she's sorry it ever ended.

They were talking about me. 'There were no teenagers in the old days. Just children and adults, and you went straight from being one to the other. Now they swarm everywhere with more money than sense.' And blah blah.

I like the idea that my life is different from theirs. That we're the first real teenagers. Good.

Mum sounds childish when she speaks to Mort. No, not that. Girlish. More girly than Bernadette, say.

As for Dad –

She couldn't think what to write about Dad, who was due to drive off back to Wycombe and leave them, thus completing the Separation.

Still in her school uniform, she went downstairs. Mort and Mum were laughing in the living room.

Dad was alone in the poky little parlour, sitting on a footstool before the television. The news was on, and he was making notes about it.

Mum's furniture, crowded in with the old lady stuff, was too big for the room. But then this was a smaller house than the one they had had in Wycombe, because it stood for Mum's half of the family savings.

The telly showed a flickering map of North America, highlighting an island south of Florida. Cuba. The Americans were agitated because the Cubans were pally with the Russians.

It was always Americans and Russians in the news, annoying each other around the world, like two gangs in a playground. It was boring. Except that if they went to war Britain would be caught in the middle, and everything would be blown up with nuclear bombs.

'Well, that's torn it,' Dad murmured. He was so close to the thick, dusty screen that silver light played on his face. Not a handsome face, she thought. Strong, though.

'Dad, can I watch *Six-Five Special*?'

He snapped, 'Can't you see how important this is?'

She flinched.

He seemed to catch himself. He turned to face her. The muscles in his neck were taut, like ropes. He always had a tension that seemed on the point of breaking. Once he had flown Spitfires in the Battle of Britain. That was probably the trouble, why the Separation had happened. He had always been in love with somebody else – the air force.

'All right, chicken.' He patted the carpet beside his stool, and she went to sit beside him. 'So how was school?'

'OK, I guess.'

'Did you make any friends?'

'Dad, I'm fourteen.'

He laughed. 'So how's Miss Wells?'

'I don't know.' She hesitated. 'Dad, do you think she looks a bit like Mum?'

He thought about that. 'Maybe.'

'She couldn't be some kind of cousin, could she? A long-lost auntie.'

'I don't think so. Your mum's family are close. Does it matter who she looks like?'

'She's a bit funny with me.'

'Life's complicated, isn't it? I'm sure you'll be fine.'

'Well, you won't be here to see one way or the other, will you?'

'No. Look – I'm sorry if I was a bit brisk with you this morning.'

It was very rare for him to apologise, even if he kept slipping into RAF jargon when he did it. *A bit brisk.*

'I just want to make sure you understand what's going on,' he said. 'Mum and I still love each other. And you. We just can't live together, that's all.'

'But you can't divorce.' Mum was a Roman Catholic from Liverpool. Roman Catholics from Liverpool didn't divorce. Even Auntie Eileen hadn't got divorced, despite her colourful life.

'No. So Mum has come home to be near her family. And I, well –'

'You've got your work.'

He pulled a face. Then, astonishingly, even though the news wasn't finished, he reached over and turned off the telly. The grey image collapsed to a white dot that slowly faded.

If he rarely apologised, he *never* turned off the news. It made her realise how serious things were.

'Yes, I've got my work. But it's not, you know, a rival for you. You're my only daughter, chicken, and you come first. But I have to keep at it. For your benefit. And Mum's, and everybody else's, in fact. And that's why,' he said, 'you have to wear your Key.'

'Dad, if you're going to start that repeating thing again –'

'I won't. But I'm going away tomorrow, chicken, and I don't know when I'll see you again, and I have to be sure you're safe. Even though I'm not here. You know what to do with it?'

She knew. She'd been told often enough. If the worst came to the worst – though Dad had never spelled out what that 'worst' might be – she was to call a phone number he had made her memorise, which would put her through to somebody called the 'Regional Director of Civil Defence'.

'Then tell him the Key's War Ministry code number.' She'd had to memorise that too. 'If you tell him my name, and tell him you have the Key, and give him that code, he will have you found and brought to safety. Make sure you always know where the nearest telephone is. And keep a threepenny bit in your sock to pay for the call. But *keep it secret*.'

She didn't know what the Key actually was. He had never said. But it was an important enough bit of military hardware that if the government or the air force or the police found out she had it, they would come looking for her and take her in. They would protect her, not for herself, but because of the Key she carried. 'They'll probably arrest you,' Dad said, 'but at least you'll be safe.'

To Laura the key was just a Magic Token that would keep her safe, even if Dad couldn't help her himself. At least, that was how Dad wanted her to think of it.

It was scary to think that Joel might actually find out what the Key was *for*. Scary, and exciting.

She'd wear the Key to keep Dad happy. But she resented all this confusion and worry.

Maybe he sensed what she was thinking. He hugged her to him, and kissed the top of her head. 'Mmm. Always did like the taste of Vosene.'

That made her giggle.

'Oh. Sorry, folks.'

Laura pulled away from her father. Mum and Mort, the American, were standing in the doorway. Both had drinks in their hands, ciggies in their lips. Mort was holding a parcel, wrapped up in silver paper.

'It's all right.' Dad stood up, supple.

Mort eyed Laura. 'We got off to a bad start, little missy. In the line for the bathroom, remember? I'll try to stay out of your hair. In the meantime –' He held out the package. 'Peace offering?'

Laura took the parcel and opened it. Inside, in a plastic box, there was a doll, with a pointy chest, long legs, beehive hairdo and high heels.

'It's a Barbie,' Mort said. 'New toy. All the rage in the States.'

Mum giggled. 'Isn't he something? He always brings such great stuff from America. Used to bring me nylons during the war.'

Laura stared at the doll with disbelief.

Mort shrugged. 'So. Did I do wrong? Look, I don't know diddley squat about kids. I guess you're more of a bobby-soxer, right?'

'Say thank you, Laura.' Mum sounded desperate.

Her bedroom was just a box with her stuff still in a suitcase, or in heaps on the floor. The wallpaper was stained yellow. It looked like somebody had smoked themselves to death in here, and maybe they had.

She threw herself on the bed and opened her diary.

Friday 12th October. 6 p.m.

It makes sense to have It here. The Mort-Monster. That's what they all say, all three of them.

It works with Dad. It is in Liverpool to see about 'civil defence preparations', whatever they are.

And It knows Mum from the war, when she was in London.

Mum and Dad were well off before they split, but now everything is divided in half and we're all poor. To keep the house, we need the rent It will pay.

How sensible.

Here's what I think of It.

She started a list of every spiteful, obscene thing she could think of to say about Giuseppe Mortinelli the Third, Lieutenant-Colonel, US Air Force.

Her diary was a thick book bound in real leather that Dad had given to her on her eleventh birthday. She was embarrassed now by the early entries with their round handwriting and pictures of horses and dogs and stupid boys' names. But the diary had stuck by her through the Separation, and was still with her, a little bit of home.

She felt like crying. None of that.

Her list of swear words looked stupid. Childish. Bernadette could surely do a lot better. She crossed it all out.

She hated Mort, though. She hated the way he had come

into her home, his murky old relationship with Mum coming between her and Dad.

And she hated the fact that her whole life was shaped by two huge wars. The German war had been over before she was born, but people like Mum still wandered around going on about it, as if shell-shocked. And then there was this scary war in the future that they all worried about, and Dad spent his life trying to avoid. Laura thought of it as a wall of hot atomic light that might end her life before she had a chance to live it. She hated living with such a horrible prospect in her future.

She needed something else to think about.

She remembered the newspaper Nick had given her. She dug it out of her inside blazer pocket. Mersey Beat – Merseyside's Own Entertainments Paper – Price Threepence. It was a fan thing, cheap and flimsy and the ink came away on her hands. She flicked through it until she found a small boxed ad:

LIVE ON STAGE
DIRECT FROM BOOTLE
JOHN SMITH AND THE COMMON MEN
&
NICK O'TEEN AND THE WOODBINES

Saint Edward's College, West Derby, Liverpool 12.
Sunday 14th October 1962. 6:30 p.m.
Admission One Shilling. No Bopping or Jiving.

She was impressed that Nick's 'group' actually existed.

She wasn't much interested in music, though. Back in Wycombe she'd been taken to a few concerts by Mum and

Dad. But they had been folk music, which was old men in woolly hats with their fingers in their ears, or trad jazz, which was old men in bowler hats belting out show tunes on trumpets. Everybody said trad jazz would be the next big thing in popular music. The sixties would be the 'trad decade'.

As for pop music, she had dutifully listened to scratchy 45s by Cliff Richard and Tommy Roe on her friends' gramophones, and had tried to do the Twist to 'Let's Dance' by Chris Montez. It didn't mean much to Laura. In fact the lilting tunes and the popstar boys' high-pitched voices mooning over their 'sweet angels' just annoyed her.

So going to this concert wasn't all that appealing. But at the end of the school day Bernadette had offhandedly told her about a coffee club where they could meet on Sunday afternoon. After Mort and his Barbie doll, it sounded a good idea. Any excuse to get out of the house.

And a chance to make better friends with Bernadette. All day Bernadette had struggled in the lessons, but she was somehow a bit more sensible than the other kids around her. Laura was glad to have her solid company.

She folded the newspaper up again. On the front page was a grainy photo of another group, four skinny young men in suits, and half of the rest of the page was taken up by a huge ad:

MONDAY OCTOBER 22ND
BACK AT THE CAVERN AT LAST
DIRECT FROM HAMBURG
THE SAVAGE
YOUNG
!! BEATLES !!

Beatles? She'd never heard of them. Stupid name. She folded up the paper and put it in the rubbish bin.

Of course the big question was what to wear on Sunday. She started to go through her suitcase.

Chapter 4

Sunday 14th October. 10 a.m.

Another sunny morning. It's an Indian summer, the weatherman says.

Hurray.

Never mind Cuba and nuclear bombs. Today I face the ultimate horror.

Sunday lunch. With Mum and Dad.

And It.

And tomorrow, he's been putting it off, Dad's driving back to Wycombe at last.

She was stuck indoors, waiting for the chicken to cook in Mum's new cooker, a Tricity Marquise. Dad and Mort sat on the deep velvet-covered settee in the parlour, minuscule glasses of sherry in their hands, not speaking.

Laura didn't want to sit with them. She roamed around the house, like a rat in a cage, avoiding the adults.

The house had cost six thousand pounds. It had been done out by an old dear, the previous owner who had died, and most of her furniture was still here. It was all thick-pile carpets and oatmeal wallpaper, and the whole place stank of Johnson's furniture polish. In the parlour, walnut bookcases held condensed editions of Charles Dickens and Agatha Christie. The phone was stuck to the wall, an old-fashioned box that you had to put pennies into to make it work. The most fun piece of furniture was a huge cocktail cabinet. When you pulled down the hatch at the front a tray inside lifted up and out, and fluorescent lights switched on.

The back garden was tiny, just a patch of muddy earth. It had been turned into an allotment. In one corner stood a wooden frame that might be the ruins of a chicken coop.

At last Mum banged a silly little gong, three inches across. 'Lunch is served!'

They sat down at the dining table. The table was polished walnut, hardly ever used. Mum bustled around in her hostess apron, and served drinks: sweet German wine for the men, dandelion and burdock for Laura, Babycham for Mum. The smoke from their cigarettes curled up to the ceiling.

The first course was prawn cocktail. Then Mum went off to the kitchen and came bustling back with her brand new hostess trolley with its heated shelves, laden with the main course, coq au vin. Laura knew for a fact she had never cooked coq au vin before. The chicken was like rubber, floating in gloopy sauce.

Mum had fussed her way through the first course, nervous and chatty, and by the time they were chewing their way through the overcooked chicken she was mildly drunk. 'Of course now we're back in Liverpool we're not eating lunch but dinner. And later we won't eat dinner but our tea.' She put on a Scouse accent. 'Isn't it funny?'

'I saw the vegetable patch out back,' Mort said gruffly.

'Everybody had them in the war,' Dad said. 'We used to eat pigeon pie for Sunday lunch. Rationing only came off – when, love, 1954?'

'You remember, don't you, Laura?' Mum said. 'When the sweets came off? I remember your little face that Christmas when you ate your first tangerine.'

Laura, embarrassed, said nothing.

'You folks had it tough,' Mort said, nodding his huge head. 'I won't deny that. Even though I was stationed over here for most of it, it wasn't the same for us, we were provisioned from home. We had luxuries. Like stockings and soap. Great gifts, right?' He grinned at Mum.

Laura saw the look that passed between them. Dad just chewed his chicken, head down.

'And even now,' Mort boomed on, 'half your houses are still bombed to bits, and your food's still crap – forgive me – and you're only just getting washing machines and vacuum cleaners. Is it true some parts of England still don't have electricity? Why, I swear you're twenty years behind us.'

Dad looked up, his expression blank. 'Of course we are. But we'd be catching up a lot quicker if your government was a little more generous over the war reparations.'

Mort leaned back and blew smoke out of his pursed lips. 'Yeah, but sooner a bill from Uncle Sam than to be owned lock, stock and barrel by Cousin Adolf. Right, Harry?'

Dad kept his mouth shut.

Dad groused about this a lot. The Americans had loaned the British a fortune during the war to keep fighting the Germans. Once the war was over, the battered British tried to recover and rebuild, but the Americans wanted their money back. And Britain had to accept American bases all over the country. 'We're just a big aircraft carrier for the bally Yanks,' Dad would say sometimes. But it was his job to work with people like Mort.

'You're always going on about the war,' Laura found herself saying.

They all turned to her.

Mort shrugged. 'Well, it was kind of a big event for those of us who lived through it, missy.' He grinned around his ciggie.

Dad said more thoughtfully, 'You're growing up in an aftermath society, Laura. Physical, psychological. Everything around you is shaped by the war. I can understand you'd get a bit miffed with that, but –'

Her mother snapped, almost tearful, 'Why are you always so difficult, Laura? I was younger than you when the war broke out. We all thought we were going to *die*. You children, the first to be born after the war, were precious. Can't you see that?'

Laura stood up. 'But there's nothing I can do about it, is there? It was all over before I was born!'

Mum said, 'Oh, sit down, you little fool.'

'I'm full, thanks. You just get on with talking about the dead and gone,' Laura said, and, though she knew she'd pay for this later, she walked out.

She got her stuff and left the house.

She was supposed to meet Bernadette at the coffee club, but not until later in the afternoon. She couldn't call Bernadette. She didn't have a number, and besides Bernadette didn't look like she came from a house with a phone.

On the other hand she didn't have anywhere else to go. So she walked, to save the bus fare, and to stretch out the time. The day was dull, the suburban streets were empty. It didn't take her long to reach the coffee club, which turned out to be the cellar of a semi in an ordinary-looking road. It had a hand-painted sign with an arrow pointing downwards:

JIVE-O-RAMA
ESPRESSO, SHAKES
JUKEBOX
FAB LIVE MUSIC
ADMISSION ONE SHILLING

The place looked closed, the house empty. But Bernadette and Joel were here, sitting on a garden wall.

Bernadette was in what looked like her school uniform, save for her blazer, but with thick black mascara and lipstick on her face. She wore bright pink stilettos that looked a foot high, and her dirty blonde hair was heaped up in a spectacular beehive. Joel was wearing his red hat, a battered old suede jacket, and baggy corduroy trousers.

'Not open yet,' Bernadette said.

'I can see that,' Laura said.

'So what you doing here?'

'What are *you* doing here?'

'Nowhere else to go,' Joel said.

'I hate Sundays,' Bernadette said. She didn't seem either glad or irritated to have Laura turn up. She looked at Laura shrewdly. 'Have *you* got any money?'

Laura didn't have much, but more than the others. They pooled what they had, and counted carefully through the coppers, sixpences and shillings.

'We could go to the flicks,' Bernadette said.

'Where?'

'How about the Abbey?'

'That's Wavertree,' Joel said.

'We could get a bus.'

‘Not enough money. Unless we bunk it. Anyway you’d wait for ever for a bus on a Sunday. It’s only a couple of miles. Let’s walk.’

So they set off, through Sunday afternoon streets. Smoke curled up from chimneys, and through open windows you could smell roast dinners. There were few people around. The odd dog-walker, boys playing football. Once a couple of little kids followed them down the road, staring at Joel. Joel just put up with it.

They saw a few knots of teenagers hanging around corners or bus stops or telephone boxes. There were places to go, church youth clubs where you could play table tennis or learn the quickstep. But there were no shops open, the pubs and coffee bars closed, nothing to do at home, nothing on the telly until the evening.

‘I hate Sundays,’ Bernadette said again.

The cinema was a big modern place called the Cinerama. They had a choice of *Summer Holiday*, a musical featuring Cliff Richard riding around in a double-decker bus, or *Dr No*, a movie about a new spy called James Bond. Laura voted for Cliff, but Bernadette made puking noises, and they chose the spy.

The cinema was packed. They didn’t have enough money for popcorn, so Bernadette swiped some Mars Bars and Milky Ways from the foyer. Laura ate hers guiltily.

The movie was about a debonair British spy taking on an evil half-Chinese warlord who was sabotaging American atomic missiles. It was colourful and fast-paced. At the end they all came spilling out, blinking in the still-bright afternoon.

‘Well, that was dead good,’ Bernadette said. She made some quick repairs to her lippy using her compact mirror.

'That fella in his suit, the casino, the posh cars. I bet there were a few wet seats in that cinema by the end.'

Laura pulled a face. In fact she hadn't liked Bond. She quite enjoyed spies, like Dick Barton on the radio, and The Saint on the telly. But something about Bond's cruelty, he shot unarmed people dead without a qualm, reminded her of Mort.

'I did like the spy business,' she said.

'Like where that old biddy had a radio transmitter hidden behind her bookcase?'

'The simple stuff. Where he put talc on his briefcase to see if anybody messed with it. And stuck a hair across that cupboard door to see if it had been opened.'

Joel snorted. 'Boy scout stuff. Didn't you ever read *The Secret Seven*?'

Bernadette laughed. 'Did you?'

He looked away.

Bernadette said, 'You know, I hate the war with the Nazis. Everything the wrinklies moan about. Rationing and bombed-out houses. *You kids today don't know you're born.* But if James Bond is what the Third World War is going to be like, it'll do. Radios and spies and satellites.'

Joel said, stern despite his limp and his huge red hat, 'Nuclear war would *not* be like that.'

Bernadette laughed at him. 'You saw the movie. They got contaminated by radiation and just showered it off!'

Joel shook his head. 'That movie was a joke. You can't shower off radiation. Nuclear war would be hell.'

Laura asked, interested, 'How do you know?'

Bernadette grabbed the lapel of Joel's battered suede jacket and turned it over. He was wearing a badge with a symbol, a circle with an upside-down Y inside. 'See that?'

she said, sneering. 'CND.'

'What's that?'

'The Campaign for Nuclear Disarmament,' Joel said.

'Posh students and Labour MPs, all jazz and science fiction, marching about in London,' Bernadette mocked. 'Ban the bomb!'

'It's more than that,' Joel said quietly. 'People just don't know. They're stupid, like you, Bernadette.'

Laura asked, 'Don't know what?'

'About what would happen if war came. People aren't told. That's what CND are campaigning for, for people to be told. And to get rid of the bomb.'

'Tell that to Uncle Joe Stalin,' Bernadette said cheerfully.

'Stalin is dead,' Laura said. 'There's a man called Khrushchev now, in charge of Russia.' *Crooss-chov.*

'You'd know, wouldn't you?' Joel said.

'What do you mean by that?'

'That Key you wear around your neck. I looked it up.'

'Where?'

'CND has found out a lot of stuff. We're like plane-spotters.' He leaned close, his big red hat ridiculous on his head. 'I was right. The Key does come from a Vulcan. A V-bomber, a nuclear plane. It's an enabler that a pilot would use. A bit like an ignition key on a car. With that Key, if you knew what you were doing, and you knew the right codes and such, you could start up a V-bomber, and fly off and bomb Moscow.'

Wow, Laura thought. No wonder she would be arrested if anybody knew she had it.

Joel stared at her. 'You didn't know all that, did you?'

Bernadette turned to Laura. 'Good stuff, Posh Judy,' she said respectfully.

Laura blurted, 'My dad gave it to me. Bern – just don't tell anybody.'

Bernadette studied her. She seemed to be making a decision. She could make Laura a friend, or use her secret as a way to impress others. 'OK,' she said at last.

'Bus!' Joel yelled.

They were a hundred yards short of the stop. Bernadette and Laura got there in time, panting, laughing, and then held the bus while Joel limped up.

Chapter 5

By the time they got back to the Jive-O-Rama it was after five and the Sunday afternoon daylight was going.

There were a couple of scooters parked outside the club, perky, bright machines. Joel lusted after these. 'That one's a Lambretta GT200. And *that* is a Vespa GS160. Very, very cool . . .'

The house itself looked as dead as ever, but the garage door was open, to reveal steps down to the cellar. Lurid pink light glowed, and music thumped out, a fast, heavy beat.

Led by Bernadette, the three of them clattered down the stairs. At the foot of the staircase a little boy sat behind a table, with a roll of tickets and a plastic cup full of change. He looked Chinese. He was only five or six. He held his hand out. 'Shillin'.'

Bernadette handed over the money. 'Here, Little Jimmy, you money-grubber.'

Joel scratched Little Jimmy's scalp. 'Some doorman you are. Mucky as a dustbin lid. What will you do if a bunch of Teds turn up looking for a ruck?'

'Bash them.' He showed white teeth, grinning, and waved tiny fists.

They passed the kid, and walked into a packed cellar full of music and glaring light.

'It's chocker,' Bernadette said. 'Stay close.' She led the way, squeezing through the crowd towards the counter.

The decor was bright-red plastic and rubber plants. In one corner a huge gleaming jukebox blared out a fast track. There were probably only fifty people down here, Laura thought. But this 'club' was only a cellar, made to look bigger by the bright coloured spotlights on the ceiling, and cheap mirrors screwed to the walls. The air was a fog of sweat and perfume and cheap aftershave, all laced with the stale tang of ciggies.

Laura had never been in a crowd like this. The boys' clothes ranged from jazzed-up school uniforms to fancy Ted or Mod outfits. The girls wore beehive hairdos, slacks or skirts, with black mascara and bright lipstick. There were a few beatnik types, in black polo-neck sweaters and thick Buddy Holly glasses. Some of them were dancing in the tiny space by the jukebox, but most were sitting around Formica-covered tables, nursing half-drunk coffees. It was impossible to tell how old anybody was. They all talked loudly, in bright, brittle Scouse accents.

The jukebox music was exciting, with a pulsing guitar riff and a hammering drumbeat. Laura had never heard anything like it before.

Behind the counter a cheerful Chinese man was working chrome machines that dispensed espresso coffees and milkshakes. He was helped by a thin, depressed-looking woman.

Bernadette shouted at the woman. 'Oi, tatty head!'

She turned, her face a slab. 'Yeah?'

'One espresso,' Bernadette called, above the racket. 'Italian style.'

'There's three of you,' the waitress pointed out.

'We haven't got enough money.'

'Not my problem.'

'Give us three straws. Italian style.'

The others laughed.

The waitress just gazed back, dully. She wore a hand-lettered name tag: AGATHA. She was a sallow, skinny woman of about forty, but with an oval face that might once have been pretty, and pale-blue eyes, and thin hair pulled back. She looked bored, resentful.

But when she saw Laura, her eyes widened. As if she recognised her.

Laura looked away, confused.

The Chinese man came over. His tag read BIG JIMMY. 'Oh, it's you,' he said cheerfully. 'Saint Bernadette. I wish you'd shove off back to Lourdes and stop causing me trouble.' His accent was pure Scouse, not a trace of the Chinese Laura had expected.

Agatha said, 'She wants one espresso and three straws.'

'Oh, give her what she wants.' He wandered off to tend to his shining machines.

Agatha just shrugged and went to get the drink.

Laura, disturbed by the interest Agatha had shown in her, watched her go. And she saw that Agatha had a thick book, bound in brown leather, jammed into the pocket of her grimy apron. The end of the spine was ripped, and the gold page ends looked scorched.

For all the world it looked like Laura's own diary.

Of course it wasn't her diary. How could it be? But she remembered how oddly Agatha had looked at her. What was going on here?

Bernadette had seen all this. 'Another one of your

cousins, H-Bomb Girl?'

'I don't know what you mean.'

'The eyes,' Joel said. 'The shape of her face. Like Miss Wells. Like *you*.'

'There really is something funny about you,' Bernadette said without malice.

Laura asked, 'Who is she?'

'Agatha? Beats me. I don't know why Jimmy keeps her on.'

'Probably for a bit of the old bayonet practice.' Nick O'Teen joined them.

'Come off it, Nick,' Bernadette said. 'Last time I saw a mouth like hers it had a hook in it.'

'Beggars can't be choosers.' Nick was in his Ted uniform, a blue suit and shoes with pointed toes. His duck's-arse hair was slicked back, and he looked sharp, clean, his bootlace tie carefully knotted. His eyes were bright, his lips full.

Agatha brought back their coffee, a tiny cup with three huge straws falling out of it.

Nick reached into his pocket. 'I'll mug you for this, Bern.'

Agatha looked at Joel. She smiled, a strange, empty expression. 'Are you Joel Christmas?'

Joel looked alarmed. 'What's it to you?'

'Nothing. Just – it doesn't matter.' She turned to Nick. 'And are you wearing make-up?'

He just smiled back. 'I'm on stage in a couple of hours.'

'You look like a clown.'

'And your name means "death", darling. Keep the change. Bern, come and join us.'

He led them to a table, where another boy was already sitting. They had to scrounge chairs to sit down. There was a bowl of boiled sweets on the table. Bernadette cadged a ciggie from Nick. He produced packets of Park Drive, Embassy, Woodbine, all more than half-empty.

Nick introduced Laura to the boy, who was in his group the Woodbines. 'Billy Waddle, drummer to the stars.' The drummer, a plump, good-looking boy with a sullen mouth, did a brief drum roll on the table top with cutlery. A couple of girls on a nearby table looked over and laughed. He grinned back.

Bernadette crowded in next to the drummer. She looked more animated than she had since Laura had met her. 'Hello, Billy. Long time no see.'

But Billy was still grinning at the other girls.

Bernadette grew angry. 'You don't half irk my shingles, Billy Waddle. Leave those scrubbers alone!'

Nick watched, his expression complicated. Joel looked at the floor. Billy Waddle didn't say a word.

Laura saw all this. There was a lot going on here, she thought. A lot of ties between these people, whose lives she had just walked into. In a way, it was just like at home. And she wasn't a part of any of it.

Bernadette changed the subject. 'Nick wouldn't like your dad, H-Bomb Girl.'

'Why not?'

'Nick doesn't like soldiers,' Bernadette said, goading. 'Do you, Ciaran O'Teen?'

Joel looked at Nick. 'Why?'

'I had to do National Service. They've scrapped it now. I was one of the last to be called up. Lucky me. Eighteen months of square-bashing and spud-peeling. Like a cross between boarding school and a loonie bin. I got thrown out in the end. They said it was *my* fault.'

Laura asked, 'What was?'

'Among other things, a broken jaw.' He rubbed his chin. 'I was a bit of a target in there. Long story. You lot have been spared all that.'

Bernadette glanced at Laura, and they said it together. '*You kids today don't know you're born.*' They laughed.

'All right, all right.'

With their one coffee drunk and Bernadette's ciggie smoked, Nick produced more money for another round.

Laura took the coffee cup back to the counter. Agatha had her back turned. Laura could clearly see the 'diary' in her pocket.

Big Jimmy took the cup, and smiled at her. 'Thanks. You new here?'

'We just moved up. My family.'

He listened to her accent. 'From where? Down south? How you fitting in?'

She considered bluffing it out. Something in the expression on his round, warm face made her tell the truth. 'Badly. Everybody takes the mick. I want to go home.'

He smiled, his brown eyes creasing. When he spoke again his accent was strong Chinese, not a trace of Scouse. 'I feel like that sometimes. I was born in Hong Kong. Emigrated here, worked at my cousin's restaurant, saved up, bought my own place. Now I do this, and other things. Out of place? Maybe everybody feels the same way. My advice is, just pretend you fit in, and pretty soon you find you do fit in. Come again. You're welcome here. But bring some money next time.' He grinned and turned away to make the coffee.

Laura didn't go on with the others to Nick's gig that night. She didn't quite have the nerve.

She got home about eight.

She had to knock. She wouldn't get a key of her own until she was twenty-one, and she was given 'the key of the door'.

Dad opened the door, one-handed. He had the phone headset tucked under one ear and was making notes on a pad. 'Yes . . . Yes, sir. And what about our own deployment? . . . Yes, I understand the decisions will follow on from the diplomatic posture we adopt, but we need to be prepared . . .'

He barely noticed her as she squeezed past him.

Her mother was sitting alone in the parlour, before the television. *Sunday Night at the London Palladium* was showing, with some dismal comedian bantering with Bruce Forsyth. Two wine glasses sat on the occasional table beside her. Mum looked vaguely drunk, her eyes glazed silver by the telly's pearl light. 'Hello, dear. Have you eaten?'

'Yes,' Laura lied. 'Who's Dad speaking to?'

'Work,' Mum said. 'Been on the phone for hours. Some crisis or other, I suppose. Do you want a cup of tea?'

'No, thanks. I could do with a bath. I've got some homework left too.'

Mum laughed. 'You leave it late, don't you?'

Mort bustled in, shirtsleeves rolled up, tie loose, wine bottle in his hand. He looked huge in the little English parlour. 'I found another Liebfraumilch, honey. Oh, hi, Laura. How's life in the land of the bobbysoxers?' He laughed at her.

Laura got out.

In her room she thought back over the events of the long day. She remembered the strange, pale woman in the coffee bar, Agatha, and the book in her pocket.

She had stuffed her diary at the back of her underwear drawer. She looked there now. The diary was intact, not scorched. But when she looked more closely, she saw that the bottom of the spine was slightly torn and folded down.

Just like Agatha's.

Chapter 6

Monday 15th October. 6 p.m.

Another day got through.

Dad hasn't gone yet.

*

Tuesday 16th October. 8 a.m.

Dad still here.

He definitely should have gone back to Wycombe by now. I think he spent the whole night on the phone. And at 5 a.m. this morning a motorbike courier brought him a packet of photos. Something is 'brewing up', as he would say. As if to the RAF the whole world is one big cup of tea.

Well, I'm glad he's here. I feel a lot safer. I hope he's still here when I get back from school.

PE again today. On Friday they let me off because I didn't have the right kit. Today I'll have to get changed. I'm worried about the Key.

And Miss Wells wants to have a 'get-to-know-you chat' in my free period. Oh good.

Bernadette didn't show up for school. Miss Wells seemed to think this wasn't too uncommon, as she entered a big 'O' in her register.

Laura could have done with Bernadette being around when it came to PE time. She would have to get changed into a singlet and short skirt. How was she supposed to hide the Key? Not in her desk, that was for sure.

As she closed the desk before PE she had an idea.

Then she thought it was stupid.

Then she decided to do it anyway.

Making sure nobody saw, she plucked a strand of hair from her head, licked it, and plastered it over the edge of her desk so it joined the lid to the main body of the desk. At first it didn't stick. James Bond's hair must have been coated with Brylcreem. There was some face cream in Bernadette's desk, so she made the hair sticky with that.

Just like a spy. She was only playing, she told herself.

Then, as she made her way down to the changing room with her PE kit, she noticed a roll of duct tape, heavy silvery stuff, left sitting on a window ledge by some workman. She swiped it without anybody seeing and tucked it under her blazer.

In the unheated changing room there was nothing but benches and a peg to hang her clothes on. No lockers.

While the girls chattered, Laura went into a toilet cubicle and locked the door. She glanced around the cubicle. The wooden door and walls didn't reach the floor or ceiling, but there was nobody peeking.

She opened her blouse. She took the Key off her neck, rolled up its chain, held the whole lot against her belly just below her bra, and wrapped two lengths of tape around her torso. It was uncomfortable. The tape pinched when she moved. But it ought to hold up for a period of PE.

Then she pulled on her singlet and hurried out of the cubicle.

PE wasn't too bad. While the boys chased a football, the girls played hockey, which Laura had played before. Because she had started the term late she had missed the selection for the school teams, and she found herself playing with a bunch of no-hopers and layabouts, resentfully monitored by a teacher whose main interest was a ciggie or two.

But the game warmed up. There were one or two players who weren't bad. As she ran around, her breath cold in her lungs, Laura managed to stop thinking about everything, just for a while.

In her free period she had to go to see Miss Wells.

The staffroom was a box of a room crammed with tatty chairs, an electric point with a kettle, and cupboards with stacks of newspapers and magazines on top. A metal cabinet of lockers, each no bigger than a shoebox, took up a lot of space. The air was stale with old ciggie smoke, and brimming ashtrays sat on the arms of the chairs.

Laura sat down on one of the grimy armchairs, facing Miss Wells. They were alone in here. Laura felt uncomfortable, sweaty in her uniform after the hockey.

And she didn't want to be here at all, facing Miss Wells, with those cold blue eyes, and a face so like a reflection of her own, in a distorting fairground mirror that made her look sixty years old. It was truly weird, she thought.

Miss Wells said, 'I suppose you're wondering where the confiscated comics are. Or the pornography. *Lady Chatterley's Lover.* The teachers take it all home. The men, anyway.'

Not an appropriate thing for a teacher to say, Laura thought uneasily. 'Yes, Miss.'

'"Yes, Miss." Funny little room this, isn't it?'

'I wouldn't know, Miss.'

'It's actually a storeroom. A cupboard, really. As the kids of your generation keep swarming in, the authorities can't expand the schools fast enough. The old staffroom was converted into a classroom, and the poor old teachers were evicted to this place. Hardly room to light your roll-up.' She smiled at Laura. 'I told you, Laura. You're a unique generation, you post-war kids.'

'Baby boomers, you said.'

'Yes. People will look back on this as an unusual time, you as an unusual cadre of kids. Making friends, are you?'

'I think so. Bernadette O'Brien. Joel Christmas.'

Miss Wells snorted, a soft, subtle breath through her nose. 'Those drones. *They* don't matter.' She leaned forward. 'Only you matter, Laura.'

Laura tried not to flinch. Drones?

'How are you getting on at home? Is your father still here in Liverpool, or has he gone back to Strike Command?'

How did she know about Dad's job? 'He doesn't like me talking about his work to strangers.'

Miss Wells laughed. 'I'm your form teacher. I'm no stranger. And what about Mum?' Miss Wells's voice seemed to catch for a moment when she said that. 'Do you think she's coping?'

Why would a teacher use the word 'Mum', and not 'your mother'? And why was she asking all these questions? 'It's not for me to say,' Laura said.

'You're loyal. Good. I remember that. I mean,' Miss Wells said hastily, 'I like that about you. But you can trust me.' She laughed, as if thinking about a private joke. 'If you can't trust *me*, who can you trust? . . . Never mind. If there's anything on your mind, you can tell me. I hope you will, in fact.'

Laura squirmed. 'Thank you, Miss.'

'I want you to think of me as a friend. Really. For instance, there are plenty of thieves around this place, what with the workmen running around. Some of the staff are a bit shifty too, let me tell you. If there's anything valuable that you're worried about, you can leave it with me. Any time.'

In that moment, even though it didn't explain all the strange things she was saying, Laura was sure that all Miss Wells wanted out of her was her Key. She felt the Key's hard edges pressed against her chest, under her blouse. She didn't look down or touch it, or do anything to give it away.

'I'll bear that in mind.'

After that she just sat there as the period wore away, and Miss Wells wheedled and probed.

When Miss Wells let her out she hurried to her class. She was the first back. She was pretty sure nobody had been in here since they had all left for PE.

But the strand of hair was gone from the desk lid. Somebody had been through her desk while she was away.

It was ridiculous. What was she thinking, that Miss Wells was a spy, after her Key? Maybe her head was too full of James Bond. But who else would be after a nuclear bomber starter key?

Maybe it would be better if Miss Wells *was* a spy, rather than something even more weird.

At lunchtime Laura asked Joel about Bernadette.

'Oh, she's always sagging off. It's usually Mondays though. Wash days. Her mum can't cope. Come on, let's go and see her. It's only a mile. If we're lucky with the buses we'll be back in time for classes.'

Bernadette lived closer to the city centre, in a suburb called Tuebrook. Laura found herself walking through streets of skinny back-to-back terraced houses separated by narrow, rubbish-clogged alleys. Some of the streets were cobbled, and grass and nettles pushed through the stones amid the fag packets and dog muck.

Kids ran around, some barefoot, some too young to be at school, some not. All the kids looked grey to Laura, as if they needed a bit of sunshine. A few women bustled about with shopping trolleys and prams, but there were no men around. A factory hooter cried like a bird.

There weren't many cars here. 'Only the doctors have cars,' Joel said. 'Stinks here, doesn't it? The pong's enough to knock a buzzard off a bin lorry.'

Bernadette had to drag at her front door to open it. The door frame was bent. She was wearing a shapeless dress of some faded flowery fabric. With her hair tied back, no lippy or mascara on her face, she looked much younger. She seemed shocked to see Laura standing there, then embarrassed. 'Come to see how the other half lives, Posh Judy? You want to watch it round here. They play tick with hatchets.'

'Come off it, Bern,' Joel said. 'Just seeing if you're all right.' He pushed his way in and took off his hat. 'Is the kettle on? I'm gasping.'

The terraced house was long and thin, like a corridor. Inside it was hot and smoky, and there was a smell of milk and boiled cabbage. Laura glimpsed a lounge, with a settee polished smooth in the places where you'd sit down, and hard-backed chairs with drying nappies hung over the back. There was a telly, even older-looking than the one at

Laura's, and a few worn-out baby toys scattered on the floor. On the window ledge sat a bottle of Hiltone hair dye, and a yellowing *News of the World*.

In the kitchen a fire was burning in the hearth. Bernadette filled a rusty kettle from the tap and hung it on a hook over the fire. There was washing heaped in the sink and hanging before the fire that made the air smell of steam and soda. There were no mod cons here, no washing machine or tumble dryer, only a scrubbing board and a mangle. Laura saw that Bernadette's hands were bright red from the scrubbing.

Laura sat down on a hard chair. Cracked lino peeled off the floor under her feet.

'Wash day,' Joel said. 'Thought so. Bernadette's mum always has trouble with wash day.'

'She seemed all right last week,' Bernadette said. 'But she's jiggered today. She's upstairs with the baby. She might come down later and watch a bit of telly.' She shrugged. 'I can do it. If I ever have a bit of money I take it all down to the coin-op. Lots of lads there.'

Laura asked, 'What's wrong with her? Your mum.'

'Nerves.'

'Where's your dad?'

Bernadette snorted. 'Even the scuffers don't know.'

Laura had to ask. 'Scuffer' was Liverpool slang for policeman.

Bernadette handed them mugs of tea, sweet, with sterilised milk. Laura saw that the dress Bernadette was wearing was cut from curtain cloth. No wonder she wore her school uniform the whole time.

Not two feet from where Laura sat, a mushroom was growing out of the wall, the size of a breakfast plate.

'You admiring the decor, Posh Judy?'

Joel poked the mushroom in the wall. 'It's not exactly *Ideal Homes*, you've got to admit.'

'If you cut it off it just grows back. The whole place is manky. Got shook up by a bomb in the war and never got fixed. Now you can't close the door, and there's a big hole out back where the rats get in.'

'You ought to get Billy Waddle to help,' Joel said. 'He's a joiner.'

'I thought he's a drummer,' Laura said.

'He's a joiner, and a drummer.'

'Billy Waddle can shove his head up his big bass drum,' Bernadette said fiercely. 'He'll take you out if he thinks he's got a chance of pulling. But he's so tight he wouldn't give you last week's wet *Echo*.'

'Ah,' Joel said. 'The great love story is over.'

'Cobblers, Joel,' she snapped. 'I don't need Billy's help. Or anybody's. Anyhow I *was* sick this morning. Nearly spewed up my ring. Old Arthur next door complained about the stink in the bog.'

So they shared a toilet with the neighbours, Laura realised.

'You should tell somebody at school,' Laura said. 'That you have to bunk off because your mum can't cope.'

'Don't be a div,' Joel said. 'She can't tell the teachers. She and her sister would just be put into a corpy home. Better this way, at least they're together. I think the teachers turn a blind eye. Except Miss Wells, who's a headcase.'

Laura jumped at something else to talk about. 'Miss Wells called me in this morning. She said she wants to be my friend.'

They both laughed at that.

Bernadette snorted. 'I still think she's a muncher.'

Laura asked, 'A what?'

'She means, Miss Wells fancies you,' Joel said.

'Not that.'

'Then maybe she's just needy,' Bernadette said. 'One of my dad's sisters lost her own baby, and then couldn't have any more. She was around here all the time when I was small. Wouldn't leave me alone. Maybe Miss Wells is like that.'

'She really could be your long-lost auntie, Laura,' Joel said. 'She does look like you.'

'I think it's more than that.' Laura struggled to put her thoughts in order. She didn't want to seem weird, or stupid. 'She doesn't *feel* like an auntie, or a mother, or a sister. We're connected somehow. But not in any way I've felt before.'

Bernadette rolled her eyes. 'You're one brick short of a full hod, girl.'

In the face of her common sense, the strange fantasies Laura had been building up about Miss Wells popped like a soap bubble.

'All right,' she said. 'I'll tell you something real, though. Somebody went through my desk.' She told them about the missing hair.

Bernadette just laughed. 'I can't believe you did the business with the hair. What do you think, that Miss Wells is a spy?'

'Well –'

'Oh, come off it. They search *my* desk all the time.'

'What for?'

'I don't know. Condoms. The pill. Whatever they think girls like me shouldn't have. You can always tell when they've had their mucky paws in there. These are teachers, remember. They aren't exactly the CID.'

Laura nodded. 'Maybe it's just something like that.'

'Yes,' said Joel. 'Maybe.'

They sipped their tea, hot and sweet, in silence.

In a room upstairs, a baby cried.

Chapter 7

When she got home that afternoon, she found Dad sitting on the hall carpet, with his ear glued to the phone. He had a military radio beside him, and there were papers and maps of the American east coast scattered over the floor. He just glanced up at Laura, then went back to work.

Deep voices boomed in the parlour. Laura glanced inside.

Mort was standing there, silhouetted in the dusty light cast through the net curtains. Mum perched on the edge of the settee, legs crossed at the ankles, nervous as ever. And there was another man, sitting in what looked like an upright chair. Laura saw medals on his chest.

Laura tried to hurry past and get to her room. But Mum spotted her and came bustling out. 'Laura,' she called in a loud, fake voice, and she grabbed Laura's hands. 'Come and meet our visitor. Or rather it's Mort's visitor . . .' All that ever mattered to Mum was not to have a scene, not to have anybody think badly of her.

She had Laura's hands locked tight. Laura didn't have a choice. She dropped her satchel in the hall, and let Mum draw her into the parlour.

There was a mechanical whir. The stranger's chair came rolling towards her. It was a wheelchair, she saw now, with some kind of motor built into it. Sitting in it was a big square man, as big as Mort. But he was old, maybe eighty or more, his stubble of hair white. He wore a suit, not a uniform, though he had that row of medals pinned to his breast pocket.

And he was stuck in that chair, she could see. His legs and torso didn't move at all. All that moved was one hand that worked a joystick to push the chair around. The hand was a red claw. Maybe it had been burned.

He smiled at her, showing gleaming teeth, surely false. 'Laura, isn't it? Mort told me all about you.' His voice was a croak, but his accent was just like Mort's. 'You're the flower of England we're over here to shelter from the atomic fire of the Soviets. Right?'

'Darn right, sir,' Mort said.

When Mort spoke, Laura saw how alike they were, the same worn-away faces, the same flat noses and deep eyes and square chins, though the old man's right cheek was marred by a long, livid scar.

She felt a bit dizzy. It had already been a strange day. 'Well, well,' she said. 'More lookalikes. More family resemblances. What a coincidence.'

The Americans exchanged glances.

Mum looked shocked. 'Laura, what are you talking about?'

'Let me guess. You must be Giuseppe Mortinelli the Second.'

The old man said, 'No, the Third –'

Mort shut him up by kicking his wheelchair.

The old man nodded shrewdly. 'You're a smart girl. Just call me the Minuteman. Everybody else does.'

Mum said, 'He's here to speak to your father, and to

Mort. There's an international crisis. Your father and Mort are going to have to work on resolving it.'

'There's always an international crisis,' Laura said. 'Boring.'

'Laura.' That was Dad coming in the door, a sheaf of papers gathered up under his arm. 'I think you ought to apologise.'

The Minuteman's face creased, though he didn't move a muscle of his body. 'Oh, no need for that. Just joshing. Weren't we, girly?'

Mort tried to take control. 'Harry, I think the Minuteman's tiring. Maybe we should conclude our business.'

'Sure. Laura, maybe you could give us a few minutes. Do you have homework?'

It would be a relief to escape. 'OK.'

'Good to meet you, little missy,' the Minuteman called after her. 'I hope we get a chance to get to know each other better. In fact,' he rumbled, 'I'm darn tootin' sure we will.'

'Yes,' Mort said, staring at Laura hard. 'We really got to make more of an effort, you and I, Laura. We'll talk later.'

It sounded like a threat.

She heard the Minuteman leave an hour later.

She looked out of the window. The Minuteman's chair whirred down the drive to his car, a huge black automobile. People came out of their front doors to goggle.

She went downstairs. Mum was in the kitchen. To her relief, Mort was nowhere to be seen. She had thought Mort was here because of his relationship with Mum. But he had seemed different with the Minuteman here, more focused on Laura. Whatever that was about, she didn't want to know.

She found Dad in the parlour with the telly on, watching the news. He was on his footstool, with his sheaves of papers and photographs spread over the floor beside him. He glanced up at Laura. 'Just give me a minute.'

She sat on the edge of the settee, and watched the telly absently.

She hated the news. It always seemed to be bad. Wars in faraway places like Laos and Thailand and Algeria. Tension between Americans and Russians and Chinese. That awful concrete Wall the Russians had built across the middle of Berlin, to divide the American west from the Russian east. And the long, posh, doleful face of Prime Minister Macmillan, droning on about international crises or the Balance of Payments. She'd much rather have President Kennedy, JFK, with his boyish good looks and glam wife and gorgeous little kids.

What was worse was that whenever the news got bad enough, Dad got drawn away into the thick of it.

At last the newsreader said, 'And in other news . . .' The screen filled up with images of gleaming cars. The Motor Show at Earl's Court.

Dad looked tired, but he pointed to a Cortina. 'Got one.'

'Dad. I need to ask you some questions.'

'Fire away.'

'What's a Minuteman?'

He counted the answers off on his fingers. 'One. A volunteer soldier in the American Revolution.'

'When they got rid of the British king.'

'Yes. The Minutemen said they would always be ready to be called out in just one minute. The kind of legend the Americans are very proud of, bless their flinty hearts. Two. A Minuteman is the codename of a new kind of missile the

Americans are deploying.'

'A nuclear missile?'

'Well, yes. And three. The nickname of that crotchety old chap who wouldn't drink the perfectly good cup of char your mother made for him.'

'He probably would have rusted.'

Dad laughed at that.

'What was he doing here?'

'He came with orders for Mort. Not me. The Americans keep some things classified, even from their closest allies.'

'Orders about what? What's going on now that's so terrible?'

He looked at her. 'Well, we're in a bit of a spot. I'll tell you the truth, Laura. This isn't just another crisis. We've never been closer to world war, since 1945. Never closer to a nuclear conflict. Not even over Berlin.'

She stared at him. 'So what's it about?'

He sighed. 'It takes a bit of explaining. It would be a lot easier if you *ever* watched the news. Look, Laura – do you know what the Cold War is?'

She shrugged. 'Americans and Russians. H-Bombs.'

'Yes. Exactly. At the end of the war the Americans, and we, marched into Germany from the west, and the Russians came from the east, and we all met in the middle of Germany, and we're still there seventeen years later, eyeball to eyeball. Only now we're all armed to the teeth with nuclear bombs and missiles. Enough to blow everybody up several times over, if it all kicked off.'

'So what's changed now?'

'Do you know where Cuba is?'

'It's a little island off the coast of America.'

'Yes. But it doesn't belong to the Americans. It's independent. And the government is Communist.'

'Like the Russians.'

'Like the Russians, yes. We, I mean the Americans, have known that the Cubans have been mucking about with the Russians all summer. Cargo ships crossing to Cuba. "Advisors on land reclamation" going over. That sort of thing. But the Americans weren't sure what they were up to.

'Now, a couple of days ago the Americans took some photos of Cuba from a spy plane. And they saw that the Russians are building missile bases on Cuba.'

'Nuclear missiles?'

'Yes.'

'Why would the Russians do that?'

'Actually it sort of evens things up. We have bases close to Russia, in Turkey for instance. If these missiles in Cuba go ahead, the Americans will be under the same sort of threat. It's fair, in a gruesome sort of way.'

'Has this been on the news?'

'No,' he said heavily. 'Not yet. This really is classified, Laura. I'm telling you secrets. *Even the Russians don't know the Americans have those photos*. Not yet. So you mustn't tell anybody about it. I'm just telling you for your own good. Promise me.'

'I promise. So what's going to happen?'

'Well, since the missiles are right on their front door the Americans are pretty miffed. Unless somebody backs down –'

'There'll be a ruckus.' She used one of his RAF words.

It made him smile, but it was forced.

'Why am I lumbered with this Key, Dad?'

He shocked her by getting up, crossing to her, kneeling on the carpet before the settee and taking her hands in his. 'Look, love, a nuclear war won't be like the last lot, against the Nazis. It took us years to slug that one out to the finish. Now we have intercontinental missiles and high-altitude bombers, and a war could be fought out in days – hours, even. It won't even be *like* a war. It will be like a great shining lid slamming down on us all.

'I'm stationed at Strike Command at Wycombe. You know that. I have a senior command position regarding Britain's own nuclear weapons, which would have to be deployed – I mean, launched against the Russians – if the worst came to the worst.'

'The V-bombers.'

'The Vulcans, yes. Even with our weapons alone we could wipe out thirty or forty Russian cities. Say eight million citizens. That firepower makes my base a prime target for Russian missiles. And, if the balloon does go up –' He looked right into her eyes. 'I'm right in the front line. *I would be dead, in minutes.* That's how fast the Russian missiles would come in. It's a sure-fire certainty. So I wouldn't be able to help you, or Mum, in whatever followed. And that's why you must wear the Key. I know it sounds loopy, but it's the best way I could come up with to be *sure* you'll be taken somewhere safe, even if I can't help you. Even if –'

She pulled back her hands. 'You're frightening me.'

'Well, I'm sorry. It's a frightening world, unfortunately.'

'Dad – what's going to happen on Saturday?'

'Which Saturday?'

'A week on Saturday. The 27th.'

He frowned. 'I don't know. Why do you ask?'

'No reason.'

Laura heard her mother in the kitchen, softly singing 'Galway Bay'.

'Why don't you give the Key to Mum? She's the adult.'

Dad looked away. 'Things are a bit tricky for your mother right now. The war was complicated for her. The evacuation. Growing up too fast in London. Coming home to Liverpool – Mort being here – has brought it all back, I think. And she's taken our separation hard. She'll get over it. But for now . . .'

For now, it was Laura who had to have the Key. Laura who would have to take charge, who would have to be the adult, if that great shining lid came slamming down.

Suddenly she couldn't bear this conversation any more, or the sight of Dad on his knees before her. She pushed him away and ran out of the room.

She threw herself on her bed and tried to sort it all out in her head.

Dad loved her. But he was hard and unrelenting. It was like being loved by a slab of rock, by a mountain. And it was a love that took him away from her. She didn't *want* to be loved that way.

And she didn't want to be vapourised in a nuclear war either.

On top of that there was all the murky strangeness about her new life in Liverpool. Her parents' peculiar relationship with Mort. The way Mort had suddenly grown a new interest in Laura after the Minuteman showed up. The way Mort looked like the Minuteman, as if the Minuteman was Mort's dad, or uncle. And the way Miss Wells looked like Mum, like Auntie Eileen, like *her*.

It was going to be hard to concentrate on her English homework.

She still hadn't washed properly since PE. She probably had time for a bath before dinner. Listless, she climbed off her bed and went to her chest of drawers to dig out new underwear.

The top drawer was open, just a little. She never left it like that.

She went through all the drawers. Nothing seemed to be missing.

She sat down on her bed. So what now? Mum, looking for contraceptives or suspenders?

Mort, stealing her knickers?

No, not that. Mort might have been in here, but not for that. But why else was he interested in her? What else did she have that he might possibly want?

The Key, the same as Miss Wells? Could he be another spy – right here in her own house?

Maybe she was going mad.

She sat on her bed for a while. Then, trembling slightly, she pulled the chair across so the door was blocked.

Chapter 8

Friday 19th October. 8 a.m.

Dad left on Wednesday.

He promised to write. Nothing's come yet.

At school, Bernadette was almost late. She ran into the playground just as the teacher rang the bell. Her face was as pale as a ghost's.

And then she had to duck out of the first lesson, maths, to throw up in the toilets. Laura was sent with her. 'Dodgy curry,' was all Bernadette would say, but Laura didn't believe her.

There was a special assembly at lunchtime that day, compulsory for everybody.

As they all sat on their hard benches the headmaster, Mr Britten, walked on to the stage. He said the school was honoured to greet a special guest. 'Lieutenant-Colonel Giuseppe Mortinelli the Third, US Air Force.'

Laura was astonished when Mort walked in, beside Miss Wells. They all had to clap. Mort, in a sharp uniform, looked around the hall until he found Laura. He pointed at her, grinned and waved. Some of the girls turned around to look at her with envy.

Laura hissed to Bernadette, 'I can't believe he's *here*.' For all Miss Wells's strangeness, she had thought of school as somewhere safe from *him*. Now that sanctuary was broken down.

'He's tall enough to wind the Liver clock,' Bernadette said. 'Do you peek at him in the bathroom? Look at that jacksie.'

'Shut *up*.'

Mort launched into a brisk slide show. He said he was here to talk about Britain and America. 'We have a Special Relationship, as your Prime Minister Macmillan calls it.' He showed slides of British and American troops fighting together in France during the war against Hitler.

Then Mort talked about the new atomic age. 'Today Americans and British stand side by side around the world, toe to toe in *nuc-ular* combat with the *Rooskies*.' Mort said he reported to the 574th Bomber Wing of the Strategic Air Command of the US Air Force. He showed a slide of a B-52 bomber, a plane that circled the North Pole for ever, waiting for war. Just one of these planes, he said, carried more firepower than *all* the bombs and shells used in World War Two. He seemed proud of this. Laura thought that was horrible.

Mort showed a last slide. It was the shield of Strategic Air Command, with its motto:

PEACE IS OUR PROFESSION

Joel just laughed. 'Fluff,' he muttered. 'Propaganda.'

Miss Wells led the applause, then asked for questions.

'Do you play football in America?'

'You mean soccer? We play our own football, which is like your rugger, I think.'

'Do you have chewing gum in America?'

'I think we invented it.'

'Do you really say "line" instead of "queue"?'

'We don't have too many queues in America.'

'Have you heard of the Beatles?' That raised a laugh.

Joel stood up. 'What about Holy Loch?'

'Excuse me?'

Miss Wells snapped, 'I didn't point to you, Mister Christmas. Sit down.'

But Joel said quickly, 'Holy Loch is a base in Scotland. Americans have nuclear submarines there. It's close to Glasgow. So the Americans have put a big British city in the front line of their nuclear war.'

There was a ripple of excited noise among the kids, as there always was when somebody did something brave, or stupid.

'It's OK.' Mort held his hands up. 'You're well informed, young man. I can't discuss operational details here. I mean, who controls what. But it makes no difference. The Special Relationship, remember. We're all on the same side. Let's take another question. You at the front with the teeth.'

'Do you want to be an astronaut?'

When the assembly broke up, Miss Wells said, 'Mister Christmas. Go straight to the headmaster's office.'

Everybody poured through the corridors on the way to afternoon class, their chatter a noise like flocking birds.

'Well, that was a laugh,' Bernadette said. 'When Joel gets back, look for his goolies stapled to his CND badge.'

'He was brave.'

'Just showing off.'

'It was creepy,' Laura muttered. 'Seeing the two of them together like that. Mort and Miss Wells.'

'Your two enemies,' Bernadette said, mocking. 'Quite a coincidence.'

'It's not a coincidence at all. It's obvious why he came here.'

Maybe they were all in it together. Maybe Mort had orders from the Minuteman. Maybe Mort had been *told* to come to school to hook up with Miss Wells, just as he had started rummaging about in her smalls drawers.

Bern was staring at her. 'What are you on about? Why would Henry Fonda out there be interested in you?'

'For my Key.'

Bern laughed. 'You're kidding. You think he's a spy too?'

'Oh, shut up, Bern. I don't know what to think.'

They reached class, and went to their desks at the back.

Bernadette said immediately, 'Somebody's been through my desk. You can always tell.'

They checked Laura's desk, and their bags, and their coat pockets. Everything had been rummaged through, searched, put back. Bernadette showed Laura how you could tell from small clues: dust traces, excessive neatness.

Bernadette said, 'Well, now we know why we were all kept in the hall over lunch. So they could search the place.'

'For what?'

'Well, that Key of yours, if you're right. What else? Just as Miss Wells searched your desk for it when you were at PE, I suppose.'

Laura looked at her. 'You said they're always searching the desks.'

'Well, they are. But it's a bit of a coincidence, isn't it? Maybe you're right. Maybe they are all spies!' She was grinning.

'You're enjoying this. You're laughing at me.'

'Well, it's better than fretting over my mum and her wash days, I'll tell you that. What would James Bond think about all this? And the question is, why *now*? What's going on?'

Laura thought she knew what this was all about. She longed to tell Bernadette about Cuba, and the missiles, and the silent, invisible crisis that was pushing the world towards war. But Dad had made her promise to keep quiet, and, ashamed, she said nothing.

The teacher walked in and everybody stood up, ready for class.

'Let's come back tonight,' Bernadette whispered.

'To school? Why?'

'I've got an idea. How we can get our own back. And maybe find out the truth about your mysterious auntie.'

Friday 19th October. 4:30 p.m.

Home from school.

Mum is in the living room with Mort. He's still in the uniform he wore at school. She is in one of her party frocks, and stiletto shoes, and bright lipstick on her face. They are laughing, wine glasses on the occasional table, dancing around to Glenn Miller.

They didn't hear me come in. Good.

Nothing done in the house all day. Dishes from breakfast still in the sink. Hoover in the middle of the parlour floor.

No smell of cooking. Friday is fish night. We always have smoked haddock. Not tonight.

Mail not picked up from the mat. But there is a letter in there from Dad.

The letter went on about Cuba.

Things had got worse. American spy planes had seen

more Russian missiles on Cuba, a more powerful kind than before. Now they were sure that Cuba could be a threat to the whole of the US, not just Florida, the nearest state.

Dad wrote, 'The question is, what's JFK going to do about it? Bomb the missile bases? Invade Cuba? If he does that he might trigger global war. Or, should he do nothing about Khrushchev planting missiles in his own back yard? Then he looks weak.

'I think he's looking for some middle way to defuse the whole situation. But his Joint Chiefs of Staff – they're his top soldiers – are pressing him to attack. The Russians will just cave in, they say. But the Joint Chiefs *always* want you to attack. Kennedy says the joke is that if he listens to them, and the world gets blown up as a consequence, none of us will be left alive to tell them they were wrong.'

Dad wrote all this down with his fountain pen in his neat, sloping handwriting. She'd always loved his handwriting. Even his signature had flourishes.

But the news was dismal. It was as if the whole world was a huge unexploded bomb that might go off any minute.

She hid the letter. She tried to concentrate on her homework.

Later, she heard Mort going out.

Laura crept downstairs.

Mum was sitting on the big settee, alone, listening to 'Moonlight Serenade' on the Dansette. She had her legs crossed, one stiletto dangling from her toe. Her face blank, her head off in some other place, she looked very young, much younger than her thirty-three years. Her lipstick was smudged.

She saw Laura, standing in the door. 'Oh, hello, love. I

didn't know you were in. Come and sit with your mum.' She patted the settee.

Laura turned down the volume on the Dansette, and sat down. Mum sighed and rested her head on Laura's shoulder. Laura had to take her weight. Mum was behaving like a child, not a mother. Laura smelled perfume, hair spray – and maybe just a hint of Mort's iron-tinged aftershave.

'I've had a lovely afternoon,' Mum said.

'I can tell. With Mort.'

'There's nothing wrong with that.'

'All that old wartime music. Dad hates it, doesn't he?'

'Yes, well, your father isn't here.' Mum straightened up, pulling away from Laura, and primped her hair. 'You might try to understand, Laura. You're so – ooh, you're so *judgemental* sometimes. Like a little old woman sitting there looking at me. Life isn't easy for me just now, you know. I like to think about good times.'

'Like the war.'

'Yes, the war. In the beginning it was quite fun, you know. I was ten when it all kicked off. The ration cards, and your own little gas mask, and blackouts, and running to the air-raid shelter in the back garden. Of course it all got a bit difficult with the bombing.'

Laura had heard the story before. Liverpool had had it hard. The docks were the main way food and supplies from overseas got into the country. In the worst of the Blitz, there were so many ships sunk in the Mersey there wasn't a single berth free for docking.

Mum, younger than Laura was now, was evacuated, along with thousands of other inner-city kids. She was sent on a train to North Wales, and lodged with a family in Rhyl. But Mum had hated it. 'I always was a city girl,' she would say breezily.

Laura had heard hints that things had been more difficult than that. Somebody had harmed Mum in some way. It happened, to vulnerable kids, lodged with strangers far from home. And Mum had always been pretty.

Anyhow she was taken back from Wales, and sent from one city to another: down to London, to be with a cousin of her father's. Peggy, a twenty-something girl, had a flat in the West End, tiny but big enough for two girls to share. Of course London had its share of bombing, but the East End and the docks had it worst, and the West End was safer than Liverpool. And at least now Mum was with family.

'London was a fairyland, as long as a bomb didn't actually fall on you,' Mum said. 'The searchlights waving across the sky like wands. The barrage balloons like great whales in the air. Star flares like fireworks. I was just about your age then, Laura.

'Even when the bombs fell it could be, well, marvellous. Sometimes a building would just jump up and settle back, unharmed, in a great cloud of dust. Or you would see waves passing through brickwork, like shaking a sheet. After a big raid Peggy and I would walk around Piccadilly or Trafalgar Square or along the Strand, just looking. Dust covered everything, making it all pink or grey.

'And whenever there wasn't a raid, in the dark – the blackout, you know – we'd go crazy. No rules! We'd dance and dance.'

'You danced with Mort.'

'Oh, yes, with Mort. The Americans in town, you know, with their chocolate and cigarettes and stockings. No rationing for them! It was all terribly glamorous, really . . . Why are you looking at me like that?'

'I'm just thinking that if *I* went with soldiers like that you'd murder me.'

'Yes, well, you're you and I'm me, you're just a little prig and I was mature for my age. You know what I think? I think you're jealous. Jealous because you live in this drab time, when everything is boring and rubbish. Jealous, because you were born too late.'

Maybe, Laura thought. For sure, if war came again, there wouldn't be much dancing.

She faced facts. She wasn't going to get any help from Mum with Mort, or Miss Wells, or any of the problems in her life. She felt resentful. She even resented the way Mum was leaning on her now.

But maybe it was just the way things were. Bernadette had to look out for her mother. If it was going to be the same for Laura, well, she'd just have to put up with it.

She stood up. 'What's for tea?'

'Oh, I don't care. Go and get some fish and chips. My purse is in the kitchen.' She settled back on the settee, her party dress splayed around her. 'And put my record back on, will you?'

Chapter 9

That evening Laura crept out of the house without her mother noticing.

She met Bernadette and Joel at the railings at the back of the school grounds. It was eight o'clock, dark, cold. They were all wearing black, at Bernadette's suggestion.

Joel looked subdued.

Laura asked, 'Did they give you a tough time after assembly?'

Joel shrugged. 'That cow Miss Wells tore into me. Mr Britten told me he approved of my "enquiring mind". I just had to channel it in the right direction.' He tried to sound casual, but Laura could see how wide his eyes were. He was no tougher than she was, really. 'He isn't so bad, old Bulldog Britten. Even if he did give me one thousand lines.'

Bernadette whistled softly. 'One *thousand*. That's an all-time record, pal. They ought to engrave your name on the gateposts. Anyway, let's get on with it.'

'Get on with what?'

'Just follow me.'

It didn't take long for Laura to realise they were going to break into the school.

First they had to get over the railings, which were eight

feet tall with spikes on the top. Bernadette was wearing a long black scarf. 'Not by accident,' she said. She threw the scarf up so it caught over a spike. Then she hauled herself up, hands on the scarf, feet walking up the railings. At the top she easily climbed over the spikes and let herself down.

Laura followed. The physical exercise, and the sense of breaking the rules, got her blood pumping.

When Joel was over, they ran across a stretch of playing field. Joel limped, but kept up.

They came to a side door that led to the changing rooms.

Joel said, 'We haven't got a key.'

Bernadette just walked up to the door and pushed. It was open. She sang, 'Ta-*da*!'

Laura hissed, 'How did you know?'

Bernadette put her fingers to her lips. Then she beckoned, and led them into the school.

The old building was a maze of corridors which Laura still hadn't got to know well, and it all seemed different in the dark. But Bernadette led the way confidently.

They came to the staffroom, the converted store cupboard. Bernadette peered underneath the door. No light showed.

But a little way down the corridor light spilled from a room, and there was a rumble of voices. Joel looked panicky.

Bernadette just pushed open the staffroom door. The three of them crept inside, into the dark, and Bernadette shut the door. Then she clicked on a torch, lighting up their three faces from below.

'Cor,' Bernadette said. 'You can tell it's the staffroom just from the stink of ciggies.'

Joel whispered, 'How did you know we could do this?'

'I knew about the meeting. Teachers and governors.

They'd leave the school open until it was done. And I knew they would meet in a classroom or somewhere, not in this poky cupboard of a staffroom.' She was grinning, and sounded smug.

Laura admired the way she had thought through all this, and the cool way she was carrying it out. Reading bored Bernadette, and she struggled in class. But she had other skills, organisation and determination and courage, that just weren't being picked up at school.

'And why,' Joel said, 'are we here at all?'

Bernadette said, 'They searched our stuff today. So tonight it's our turn.'

'What are we looking for?'

'Proof of what they're up to. That or ciggies.' She grinned.

It really was all just a laugh to her, Laura thought. It was a huge risk to be taking. But at least they might find out a bit more.

Bernadette used the torch to find Miss Wells's name on a locker. The locker was padlocked, as they all were. But Bernadette was prepared for this too. She pulled a hairpin from the lapel of her jacket, and stuck it inside the lock, wiggling it back and forth.

Joel said, 'How come you know how to pick a lock?'

'To get money off my mother. She might live on gin. I can't, or the baby. Mind you we're that skint we switch the gas off when we turn the bacon over.'

'Oh, you're funny,' Joel hissed, tense.

There was a soft click. 'Aha,' Bernadette said. Delicately, trying not to make a noise, she opened the padlock and lifted it away from the locker. 'Open Sesame.' She pulled back the locker door.

She began to lift stuff out. Some of it was uninteresting. A scarf, a pair of tights, pens, a box of chalk. A comb, a 'biddy rake', as Bernadette called it.

Then she found a little leather wallet, which folded out to reveal plastic cards.

They inspected the cards by torchlight. 'This one's pretty,' Bernadette said. 'A "credit card". But what does "chip and pin" mean?'

'Beats me,' Joel said.

'This one says it's a driving licence,' Laura said. It was a little pink card with a photograph of Miss Wells on it. 'I've seen my dad's driving licence. It's a big bit of paper. *This* isn't a driving licence. And what's this on the back?' It was a row of vertical black lines, all different thicknesses.

'A code, maybe,' Joel said. 'A code made of bars.' His voice was quiet.

Bernadette rummaged about some more, and pulled out what looked like a wristwatch, with a gold strap and glass cover. But it had no hands. On its face were numbers that changed as they watched. *20:38:04. 20:38:05. 20:38:06 . . .*

Even Bernadette sounded spooked now. 'What do these numbers mean?'

Laura couldn't help smiling. 'It's the twenty-four-hour clock. My dad uses it in the air force. 20:38. That's, oh, nearly twenty to nine.'

'It's a wristwatch.'

'Yes.'

Joel held it to his ear. 'I can't hear the clockwork.'

'Whoah.' Now Bernadette pulled out a silver case, the size of a small cigarette packet. 'Look at this. It's cracker.'

'What do you think it is?' Joel asked. 'A ciggie case?'

'Maybe. Look, it's got a hinge.' Bernadette delicately

pushed her fingernail into a seam. The gadget opened up easily, and it lit up, silver-blue. In its top half it had a little screen, like a tiny telly, and there were buttons in the bottom half with the numbers 0 to 9 set out in a square, and other buttons with arrows and other symbols. Each button glowed individually, like a tiny jewel.

The soft blue light lit up their faces. Bernadette said, 'I *want* one.'

Joel said, 'They don't even have stuff like this in America.'

Bernadette said, 'You know, H-Bomb Girl, I thought you were cracked. I only came here for a laugh. I didn't think we'd find anything in here but a half-bottle of gin. But there really is something going on, isn't there?'

Joel was peering at the screen on the little gadget. 'But what *is* it? Look. There's writing. Beside that green phone symbol.'

Laura looked. There were two lines of text.

PEACE THROUGH WAR
2 incoming calls

'"Peace through war"? What does that mean?' Bernadette asked.

'No idea,' Laura said.

'And, calls? What kind of calls?'

Joel shrugged. 'Phone calls, maybe.'

Bernadette snorted. 'Don't be a divvy.' She pointed to the clunky staffroom phone that sat on the table in the middle of the room. '*That* is a phone.'

'Then you tell me what this little green phone-shaped sign means –'

The door opened. Light flooded into the room. Bernadette snapped the 'phone' shut. The three of them ducked behind the table.

Somebody came in, singing 'Livin' Doll'. Laura recognised the voice. It was Mr Britten, the head. He crossed to the table, picked up something, turned and left, still singing as he closed the door.

Joel blew out his cheeks. 'He just picked up his fags. He didn't even notice the locker door swinging open.'

Bernadette shrugged. 'People see what they expect to see.' She looked at the 'phone' gadget, which nestled in the palm of her hand, slim and beautiful. 'I'm having a souvenir.' She slipped the phone into her pocket.

Laura hissed, 'Bern, put it back.'

Bernadette put her fingers to her lips. 'They'll hear you.'

Joel was stuffing the cards back into the leather wallet. And he looked again at the 'driving licence'. 'Laura,' he said. His voice was flat. 'You ought to have a look at this.'

'We need to go –'

'I mean it. *Look.*'

Beside the picture of Miss Wells there was a list of details. There was a name, but it wasn't 'Wells'.

1 Mann
2 Laura Mary
3 Date of birth 6-9-48 United Kingdom
4 Date of issue 12-3-07 . . .

Bern looked at this, and at Laura. 'Let me guess what your birthday is.'

'Shut up.'

'And what your middle name is. And you must have been born in 1948, the same as me –'

Laura couldn't deal with this. 'Shut *up*.'

'What about this other date?' Joel whispered. 'Do you

think this means 1907? No, of course not. *Two thousand* and seven. Forty-odd years from now.' He looked at Laura. 'When you will be about sixty.'

'Like Miss Wells,' Bern whispered. 'Blimey, H-Bomb Girl. Miss Wells isn't your auntie. She's –'

There were footsteps.

Bern shoved the wallet back in the locker and slipped on the padlock, and they all hid in the shadows.

Friday 19th October. 9:30 p.m.

Just in from the school.

The front door had been unlocked. There was no sign of Mort. A wireless boomed out from upstairs, Mum's room. Mum was probably sleeping off the wine she'd drunk during the day.

Laura wrote down her thoughts as they came to her.

I can't believe it.

What if it's true?

It would make sense. All those times when Miss Wells said things like, 'One day they will call you baby boomers.' As if she knew about the future.

And, 'Who can you trust if not me?'

And when she talked about Mum she called her 'Mum'.

How can she be here? I mean, how can I be here? What do I want?

Why do I hate her so much?

It had been easier when she had just thought Miss Wells was a spy.

She wished she had somebody to talk this over with.

Restless, she went downstairs. She made herself a cup of tea, and a jam sandwich. Alone in the parlour with the telly, she glanced at a newspaper, the *Liverpool Echo*, to see what was on. *Steptoe and Son.*

She couldn't be bothered. She was too shaken up for the telly. She prowled around the living room, and the parlour, avoiding all Mort's neatly stacked stuff, his shirts and his socks. She walked past the old dear's rows of books on their shelves. Unread *Reader's Digest* editions of classics, Dickens and Jane Austen.

Something looked different.

She ran her finger along the shelf before the books. There was plenty of dust. It had been dusty when they moved in, and nobody had done much housekeeping since.

But there was a space where there was no dust at all.

She stood back, just looking at this gap in the dust, about eighteen inches long. She pulled the books off the shelf, stacking them on the coffee table.

There was something tucked away behind the books.

She reached in. It was a kind of tile, eighteen inches square, made of black plastic. It had a couple of symbols on it, an apple with a chunk bitten out of it, and a little silver panel that said 'Intel'. Laura thought it was solid at first, but it had a seam running around its edge.

Remembering Bernadette and the phone, she stuck her fingernails into the seam, and carefully prised the tile open.

It was like a giant version of the 'phone', with a flat screen in the lid, and buttons in the base. No, not buttons. They were keys, set out in the QWERTYUIOP layout of the typewriters she was learning to use at school. But the keys were just flat pads.

And, after a couple of seconds, just like the phone, the

screen lit up. Swirling patterns ran across it, in *colour*, unlike the silvery black-and-white of the telly. Images coalesced, of a green Earth in an iron fist, and a slogan written underneath: PEACE THROUGH WAR.

Whatever it meant, whatever this gadget was for, the slogan proved Mort really was working with Miss Wells.

Then a message appeared: 'Computer ready, Colonel Mortinelli. Wireless link established to central server. Please enter password.'

Laura had seen computers. Her class in Wycombe had been taken to a bank processing centre in London. Computers were boxes the size of wardrobes with lights and dials, and with tapes and punched cards and paper tapes whirring away. This couldn't be a computer. So what, then?

Half of her didn't believe this was happening. It was so like a scene in James Bond it wasn't true.

She would much rather have found nothing but dust behind these books, just as she would rather have found nothing but fag packets in Miss Wells's locker. With every new bit of evidence she found, it became more obvious that something very odd was happening to her, that she was the centre of a strange and silent conspiracy, even at school, even in her own home.

And she was becoming more and more convinced that it was all about the Key, a nuclear bomber starter key that she wore around her neck, on the eve of a nuclear war.

She folded up the 'computer', put it back on its shelf, and restored the books.

Then she washed the last dishes, locked the front and back doors, checked all the downstairs windows were closed, and went to bed.

Chapter 10

Saturday 20th October. 9 a.m.

One week to Black Saturday. And then what?

Here's a spooky thought. If Miss Wells is me from the future, then she must know what happened on Black Saturday. Or will happen. She's not just guessing.

I'll find out in a week. I don't think I want to know.

Phone call at 7 a.m. Ran downstairs to make sure it was me who took the call.

It was Dad. I asked him to give me a number to call him back. I want to be able to talk to him without anybody else listening in. After all, it's his Key. He didn't argue. I wrote the number on my hand. Then he rang off. It can't have been more than a ten-second call.

At breakfast Mum asked me who rang. Wrong number, I said.

Mort came in from the parlour, wearing a crisp white shirt. Who rang? Wrong number. He stared at me.

He knows I'm lying. And I know the truth about him. Some of it anyway. And he knows I know.

All these secrets, all these lies, in my head, and in Mort's. I hate it. I don't think I'm cut out to be a spy.

Mort hasn't read this diary yet. Well, I don't think so. After I found he'd been searching my room I put the diary at the back of my chest of drawers, and used the Boy Scout hair trick again. Of course Mort could have stuck the hair back to fool me. But he was stupid about the dust on the bookshelf. I'm keeping the diary with me from now on, in my satchel or a coat pocket. Mort can rummage through my grubby socks all he likes.

I don't think Mum has a clue what's going on. She's stuck in some fantasy about 1944. She's no help.

This morning I'm meeting Bern and Joel in town. The longer I can stay out of this house the better.

She got off the bus outside Saint George's Hall, the great black acropolis near Lime Street Station.

She stopped at the first free phone box she found. Feeding the slot with coins, she called Dad with the number written on her palm.

Dad got straight to news about Cuba, where things were getting tight. The Americans were preparing for an invasion, which would mean war with the Russians. But the good news was that it might not come to that. President Kennedy had come up with a plan.

Dad said, 'He's sending out his navy to stop more Russian ships coming to Cuba. They're calling it a "quarantine". It sounds less aggressive than a blockade.'

'Do the Russians know about it?'

'Not yet. Kennedy will go public in a day or two.'

'Dad, I don't see how this is good news.'

'Because it's a middle way. Kennedy hasn't just given up. On the other hand he hasn't started shooting. He's talking, really. "Look here, Khrushchev old bean, that's far enough with your ships and what-not. Now let's talk this over like sensible chaps."'

'Why not just phone?'

'Well, there's no way to do that,' Dad said. 'No direct line between Washington and Moscow. But while the ships are facing each other out in the ocean, the politicians and ambassadors are at it behind the scenes.'

'But it could still go wrong.'

'Oh, yes. It's the other side of the world from Russia. Communications aren't always very good. If some hothead on either side decides it would be wizard to take a pot-shot – well, the balloon could well and truly go up. But I'm hopeful, Laura. There are still ways to back out of this without anybody getting killed. Still time, too.

'Look, Laura, you understand I'm only telling you this because, you know, if the worst comes to the worst you might have to get along without me. But you must try not to worry.'

'I'll try.'

There was a silence, except for crackles on the line. 'Are you sure everything's all right, chicken? You sound a bit down.'

She longed to tell him the truth. Or what she believed was the truth. About Miss Wells and Mort and the Minuteman. 'It's just that things are a little spooky, Dad. And Mum –'

'I know. She has her own issues. Look, Laura. The situation with Mort is – well, it's complicated. But he's a soldier and he's a decent man, and if the worst comes to the worst he will do the right thing by the two of you. That's one reason I was willing to let him lodge with you. So you must try not to be anxious, even though I'm not there. And you always have the Key.'

But the Key, she thought, was the source of all her problems.

She found herself saying, 'Yes, Dad, I'm fine, I'm not worried.' There was a corner of her mind that said, I shouldn't have to be doing this. The adults are supposed to reassure *me*. But this was the way things were, and she just had to get on with it.

They talked a little more, about school and Mum and telly shows. Then he was called away.

She hung up the phone handset. She rubbed her hands to get the number off her palm. But she memorised it first.

She walked down Whitechapel towards Church Street.

It was a bright, sunny Saturday morning, and the city centre pavements were swarming. There were fashion stores with windows full of slim plaster dummies modelling leather coats and finely stitched blue jeans. There were Italian cafes and espresso bars, full of gleaming coffee machines and chatting teenagers. And there were record stores like NEMS, the giant three-floor store on Whitechapel run by the man who, it was said, managed the Beatles, the most popular beat group in the city.

Laura felt distant from all this. Since finding out who Miss Wells really was, she had felt differently about things. Now it was as if she saw these shopping streets through Miss Wells's eyes. As if she was *remembering* this day, when she was nearly sixty years old, off in the year 2007.

To the shoppers, it was as if this sunny Saturday morning, with money in your pocket and stores piled high with goods, was the way the world had always been, and always would be. But the last war was only seventeen years ago.

And the next war might only be a week away. *That* was reality. All this stuff, the shops and the laughing crowds, was a kind of dream, between the waking-up of wars.

She found Bernadette and Joel waiting for her outside C&A, as they'd promised.

Bernadette shot at her, 'You've got a face like a farmer's arse on a frosty morning. I don't know why we bother with you.'

'Neither do I,' Laura said defiantly. 'Haven't you got any other friends?'

'None as interesting as you,' Joel said. 'H-Bomb Girl.'

Nobody liked a misery. She'd learned that at her old school, when her parents had started to go through the Separation. Unhappiness was a bad smell people ran away from.

So she smiled, and linked their arms. 'Let's hit the shops.'

Joel snorted. 'Yeah. And gawp at all the stuff we can't afford.'

They started off in C&A Mode, a fashion department. Bernadette nearly wept over a leather coat, three-quarter length and chocolate brown. But it cost seventeen pounds, more than a good weekly pay packet. Still, she tried it on, and for two minutes walked around like a movie star, while Joel wolf-whistled.

Bernadette looked terrific, Laura thought. She was tall enough to pass for a few years older, and her face, while not beautiful, had good cheekbones and a strong mouth. Her make-up was bold and skilfully applied, and her blonde hair was swept up in a neat beehive. She was pale, though, under her make-up, and Laura remembered her throwing up earlier in the week.

They went to a Wimpy Bar for lunch. There was actually

a queue outside, and they had to wait for a table. It was a fun place, all Formica tables and brightly painted walls. On the table was a wipe-clean menu with pictures of the food you could buy, and a plastic squeezy tomato that you could squirt ketchup out of. Pop music blared out of speakers in the ceiling, Adam Faith and Cliff Richard.

There was nobody over about twenty in here. Everybody seemed to like the new American-ness, compared to the drabness of most British stuff.

They ordered hamburgers, cheeseburgers, and Pepsi Colas, and Laura thought she might have a knickerbocker glory to follow.

Nick O'Teen strutted in. He sat down and sipped Joel's Pepsi. 'Ugh. That's so flat they should sell it in envelopes.'

'Buy your own,' Joel said.

Laura looked at Nick curiously. Today he wore a long, threadbare frock coat, cowboy boots and drainpipe trousers. He looked a classic Ted, but not aggressive. He was too neat for that, too clean, too intelligent-looking. But the waitress, a big woman with arms like Henry Cooper's, glared at him. *We don't want any trouble.*

Joel watched Laura watching Nick. 'She fancies you,' Joel said, teasing.

That made her blush.

And Nick and Bernadette exchanged a glance, a small smile. If Laura had secrets, so did they.

Actually, she thought, looking at Nick's thin, handsome face, she didn't fancy him, not like that. He was good-looking, but something about him made her feel more as if he was a brother, say.

She asked, 'How was your concert on Sunday?'

'We got chucked out. We all leap about, you see. The

groups picked it up in Hamburg. Like the Beatles, and Rory Storm and the Hurricanes. You play for eight hours at a stretch, in front of the drunken sailors and the Anytime Annies. They shout at you if you're boring. "Mak show! Mak show!" That's before the bottles start flying.'

'He didn't stay long in Hamburg,' Bernadette said slyly. 'Couldn't stick it out, could you?'

'I got addicted to Prellies.'

'To what?'

'Preludins. Slimming pills you pop to keep yourself awake. Otherwise I was living off beer and fags. Not healthy, really.'

'I heard,' Bernadette said, 'that somebody broke your heart out there.'

'Shut it,' he said mildly. 'So what are you losers doing sitting here?'

'We've got a secret,' Bernadette said.

'Oh, yeah?'

Laura glared at her, but Bernadette rummaged in her bag. 'Oh, come on, it's *Nick*. We can tell him. Look at this.'

She put the phone gadget on the table. She had them all huddle close so nobody else could see. Then she opened up the lid, and the little numbered buttons glowed blue.

'Wow,' Nick said, impressed. 'What is it, a toy?'

'We think it's a kind of phone,' Joel said.

'*You* think that,' Bernadette said.

'There are radio phones,' Nick said. 'Walkie-talkies, like the police have. But I've never seen anything like this.'

Joel pursed his lips. 'I think we've got an idea about that.'

'Which is?'

'*It's from the future.*' And he ran Nick through their evidence that Miss Wells wasn't just a lookalike or a long-lost auntie, but was, somehow, a version of Laura from the future. 'How wacky is *that*?'

Nick sat back and looked at Laura. 'You keep surprising me, H-Bomb Girl. I don't know whether to laugh, cry, or burst out in pimples.'

'So you don't believe it,' Laura said.

'I didn't say that. It's wacky, but we live in a wacky world.' He pointed to a speaker. The record playing was a pacy instrumental, full of electronic noise. 'That's the current number one. "Telstar", by the Tornadoes. A record with a made-up sound, about a satellite in space that is going to let us watch what's going on in America or Japan, live on telly.' He touched the phone gadget. 'This doesn't seem so fantastic to me.'

He was that bit older than Laura and the others. Somehow having him take this seriously reassured Laura.

'But still,' Bernadette said. 'Time travel?'

Nick drummed on his teeth with his fingernails. 'Have you ever thought why Miss Wells is called Miss Wells?'

Bernadette said, 'She couldn't call herself "Miss Mann". Bit of a giveaway.'

'But why Wells?' He looked at Joel, letting him work it out. 'You're the science fiction fan.'

'My God. Herbert George Wells.'

Bernadette asked, 'Who?'

'You know. H. G. Wells! He wrote *The Time Machine*, the most famous time-travel story ever written.'

Bernadette said, 'Isn't that a bit obvious?'

'It fooled you,' Joel shot back.

'Miss Wells is arrogant,' Laura said. 'She thinks she's smarter than us. So she can play little games like this, thinking we won't understand.'

'Yes,' Nick said. 'I know a lot of people like that. They tend to make mistakes. But, arrogant? You don't like yourself very much, do you, H-Bomb Girl?'

'No, I don't,' Laura said, feeling grim.

'Maybe she *wanted* us to figure it out,' Joel said. 'The clue in her name. Have you thought of that? And maybe she wanted us to find this phone thing.'

'Why?' Bernadette asked.

Joel shrugged. 'Because, like Laura says, she's playing a game, and we're all just pieces on the board.' Joel always seemed to think things through that bit further.

'Well, that's a jolly thought.' Nick pushed his chair back. 'Come on. That waitress with the hairy arms is giving me funny looks. Let's go down the Jive-O-Rama, I'm meeting the group there.'

'Don't even think about doing a runner,' the waitress said, hearing every word, though she was yards away.

Chapter 11

They shuffled down into the Jive-O-Rama. At the door, Nick had a mock boxing match with Little Jimmy.

The club was as crowded as ever. Bernadette recognised the other Woodbines, who sat languidly around a table, their long legs stretched out. She walked over, with Joel in tow.

Laura went to the counter to buy some coffees. Big Jimmy grinned at her as he took her order. 'Oh – hey, Agatha,' he called to the back. 'She's in.' He clicked his fingers and pointed at her. 'Forgot your name.'

'Laura.'

'The new girl. Laura's in. There's something Agatha wants to say to you,' he said with a wink.

Agatha came out from the back, a tea towel in her hands. She took Jimmy's scribbled slip and started to make up the order, for four espressos.

Laura asked, 'So?'

Her back turned, Agatha said, 'So what?'

Laura felt deeply uncomfortable around this skinny, thin-haired, forty-year-old woman with a face like an older sister. 'What do you want to say to me?'

'They've been in. Searching.'

'Who have?'

Agatha shrugged. 'Men in suits. Believe me, we don't get too many men in suits in here. There was a black car outside.'

Mort. It must have been.

'They asked questions. They bribed the kids, with sweets, comics. A few ciggies. Copies of *Health and Efficiency*.' That was porn. Agatha sneered. 'You'd think you kids had so much *stuff* you wouldn't want any more. But there you go.'

'Questions about *what*?'

'You,' Agatha said. 'Where you go, who you go around with, how often you come down here.'

Laura felt cold, despite the sweaty fug of the cellar. Mort must have got frustrated digging around at home, and at school, and now he had followed her here. After all it wasn't just the Key he would want but the codes she had memorised. 'Did anybody talk?'

'Well, that's a stupid question. Of course they did. But nobody knew anything worth telling.'

'Why would you help me? I don't even know you.'

Agatha looked at her. 'But I know *you*.'

'How?'

'You don't want to know. Four espressos. Two bob, please.' She wouldn't say anything else.

At the table, things were tense.

Nick introduced Laura to the four Woodbines, the other members of his group. They were all about eighteen.

'Bert Muldoon, rhythm guitar.' Berk in a sheepskin jacket and sunglasses.

'Paul Gillespie, lead guitar.' Intense musician-type.

'Mickey Poole, bass. He's a Manc, but don't hold it

against him.' Shy, young. Laura knew 'Manc' meant he was from Manchester.

'And you know the famous Billy Waddle.' The drummer was the best-looking, his face set in a constant sulky sneer. He looked Laura up and down, sizing her up.

Bernadette was sitting right next to Billy, arms folded, glaring as he ogled Laura. There was obviously something going on between them.

'You're never in when I call, Billy,' Bernadette said now.

'Been out. Gigs, you know.'

'Yeah,' sneered Mickey Poole. 'That and overtime at the bottle factory in Bootle.'

Nick's expression was complicated. He tapped the tabletop with a fingernail, his glance darting from Bernadette to Billy and back. Laura didn't understand how he fit into any relationship between Bernadette and the drummer.

Billy sipped Coke from a wasp-waisted bottle. 'Anyway I'm cool with things between us. Aren't you?' Before Bernadette could have another go, he turned to Laura. 'Haven't I seen your face before?'

The other boys rolled their eyes. It was an obvious line.

Laura said, 'Well, I was here on Sunday. At the club.'

'I remember you now.'

'Sure you do.'

'She's a rock and roll virgin,' Nick said.

Billy leered. 'Is there any other kind?'

Without warning Bert Muldoon launched into an impromptu performance of a song. Laura worked out from the lyrics that it was called 'Tutti Frutti'. In his sunglasses and moth-eaten coat, Bert was like a scruffy cartoon bear, who only came to life from time to time. The others joined in, slapping the tabletop for rhythm.

There was ironic applause from the other tables in the crowded cellar.

Laura looked around the walls, at the yellowing posters for concerts in town halls and schools and church fetes, and ice rinks and ballrooms like the Locarno and the Rialto, featuring local groups with names like Gerry and the Pacemakers, Derry and the Seniors, John Smith and the Common Men, Bob Tanner and the Threepenny Bits. The freshest poster announced that the Beatles would be playing at the Cavern on Monday night, supported by the Woodbines. It was the concert she had seen advertised in *Mersey Beat.*

All these names, all these hopefuls. Would any of them be famous this time next year? Would any of them still be known in whatever year Miss Wells came from? But that didn't matter. Their music was something completely new in the world, here and now. And she, just by chance, had found herself in the middle of it. It was exciting, despite the dark cloud of her problems.

Agatha stood over them. Nobody had heard her approach. She looked straight at Laura. 'They're back. Big Jimmy is holding them up.'

Turning, Laura saw shadows at the head of the stairwell, muscular, brisk.

'Drug bust,' Bert said. Nobody contradicted him.

Everybody stood up.

Bernadette asked, 'Is there a back way out?'

Agatha said, 'This way.' She walked off.

Joel glared at Laura. 'Do you trust that woman?'

'No. But what choice do we have?'

Nick looked at her. 'More dodgy stuff, H-Bomb Girl? Well, come 'ead.'

They moved, Laura and Nick following Agatha, then Bernadette and Joel.

All the Woodbines came after them. 'I'm not missing this,' said Bert Muldoon.

Agatha led them around the counter, to the small kitchen area at the back of the cellar. Lit up by a single fluorescent strip, there was a sink, a fridge, a chopping board with white-bread sandwiches stacked up.

And at the back, Agatha pulled away a piece of stained hardboard to reveal a hole in the brick wall.

Bernadette stared into darkness. 'You had this prepared.'

Agatha said, 'Where I come from, you always need an escape route. They're coming. Let's go.'

Bernadette led the way. The others followed, Laura and Joel tense, the group members giggling and joking.

Bernadette's stomach seemed to be hurting. She worked her way through the hole with one hand on her belly.

They were in the cellar of the house next door to Big Jimmy's. It was disused, blocked off. It had been easy for Agatha to pull away the stones in the dividing wall, as the mortar was old and rotten.

Agatha left a chink of light while they found places to sit, all nine of them, on dirty old boxes and heaps of stone from the wall. Then Agatha put the bit of hardboard back in place, and they were sealed in darkness.

Laura helped Bernadette to sit, but Bernadette waved her away. 'Just cramps.'

They huddled together, their knees touching.

Bert Muldoon asked, 'Can I have a ciggie?'

'Don't be a div,' Mickey Poole said.

'I smell damp,' Paul Gillespie said.

Nick said, 'That's Bert's coat.'

The group members giggled explosively.

Bernadette snapped, 'Shut up or bog off.'

Laura, Bernadette, Joel and Nick put their heads together, a little away from the others.

Nick said seriously, 'Tell me what's going on, H-Bomb Girl.'

He already knew about Miss Wells, Laura from the future. Now Laura told him as much as she could, that she was apparently being pursued by Miss Wells and the American military. Bernadette and Joel listened intently, knowing some of this.

Nick laughed. 'H-Bomb Girl, you're more trouble than a camel in a sweetshop.'

'I'm glad you think it's funny,' Laura said. She was genuinely scared now, here in this dark hole; she felt panic brush her mind.

'Well, you can't go around hiding like this for ever.'

'It's the Key they want,' Joel said. 'The V-bomber Key.'

'Maybe we should hide it,' Bernadette said. 'We could bury it down here. Or take it somewhere else.'

'No,' Laura hissed immediately. 'I can't take it off.'

'Why not?'

'My dad made me promise not to.'

There was a silence.

Nick said, 'There's still a lot you're not telling us, isn't there, H-Bomb Girl?'

There was a hand on Laura's knee, in the dark. It felt like a hot, muscular spider. It slid up her thigh and under her skirt.

She grabbed a little finger and yanked it back. Somebody yelped and the hand pulled back.

Nick snapped, 'Who was that?'

Laura hissed, 'The letch with his hand on my leg.'

Somebody sniggered. 'It was worth the pain, sweet cheeks.'

Bernadette poured all her anger into a hot, tearful whisper. 'Billy Waddle. You sod. Oh, you lousy faithless sod. I'm sitting right here and you do that –'

Laura heard a scuffle, the soft sound of blows landing, muffled ouches. The others piled in to separate the fighters.

When they were calm again, Laura said carefully, 'Are you crying, Bern?'

'No. Bog off.'

Laura hunted for a tissue and held it out. 'Come on. I've never heard you cry before.'

'And nor,' Nick said, 'have I, and I've known her a long time. Heart of stone, our Bern.'

'She's pregnant.' That was Agatha's flat voice.

There was a stunned silence.

Then Nick said, 'Wow. This is turning out to be quite a day.'

'Bog off,' Bernadette said.

Laura said, 'The stomach cramps. The throwing up.'

Bernadette hissed, 'All right. I'm in the club. Happy now?'

Billy laughed softly.

Laura asked, 'How long, Bern?'

'Don't know. About a month, I think.'

'Agatha – how did you know?'

'I have an instinct for these things.'

'How come? Have you got kids of your own?'

'No.'

Nick said bleakly, 'And the proud father, I suppose, is the

drummer who's head I've just been sitting on.'

'Got it in one,' Bernadette said.

'Rang the bell, did you, Billy?'

Billy said, 'Could be me. Could be somebody else. Have to see if he's got my rhythm when he comes out.'

'Don't you joke, Billy Waddle,' Bernadette said. 'I lost my virginity to you, you sod. It could only be you. And as soon as you got a sniff of a baby you bogged off, didn't you?'

Laura reached out in the dark until she found Bernadette's hand. 'How did it happen? Didn't you use anything?'

Bernadette whispered, 'When we started, Billy said we'd be OK, we could take a chance.'

'I got off at Edge Hill,' Billy said. 'Usually works.'

'I didn't know any better. How stupid I was.'

Laura wouldn't have known much more herself. All she knew about sex and contraceptives and pregnancy she'd learned from whispers and rumour, from classmates, people her own age.

'Not my problem,' Billy said. 'Up to the judy to stop a kid.'

Nick said, 'You really are a piece of work, Billy.' The hurt in his voice surprised Laura, as if he'd been betrayed himself.

'I think that's why they've been searching my stuff at school,' Bernadette said. 'They can smell a bun in the oven a mile off.'

'Have you been to the doctor?'

'For what? A lecture?'

'What will you do?'

The options were bleak. Abortions were illegal. You could always find somebody to do it, some struck-off doctor maybe. But it was dangerous, even lethal. And if you had the kid, it might be taken away for adoption.

Bernadette blew her nose. 'You think you've got problems, H-Bomb Girl.'

'Yes,' Laura said. All she had to worry about was meddling from the future, and the end of the world. Somehow all that paled compared to *this*.

'We'll help you,' Nick whispered.

'Yes,' Joel said. 'You're not alone, Bern.'

Bernadette was silent. Then she said, 'Thanks.'

'But I'm alone.'

That was Agatha. In the dark she had come to sit next to Laura, moving silently again. Laura felt her cold, thin frame next to her body. A hand pressed against Laura's arm.

Laura took it, feeling a bit frightened. 'Agatha? Are you OK?'

'You asked me if I have kids. I can't have kids. Bernadette doesn't want her kid, and I can't have them. Funny that.'

Laura didn't know what to say to this forty-year-old woman, holding her hand like a little girl. 'I'm sorry.'

'You should be happy in this age,' Agatha whispered to Laura. 'This year. All of you. You have so much, your health, all the *stuff*. This time you've been given. It's different after the war.'

Nick asked, 'You mean Hitler's war?'

'No,' said Agatha, 'the Sunday War. The war to come.'

There was a long silence.

Bert Muldoon said, 'Am I the only one who's confused here?'

Somebody tapped on the hardboard cover over the hole. Big Jimmy called, 'They've gone. Come on out.'

'Good,' Bert said. 'I'm dying for a burst.'

They all started to move, with relief.

Agatha held Laura's hand for one second longer. She whispered, 'I'm sorry, Mum.'

Then she climbed out through the hole.

Laura sat watching her, stunned.

Chapter 12

Monday 22nd October. 7:45 a.m.

No phone call from Dad this morning.

Stayed in yesterday. All that stuff on Saturday was just too strange.

Especially Agatha. I don't want to think about her.

Bert was sort of right on Saturday, when he guessed it was a drugs bust. The official story was that the raid on the Jive-O-Rama was a drugs raid by plain-clothes scuffers.

I think they want the Key, and I suppose the code numbers in my head. But they have to sneak around to get it, rather than just take it. Why, I don't know. For now it's helping me.

But Black Saturday's only five days away. This kid-glove stuff can't last for ever.

Nice surprise this morning (sarcasm). Mort has hired us a new telly. It was delivered early. Nineteen-inch screen. He said he wanted to help make the house a home.

We all sat in the parlour and looked at the test card. I hate being in that room first thing in the morning because it smells of Mort and his aftershave, where he's been sleeping.

If he thinks he can buy me off with a nine-bob-a-week Red Arrow Rentals telly he's got another think coming. Stuff him.

Good picture though.

It was a damp, cold Monday morning.

At school everybody seemed in a bad mood.

In the break the three of them, Joel, Bernadette and Laura, huddled together in the yard, arms around their chests. The sky was a solid lid of cloud, and everything seemed washed out, colourless. Very Monday morning, Laura thought.

'I thought of coming over yesterday,' she said to Bernadette.

'What for?'

'To see how you were.'

'Well, I'm still up the duff.'

'Saturday was very weird.'

Joel said, 'Perhaps we all needed a day off from each other. It only all kicks off when we're together, doesn't it?'

'It kicks off,' Bernadette said viciously, 'when we're around Miss H-Bomb 1962.'

Laura shot back, 'It's not my fault you're pregnant.'

'I don't need *you*, or anybody.'

Joel said, 'Bern, you've got a lot of anger to get rid of. But –'

'Oh, what do you know? You're always sniffing around me. Get your own life.'

Joel looked devastated.

And Laura suddenly saw that he had feelings for Bernadette himself. Well, why not? Laura thought of Joel as reserved, a swot, a bit too earnest. But he had the same juices flowing as any other fourteen-year-old.

In that case, this whole business about Billy Waddle and the baby must be hurting him hugely.

It wasn't the right time to mention how she was fretting about Agatha, a forty-year-old woman who had called Laura 'Mum'.

Miss Wells approached them. She wore a huge quilted overcoat and a woollen hat. It wasn't that cold. Maybe where she came from, Laura thought, where or *when*, the world had got warmer, and 1962 seemed cold to her.

'So,' Miss Wells said.

'Miss?'

She looked them in the face, one after the other. 'We all have secrets, don't we?'

'Don't know what you mean, Miss,' Bernadette said brazenly.

'I think you do, O'Brien. How's the morning sickness? Your condition's pretty obvious, you know. Oh, don't look at me like that.'

'I'm all right on my own.'

'No, you're not. You don't need to talk to me. See Mrs Sweetman.' The deputy head. 'She'll sort you out. And she won't judge you. You're not the first gymslip mum, you know.' Miss Wells looked directly at Laura. 'We all operate under constraints. But we're here to help you. *I* am.'

Then just tell me the truth, Laura thought. If you're me, if there is any of *me* left in *you*, then show some compassion, and tell me the truth, about who you are, and what you want.

But Miss Wells just looked back at her, with eyes that were her own and yet weren't, and said nothing.

The bell rang.

When Miss Wells was out of earshot, Laura asked, 'So

will you talk to old Sweetcheeks?'

Bernadette grunted. 'What do you think? Listen. Cavern. Tonight. I've got tickets. Nick's playing, and the Beatles. Stuff the rest of it.'

Monday 22nd October. 6 p.m.
Mort came after me as soon as I walked in the door.
Keeps trying to get me alone, in the sitting room, on the stairs. I've stuck to Mum, or I've run to the bathroom, or hid in my bedroom with the door closed.
He seems to want to keep it all a secret from Mum, for now, and that's saving me. But I can see he's getting mad. I don't know what he'll do then.

Later, as Mort and Mum sat watching *Z-Cars* on the big new telly, Laura put on her best black dress and a bit of make-up. Mum didn't even know she'd blown her savings from her pocket money on creams, compacts, mascara and lipstick.

She slipped out of the house without asking, or waiting for her tea.

She took a bus to the Pier Head and walked up from there.

In town, she felt as if everybody was staring at her. Especially the men. But it was a different sort of stare. Less threatening, somehow. Maybe the make-up made her look older.

The Cavern was in Mathew Street, a narrow lane just around the corner from the shopping street called Whitechapel. This area, a few blocks from Canning Dock, was all Victorian warehouses. By day, the street would be full of traffic, with hoists working from the warehouses unstacking lorries. Now, after dark, everything was closed up, and Laura had to pick her way through rotting fruit and old vegetables crushed into the black dirt.

And as she walked she heard guitars echoing between the steep brick walls. She had learned from Nick and the others that the music was everywhere in Liverpool. There were other clubs in the area, like the Iron Door in Dale Street around the corner, and the Downbeat, and the Mardi Gras. All the dance halls had beat groups playing, and the ballrooms, even the ice rinks.

From under a crudely made sign reading THE CAVERN, the queue went right down the street, all the way past a bricked-up bomb site with a tangle of barbed wire. There were girls with beehives and heels and livid make-up, and boys in jeans or drainpipes, and a few full-blown Teds and Mods.

Immersed in noise, with thousands of fans swarming all over this grimy city centre, Laura felt her heart beat faster.

Here was Bernadette, with Joel at her side, in the queue. 'Posh Judy. So you came.'

'I couldn't miss Nick's big night.'

Bernadette snorted. 'Don't get your hopes up.'

'But all these fans lining up.'

'Not for the Woodbines,' Joel said dryly.

Bernadette pulled Laura back into the shadows. 'Business first. Normally I'd take an hour getting ready. But today's an emergency, I suppose. Want a ciggie?'

'No, thanks.'

'Let's see what we've got to work with.' Bernadette briskly opened Laura's coat and inspected her dress. It was black, cut below the knee, with a white cotton panel buttoned up at the throat. Bernadette snickered. 'Who buys your clothes? Your mother?'

'Well, yes.'

'You need to get some money of your own, kid. In the meantime it's make do.' She undid the buttons at Laura's throat and tucked the white cotton panel inside the black main body of the dress. 'In all black you'll look like a beat girl. In the dark, anyhow. You need to lose this.' Bernadette fingered the Key on its chain.

Laura couldn't quite bear to take it off. She tucked it out of sight. She glanced down at her chest, embarrassed. 'Aren't I showing too much?'

'No. Not that you've got anything to show. Here.' Bernadette dug into her bag and pulled out a handful of tissues. 'Give nature a helping hand.'

Laura goggled. 'Are you joking?'

Bernadette cupped her own chest proudly. 'How do you think I came by these? They won't let you in if you look too young.'

'All right.' Laura took the tissues and, turning her back, stuffed them inside her Marks & Spencer bra. When she was done, she let Bernadette put more lipstick on her mouth and mascara around her eyes.

Bernadette said, 'We'll do a better job next time. But nobody will notice in the dark, nothing but the lippy.'

When they came back out of the shadows, Joel looked away, comically embarrassed.

The queue was long but fast moving. Everybody was excited, chattering, the air thick with cheap perfume and hairspray. Some of the boys took nips from hip flasks.

They reached the entrance itself, next to a washing-machine factory. It was just a hatchway, lit up by a dangling naked light bulb. You wouldn't have known it was there save for the big bouncer at the front.

Laura found herself going down eighteen dank, slippery steps. She could feel the heat and damp climbing up her legs like a tide.

At the bottom of the steps a plump brunette called Cilla took their money. Cilla normally worked the cloakroom, but tonight 'Jed' was off sick, she said. It was one and six for non-members, but because Cilla knew them and they were friends of Nick's, she gave them the members' rate of a shilling.

The Cavern really was just a cellar, dark and poky, all narrow tunnels and alcoves and high vaulted pillars. It was oddly like a church, Laura thought.

From the last couple of steps she looked down over a sea of heads. The place was already full, even though more fans poured down the steps behind Laura. At the far end of the central tunnel there was a stage where lads were setting up equipment and fooling around. Some of them were Woodbines. She recognised Billy Waddle with his drum kit, and Bert Muldoon. The others must be Beatles. A skinny young man with a broad face and a sardonic voice was at the mike. 'One two, testing one two, one bogging two, can you hear me mother . . .?'

As Laura reached the bottom of the steps the air hit her, dank and hot and wet. There was a stink of rot and stale beer and dead mice. The walls dripped with condensation, and the floor was black and slippery.

'Whatever you do,' Bernadette said, '*don't* put your handbag down on the floor. It comes up black. Come 'ead. Let's find a good speck.'

She led the way, with liberal use of elbows and swear words. Laura followed, already breaking into sweat. The long tunnels were narrow and crowded.

Away from the stage itself the light was patchy, and in the dark Laura was surrounded by exotic creatures with quiffs and sideburns, sequinned cowboy boots and studded leather coats. There were a lot of bikers in the crowd, in leather coats with metal studs, and greasy slicked-back hair. And there were Teds among them, she saw, but they were not like Nick, not young, neat, smart. These were older men, maybe as old as thirty. Narrow-eyed and stinking of beer and ciggies, they sidled through the crowd like sharks. And there were bouncers, big fat blokes in suits on the door and lined up in front of the stage. They watched the Teds carefully.

Laura's head filled with the stink of ciggie smoke, and there was booze on a lot of breaths. She had never been anywhere like this in her life. She felt a thrill of danger.

But then some of the bikers noticed Joel. They closed in and began poking him. One of them grabbed his hat, but Joel held on to it. Laura could hear what they were saying. 'Niggy, niggy. Niggy nigritta.'

Bernadette moved in, tall, commanding. 'Hey, face ache. Leave him alone.' She said to Laura, 'There's going to be bother tonight. You can just feel it.'

Somebody twanged a guitar, a single electrical chord that crashed out of the loudspeakers stacked up on the stage.

A shock ran through the crowd. Everybody roared, and pushed forward. Laura had to struggle to stay with Bernadette and Joel.

The stage was only about ten feet wide. The back wall was painted with big slabs of colour, covered in graffiti: signatures of the groups in marker pens.

Near the stage, the floor was just packed with girls. They were too jammed in to dance, or even to breathe probably,

Laura thought. But they wanted to be close to the groups. The lads on stage reached past the bouncers, touching the girls' hands. Some of the girls stuck bits of paper into the pockets of the lads' jackets. Phone numbers, maybe.

Laura was crushed in among taffeta dresses and cheap serge suits. Big fat drops of condensation dripped off the roof and hit Laura on the head and shoulders.

'Don't mind the rain,' Joel shouted at her. 'Sometimes it shorts out the amps.'

Some of the girls were chanting. 'Bring back Pete! Bring back Pete!' or, 'Pete for ever! Ringo never!'

Laura tugged Bernadette's elbow. 'Who's Pete?'

'Pete Best.' It wasn't Bernadette who answered, but Nick. He smiled at Laura, his teeth white in the gloom. Compared to some of the tough-looking Teds he looked very young. He leaned towards her and shouted, 'He was the Beatles' drummer, and they sacked him because he was useless.'

Bernadette came between them. 'No, they sacked him because he was too good-looking. Even though it was his drum kit. What's the new bloke called, with the big nose? Bongo?'

'*Ringo*, you div. Glad you came, Posh Judy? What about you, Bern? Do you want me to autograph your bump?'

'Bog off.'

That sardonic voice came from the stage again. 'A one two one two testing. Is there anybody there? Hard to see without me goggles.'

There was a huge roar, and the crowd crushed forward again. Laura was swept up. Laughing, she grabbed Bernadette and Joel by the hand.

'All right, thank you, Beatle John.' An MC character, a

bustling little man in a crumpled suit, grabbed the mike. 'We'll be seeing plenty of you later, and the other boys. Go on, clear off.' Now he shouted, his voice booming around the arched roof, 'First of all, hello Cavern dwellers, and welcome to the best of cellars, as I always say, ha ha!' He got whistles for that. 'In the break you can buy water, coffee and pop from the tables over there. I think there's a bit of soup left over from dinner if you fancy that. We've got a great show for you tonight. You'll get plenty of Beatles later, don't worry. But first, let's give a big warm Cavern welcome-back to – Nick O'Teen and the Woodbines!'

Nick was up on stage. He grasped the mike stand, as the Woodbines clattered their drums and tuned up their guitars behind him. 'Good evening, troglodytes! It's wonderful to be back from Bootle. As if we've never been away. We'd like to play for you a song by a good friend of ours, a Mister Chuck Berry. You can never go wrong with a bit of Chuck, can you, lads? Eh, Billy?' He looked around, but Billy Waddle just ignored him, and, chewing gum, grinned at the girls at the front of the crush.

Nick called out, 'This is a number called "Johnny B Goode". A one two three –'

The guitarists crashed out their chords, and Billy hammered his drums, and Nick leapt about the stage cradling his mike stand.

The sound was huge, and it just walloped out of the big speakers on stage, so loud the walls shook, and bits of white paint drifted down from the roof, like snow. Laura had never heard anything like this before. It was music transformed into a battering ram. She was electrified.

You couldn't dance here, it was so tightly packed, but everybody yelled and jumped, following the rhythm as best they could, and Laura jumped with the rest. One girl fainted, and had to be passed over the heads of the crowd to the back.

Nick sang raucously but clearly, and Laura could hear every word. There was a line about guitars like a ringing of bells, which she thought was better poetry than most of the stuff she had to swot up at school.

And when Nick yelled out the chorus line, urging 'Johnny' to 'go go go', the Beatle called John came mucking about on stage, doing the Twist, jiving like a madman, even goose-stepping up and down behind Nick. The crowd screamed, and went even more crazy.

That was when the Teds kicked off.

It was planned. They had worked their way to the front. Now a dozen of them surged forward and made for the stage. The bouncers went for the Teds without hesitation. One huge man stood firm, and a Ted just caromed off his belly and went flying back into the crowd, knocking screaming girls for six. But three, four, five of the Teds got through and leapt up on to the stage. The music dissolved in a jangle of broken chords.

One of the Teds shrieked, 'Bash the queer!' And he threw himself straight at Nick, who went down under flying fists. Another Ted joined in, and another.

Billy Waddle cowered behind his drums at the back of the stage. Bert Muldoon smashed his rhythm guitar down on one Ted's head. Mickey Poole dropped his guitar and leapt at the tangle around Nick. But another big Ted held out his hand and shoved his palm into Mickey's nose. Mickey went down screaming, blood pouring from his face.

On the dance floor it was chaos. The fighting spread everywhere as bouncers fought with Teds, and the girls tried to get on to the stage, and other gangs and clans took the chance for a ruck. Laura watched amazed as a table flew through the air and smashed against a wall.

But on stage the Teds still worked at Nick, their firsts and boots flying into his body. They meant business, Laura realised.

'We've got to help him,' she yelled.

Joel held Bernadette's arm. 'Your baby!'

Bernadette shook him off. 'He'll survive. Come on!'

She pushed her way forward. Joel and Laura followed, shoving squabbling fans out of the way.

It wasn't hard to get on the stage. Girls milled around, screaming. The other Woodbines, Bert, Paul and Mickey, were wrestling with the Teds. Only Billy stayed back.

Nick was a shapeless mass on the floor, surrounded by Teds.

Bernadette screamed. She leapt at one of the Teds, landing on his back. She dug her nails into his cheeks and pulled. She was a tall, heavy girl, and as her nails dragged through his flesh the Ted came off the heap over Nick, yelling and waving his fists.

As another Ted tried to join the assault on Nick, Joel went to get hold of his jacket. Bernadette yelled, 'Not the lapels!' But it was too late.

When Joel grabbed the Ted's lapels, he screamed. He couldn't get free, his fingers somehow snagged. The Ted, a foot taller than Joel, grinned. 'Have a mouthful of dandruff, soft lad.' He casually head-butted Joel. Joel went down, his hands torn away, and Laura saw his fingers had been ripped open.

Laura looked for Nick. He was still on the floor, curled over like a baby in the womb. Now a huge Ted was taking paces back, running up, and kicking Nick's head like a footballer taking a free kick.

Nick's mike stand lay beside him on the blood-stained stage. Laura grabbed it and felt its weight. It was only flimsy, but it had a heavy, weighted base.

She really didn't want to kill anybody. But that Ted looked relentless.

As the Ted went to take another kick she swung the mike stand up between his legs, from behind. The heavy base slammed into his groin with a crunching sound. The Ted's eyes went wide, and he grabbed his crotch. 'Oh, me mutton dagger!' He fell over as if chopped down.

Laura ran forward to Nick. He lay motionless, in a pool of blood.

With a flash and a pop, the amps cut out. The crowd's fighting stopped as if a switch had been pulled, and there was a collective groan.

Beatle John clambered back on to the stage, his hair a tangle from the ruck. But his voice, unamplified now, carried over the crowd. 'Oh, well. What shall we do while we wait for Uncle Albert to change the fuse on the Vox? How about a singalong? *She'll be coming round the mountain when she comes*. Honk! Honk! . . .'

The crowd joined in, Mods and Rockers, bikers and schoolkids alike.

They're all mad, Laura thought. I must be mad to be here.

'Come on,' said Bernadette. 'We've got to get Nick out of here.'

Chapter 13

Pooling their money, they took a taxi to Broad Green Hospital, although Nick insisted he didn't need a doctor.

At the hospital they had to wait, with mothers with sick children, and half-asleep drunks.

Laura and Bernadette had a couple of bruises, and Laura had ruined her school tights. Joel had had his fingertips ripped open by fish hooks embedded in that Ted's lapels, put there to trap anybody who attacked. His hands were so swathed in bandages from the Cavern's first-aid box it looked like he wore white gloves.

Of course Nick was the worst. His face was so battered it was purple and swollen, his lips cut, one eye closed. His body was a mass of bruises too.

They were all streaked with black, where they had fallen on the filthy floor of the Cavern.

Nick ran his tongue around his mouth. 'I'll need National Health choppers after this.'

'You're going to need a new drummer too,' Bernadette said. 'Once I get my hands on that coward Billy Waddle.'

'You should have stayed out of it, Bern. A lady in your fragile condition.'

'You'll feel fragile with my fist in your gob.'

'So,' Joel said, his hands huge. '"Bash the queer."'

Nick said, 'Funny how a bunch of head-the-balls can be so perceptive.' His eyes were closed, his voice a flat whisper, as if he was half asleep.

'You knew,' Laura said to Bernadette.

Bernadette shrugged. 'It was Nick's business.'

'It is the business of my group, though,' Nick said. 'They've taken their share of queer-bashings on my behalf before. But they look after me.'

'Even Billy?' Bernadette asked sourly.

Nick looked away.

'So how did the Teds know?' Joel asked.

'They might just have seen me around town. There are places you can go. There's a pub called the Magic Clock, behind the Royal Court theatre. And a hotel called the Stork, where they turn a blind eye.' He put on a Colonel Blimp voice. 'Because what we deviants get up to is illegal, you know, by God and Her Majesty.

'Anyway I've had worse. National Service was tougher. Got my jaw broke in there. Stopped me singing for a month. That sarge was a music lover, probably. Or he might have fancied me. Some of the worst of them do.'

Bernadette teased him. 'I always wondered if you liked a bit of rough.'

He grimaced. 'Not that rough. I'm a romantic, me. I fall in love. Isn't that stupid?' He looked at Laura through his one good eye. 'So do you think less of me?'

'Why should I?'

'Have you met anyone like me before? A queer, a gay?'

She thought it over. 'Probably.'

Nick said, 'We've all got secrets, haven't we, H-Bomb Girl? I'll tell you the irony. I've never gone in for bashing myself. But I've stood aside and let others take it.' He looked at Joel as he said this. 'Even queers. If you're a target yourself it makes you feel better to see somebody else getting his head kicked in. Maybe I deserved this.'

At last the doctor came. Nick insisted he felt fine. But the doctor decided Nick would have to stay in overnight to have his head injuries checked out, and the rest of him explored for internal injuries. Joel was going to need stitches, and would be kept in too.

It was gone eleven by the time Laura and Bernadette left the hospital.

'We're dirty stop-outs. And on a school day too,' Bernadette said mockingly.

'Yes. And we missed the Beatles.'

Bernadette asked quickly, 'Can I come home with you?'

'What? I mean – yes. Of course.'

'If I get home this late my mum will kick off. Better to let her sleep off the mother's ruin. Anyway, I'd like to see your Mort in his undies.'

'Don't even joke about it.'

They walked to a bus stop. They picked at the dirt on their clothes, the bruises on their arms.

'Bern, when I met you, I thought there was something between you and Nick.'

'How wrong you were. Nick's as bent as a nine-bob note. But he's the only boy I ever met I could trust.'

'What about Joel?'

'Oh, yes, *him*. But he doesn't count.'

Laura felt very sad for Joel.

The bus came. It was the last service, and the bus smelled of pee and ciggie smoke.

At home, Mum answered the door. Laura could hear the telly in the background. She expected a chewing-out. But Mum looked troubled.

Mum asked, 'Who's this?'

'Bernadette. From school. I said she could stay.'

'Oh, did you? Well, I suppose you'd better come in.'

In the house, Mort was sitting in the parlour before the telly, which showed a grave talking head.

Bernadette said, 'Wow. Nice set.'

'Shut up,' said Mort casually, without looking round. Though it was midnight he was in his uniform shirt and tie.

Laura recognised the man speaking on the telly. It was President Kennedy.

'Uh oh,' she said to Bernadette. 'Cuba.'

'What?'

The telephone rang in the hall. Mort got up smartly, and went out to take the call. Then he came back in. 'It's for you,' he said to Laura, irritated.

Laura hurried to the phone. Bernadette followed.

It was Dad. 'You've been out late, haven't you? I phoned earlier.'

'What's going on, Dad?'

'Well, they're going public. The Americans. Kennedy is speaking to the nation right now about the crisis.'

'I know. Mort's watching him on telly.'

'How does he look to you?'

'Who, Mort? He's a git.'

Dad suppressed a laugh. 'Not him. The president.'

Laura peered through the door at the pale, ghostly face. Handsome, strained. 'He looks ill.'

'I've met people, our senior chaps, who've met *him*. He's only a young man, you know. Mightn't seem young to *you*.

But he's got a crippling back injury, and a bad bowel, and glandular problems. He gets through the day with a suite of drugs and painkillers. Now Khrushchev is quite different. A peasant. Fought the Nazis at Stalingrad, a bloody mess that was. Then he had to survive Stalin's purges, and fight his way to the top. Bit of a shower by all accounts. These things are never about bombs and missiles and submarines and airplanes, you know. It's always the people.'

'What's Kennedy saying?'

'He's told the public something about the Russian missiles on Cuba. He's sent sixty-odd nuclear bombers off to fly around the North Pole. And he's announced that he's blockading any more ships going to Cuba. He's put the US forces on DefCon 3. That's a state of alert, a "Defence Condition". There's another stage called DefCon 2, and then DefCon 1, which means war.

'He's speaking to America, but he's speaking to the Russians too. He's standing firm, but he's still trying to find a way to let everybody back down without losing face.'

Laura listened in to a bit of what Kennedy was saying. He talked about the risks of a worldwide nuclear war, '. . . in which even the fruits of victory would be ashes in our mouth'.

Bernadette was staring at the telly, and at Laura. 'You really do have secrets, don't you, H-Bomb Girl? Did you know about this stuff?'

Cradling the phone handset, Laura admitted, 'Sort of.'

Dad began talking about the Key, once more running over her instructions on how she had to use it 'if the balloon goes up': the phone numbers, the enabling code.

There was a high-pitched warble, like a small bird. It was coming from Bernadette's bag.

'Dad, I'll talk to you in a minute.'

They crept to the stairs and sat on the bottom step, out of sight of Mort and Mum in the parlour. Bernadette dug into her bag, and pulled out the 'phone', Miss Wells's little gadget. It was glowing blue, and chiming.

Bernadette stared at it. 'It's vibrating.'

Laura hissed, 'Shut it off. They'll hear.'

'I don't know how.' She flipped it open, and the noise stopped. There was a message on the little screen. Bernadette looked at Laura, amazed. 'This is for you as well.'

Laura stared into the screen.

Text Message
FROM: Miss Wells
TO: Laura
MESSAGE: Don't be afraid.

Chapter 14

She was woken by the sound of the wireless from downstairs.

'This is the BBC Home Service. Here is the seven o'clock news for today, Tuesday 23rd October. Following President Kennedy's television address to the American people last night, there has been no lessening of tension in the international waters around Cuba. Urgent negotiations are underway at the United Nations in New York. The Russian Premier Mr Khrushchev has yet to respond to the president's announcement of a "blockade". At home, Prime Minister Harold Macmillan is expected to speak to the nation later today. In other developments –'

'Oh, how dull.' That was her mother. *Click.* Jolly marching music.

Bernadette had slept on Laura's bedroom floor. But she'd gone before Laura woke.

Laura had to wait ages for a bus. There was a long queue at the stop.

At last a bus came. The queue patiently filed on, but the conductor lowered his arm like a barrier before Laura got to the front.

A woman complained, 'What's going on? Where's all the buses? This is disgusting.'

'Requisitioned, love. For official purposes. Shipping soldiers about, I shouldn't wonder. Don't you know there's a war on?'

The bus drove off, packed.

There was no point waiting. Laura walked.

The traffic was heavy that morning. Lots of police vehicles, and green army trucks rolling along in convoy. A bunch of squaddies sitting in the back of one truck leered at Laura and whistled.

There was a new air, she thought. Army lorries rolling through suburban streets. A sense of urgency. But people didn't seem to mind. Most of the older folk looked quite happy, in fact. As if it was a holiday.

But on the other hand there were queues outside all the churches she passed. People wanting to make their confessions, she supposed.

There was a special assembly this morning, and all the kids streamed into the hall.

Laura found Bernadette and Joel. She was faintly surprised Bernadette had turned up at all, and it was a miracle she had managed to smarten up her one and only school uniform, which she'd been wearing down the Cavern.

They inspected each other's battle scars. Bernadette's worst problem was broken nails. Joel's gouged fingers were out of their bandages but were swathed in Elastoplast. 'Not as bad as it looks,' he whispered. But he had a big purple bruise on his forehead where that Ted had head-butted him.

Everybody stood up as the head walked on to the stage. The senior staff followed, Mrs Sweetman the deputy head, Miss Wells, the others. The teachers actually marched, like soldiers in the war they all remembered so well.

And they had a guest. A policeman in a black uniform and an officer's peaked hat. He had a gun, a revolver, in a black holster at his waist.

A stir went around the hall. Outside her Dad's military bases, Laura had never seen anybody carry a gun before. This big grey-haired scuffer with a gun at his waist, strutting across the stage of a school assembly hall, was a genuinely frightening sight.

Mr Britten led the school in brief prayers. The policeman joined in, hands clasped, head bowed.

'I'm sure you've all heard the news this morning,' Mr Britten said. 'There's a situation developing between the Americans and the Russians over Cuba. Well, it's Britain's duty now to stand firm with our ally. And it's *our* duty, here at Saint Agnes's, to do what we can to help the war effort.' He was a small, round, pompous man with tiny National Health specs. He looked pleased with himself at being able to make such a grave announcement. 'You mustn't be concerned. We're here to guide you. All of us up here have been through this before, when old Hitler thought he could pull the tail of the British lion. Well, we showed Jerry and we'll show comrade Khrushchev too.' There was a reluctant rumble, like a muted cheer.

'Now I'll introduce you to our visitor. Chief Inspector Robert Gillespie, of the city constabulary. I'm sure you're going to treat him with the usual Saint Agnes's courtesy. And if you don't you'll be seeing me.' Just for a second there was a glimpse of the usual 'Bulldog' Britten.

The scuffer remembered to smile. It was a horrible expression that looked as if his cheeks were being dragged back by wires.

'Gillespie,' Laura murmured. 'Where do I know that name?'

Joel whispered, 'His son plays lead guitar for the Woodbines.'

'Paul. Oh, yes.'

'Don't know who's more embarrassed, father or son,' Bernadette said.

'Now then,' the chief inspector said. 'You heard what your headmaster said. Things are looking grave, and we must be prepared. That's why I'm here today, with some of my officers. To help you prepare.

'Things are going to be different as long as the crisis lasts. As I speak the Houses of Parliament are meeting to pass an Emergency Powers Act. Everything will be reorganised, from the structure of the government itself, down to what we eat, and even what we watch on television.

'But while all this is going on, remember one thing. "Business as usual!" That's going to be your motto. Life will be harder in some ways. But you must keep up with your schoolwork. That's your duty. For, you see, somebody is going to have to run the country when we all retire.' That ugly smirk again. 'We'll be seeing you all individually during the day.'

Bernadette murmured, 'Why do they need to do that?'

'In the meantime, keep calm, do your duty, pull together, and we'll see this thing through with our essential British liberties preserved.'

Joel stood up. 'Like free speech?'

'Be quiet!' thundered the policeman.

'See me!' yelled the headmaster.

That morning, normal classes were suspended.

Mrs Sweetman, the deputy head, took Laura's class. She

had a copy of a slim government Civil Defence booklet called 'Your Protection Against Nuclear Attack', and she read extracts to the class.

If the sirens sounded, she said, that would mean Russian missiles had been spotted by radar on their way to Britain. 'You will have four minutes' warning before the first missiles land.'

Joel stuck his hand up. 'Actually it would be more like three minutes. Perhaps as little as two and a half minutes.'

'Mister Christmas –'

'And if they launch from submarines off the coast, we might have no more than thirty seconds.'

'You may be right, Mister Christmas. But I have to give you the official figures.'

Bernadette put her hand up now. 'Miss. Why are you reading this out? Why don't we all have a copy?'

'Well, they aren't about to give it away for free. This booklet cost ninepence, you know. Let's get back to the sirens.'

'Mrs Sweetman,' Joel said.

She sighed. 'Yes, Mister Christmas?'

'What if you're deaf, and can't hear the sirens?'

Mrs Sweetman flicked through the leaflet. 'It doesn't say. You would have to ask a hearing person what's going on, I suppose.'

'Won't they be in a bit of a rush? They'll only have the four minutes.'

The class were enjoying watching Joel wind up Mrs Sweetman. But Laura felt sorry for her. About forty, plump, her hair grey, she seemed to be a decent woman, being asked to do a horrible thing to the children she was in charge of.

Laura asked, on impulse, 'Do you have kids, Miss?'

'Yes. Younger than you. I'd rather be with them, frankly. But we've all got our jobs to do, haven't we? Let's get on with this. Next. How to construct a fall-out shelter . . .'

They were trained on what to do if the sirens went up while they were at school. *Duck and cover.*

'You kneel down under your desk,' Mrs Sweetman said. They all obeyed, with a shuffle of desks.

'I'm too big for my desk.'

'Shut up, Deborah Sweeney. Crouch down. Done that? Next. Put your hands over your head. And kiss your jacksie goodbye.'

Bernadette looked up. '*What* was that, Miss?'

'You didn't hear it. Now. Whitewash.'

The school caretaker delivered a wheelbarrow-load of decorating sheets, brushes, and cans of whitewash. They all put on filthy old smocks that they used in art classes. The sheets hadn't been used since the last time the school was painted, which was evidently a long time ago. They cracked as they were unfolded.

When the desks were covered up the whitewash cans were opened. It wasn't paint, just a gritty, stinking mixture of quicklime and water. The pupils took their brushes, climbed on the desks, and began to slap this stuff on the classroom windows.

'"The whitewash will reflect the blast of a nearby atomic explosion,"' Mrs Sweetman read gravely. 'We will begin with the windows that face west, because the first bombs are likely to fall on Liverpool docks, which are that way.'

'I've read about this through CND,' Joel said, as he splashed his brush up and down. 'It's pitiful. I can't believe I'm actually standing here doing this. It's beyond satire.'

Laura found this irritating. 'You're a bit smug, you know, Joel. Why do you think you know better than all the experts in the government? They wouldn't make us do this if it wasn't going to do some good.'

'It's all a big lie,' Joel said. 'Just to keep us busy and stop us panicking. You could defend yourself against the bombs in the Second World War, with luck. You can't defend yourself against an atomic blast. That's the truth. Ouch, my fingers are killing me. The quicklime's getting in the cuts.'

Bernadette said, 'And the smell of it's making me heave.'

'We're not going to do very well in an atomic war,' Laura said, 'if we can't survive a night in the Cavern.'

Mrs Sweetman came along the line of windows. 'You missed a bit, Mister Christmas. We don't want those Communist megatons leaking into school because you were lazy with your paintbrush, do we?'

Joel grinned. 'No, Miss.'

Bernadette said, 'You look as if you're dying for a ciggie, Miss.'

'Gin and tonic, more like.' She walked on.

Joel filled in the last corner of his window.

At lunchtime they met Nick at the railings. He wore dark glasses and had a black scarf wrapped around his mouth. But his face was still puffed up.

'You look terrible,' Bernadette said.

'You're the one with whitewash on your nose.' His voice was gravelly and slurred. Maybe his broken teeth were giving him trouble. He seemed worse than the night before.

Bernadette reached up. 'Let's take off your shades and have a look.'

'No.' He pulled away and winced. 'My head's killing me.

Probably a hangover, right?' He touched his forehead, gingerly. 'I took some aspirins.'

Joel asked, 'What did they say at the hospital?'

'I didn't stick around.'

Bernadette snapped, 'You what?'

'Never did like hospitals. Anyway, haven't you heard? It's on the wireless. They are clearing out the hospitals. They're even sticking scuffers in there to kick out all the dockers with bad backs. Getting ready for war casualties,' he said in a graveyard voice.

A car drove through the school gate. It was silver, and it had a Stars and Stripes fluttering from its bonnet. A couple of people got out, white-coated like doctors, and they carried equipment into the school.

'That's a Jag,' Joel said. 'One of those new E-types. Dribble.'

'Americans,' Bernadette said. 'Always flash.'

'Just like their wars,' Nick said, 'Flash bang wallop! They're dragging us into this one, and it's nothing to do with us. I don't even know where Jamaica is.'

'Cuba,' Laura said.

'Who cares?'

Laura had never known Nick to be quite so sour and aggressive before. Maybe his mood had been affected by the kicking he'd taken.

Nick said now, 'Have you noticed how *happy* some of them are? The old folk. Anybody over about thirty. They complain about Hitler's war all the time. But now it's back on the telly, they can chuck all the rules out of the window and be a hero again.'

'The trouble is,' Bernadette said, 'we'll grow old too. And we'll probably be just as bad, if we're still around in 1980 or 1990 or the year 2000.'

'You're old before your time, Bern,' said Nick. 'Anyhow *I'll* still be around here when you kiddies come out of your afternoon classes.'

'Why?' Bernadette asked.

'Because if the bomb really is going to drop, I want to be close to the only two people I know who might have a way to stay alive. Which means you.' He pointed to Joel. 'Mister Junior CND cub scout.'

Joel said, 'You always laughed at me before. Nobody's bothered about that stuff, *you* said.'

Nick just ignored him. 'And *you*, Laura. You're the H-Bomb Girl. We worked that out from the moment we met you. But you've never told us the whole truth, have you?'

Laura saw the way they all looked at her. This was a crisis that was bound to come, she supposed. A test of loyalties, and their new friendship.

'Did you know about Cuba?' Joel asked.

'For a few days. My dad told me some of it.'

'So why not tell us?'

'He made me promise not to.'

'But we've helped you,' Nick said. 'We've saved your bacon a few times.'

She felt her face redden. 'Look, it was impossible for me. Whether I told you or not I'd have let somebody down. I'm glad it's all out in the open, and there are no more secrets. Anyway I've helped you too. I knocked that Ted off you, didn't I?'

'Fair enough.' Bernadette touched her shoulder. 'You're not bad for a Posh Judy.'

Nick kept up his hard stare. But his face crumpled, as the pain in his head returned.

Chapter 15

That afternoon they sat through normal lessons. With its windows whitewashed the classroom was dim.

Nobody was let out for games. They were being kept in the school building.

And, one by one, they were called out of class. You were escorted away by a teacher, and brought back. The boys had to report to Mister Britten, and the girls to Mrs Sweetman or Miss Wells. The rumour quickly spread that you would be stripped and searched.

That sent Laura into a panic. The Key was around her neck. What was she going to do now? She longed to talk to Bernadette.

But there was no chance to say anything before Madame Minet came to the door and, following a strict alphabetical order, called Laura out.

She was marched down the corridors. Helmeted scuffers stood at the corners, in case some rogue kid made a run for it. The school was more like a prison, this afternoon.

Minnie Mouse was as kind as ever. 'All to do with the emergency, you know. Not to worry.'

But Laura had absolutely no doubt that all of this was happening, not because of the emergency, but because of her.

Laura wasn't surprised to find Miss Wells sitting in the staffroom, waiting for her. A screen had been set up, like a doctor's surgery. There was also a lady in a white coat with scientific-looking equipment, anonymous white boxes, and a female police officer. The white-coat had arrived in the Jag with the American flag.

Miss Wells said, 'This is Doctor Smythe, and WPC Bryant. They're not here to hurt you. They're here to help you. We all are.'

'How does a strip-search help me?'

The WPC said gravely, 'The Emergency Powers Act has been passed by Parliament this morning. Part of the police's job is to screen out subversives.'

'Oh, yes, the fourth year is full of subversives.'

'Don't be mouthy, Miss Mann,' Miss Wells said sharply. 'Is there anything you want to tell us yourself? Anything you've seen or heard that strikes you as strange? *Anything you have in your possession that you shouldn't?*'

'Don't you remember?' Laura snapped.

Miss Wells glared. The WPC and the lady doctor exchanged glances, then shrugged. A nutty kid.

Miss Wells said, 'Go behind the screen. Pass out your clothes for the WPC to inspect. The doctor will come behind the screen to examine you.'

'Have you got our parents' consent?'

'We don't need it,' said the policewoman. Her voice was hard now. 'It's a national emergency. Please don't make trouble, miss.' And somehow, without moving, she drew Laura's attention to the gun at her waist.

Laura didn't have a choice. She went behind the screen and begin to strip off. When she handed out her blazer to the WPC she heard a clicking noise. She peeked over the screen. The scuffer was passing a kind of plastic wand over her blazer. It was connected to a box with a dial.

'What's that?'

'You wouldn't understand,' said Miss Wells.

'I've seen James Bond. That's a Geiger counter. Why are you worried about radioactivity, Miss Wells?'

The WPC said evenly, 'Get back behind the screen please, miss.'

She didn't see any way out. There was nowhere to hide the Key, which would be exposed when she took her blouse off. Laura played for time, messing about with her school tie, hoping that something would turn up. Nothing did.

She unbuttoned her blouse. The Key wasn't there.

When she thought it over she knew exactly what had happened.

She submitted to the rest of the examination with a grin of triumph. The WPC searched every scrap of her clothing. The doctor briskly searched her too, even looking inside her mouth, and she passed peculiar-looking instruments over her skin. She found nothing.

By the end of it, Miss Wells's face was like thunder.

When she got back to class, Laura whispered to Bernadette, 'How did you do it?'

'What?'

'Get the Key off me, without me even noticing?'

'That would be telling.'

'Where have you put it?'

'You'll only blab. We'll fetch it at the end of the day. And Miss Wells's phone. One-nil to us, our kid.'

'They're getting tougher, Bern. That policewoman had a gun, and banged on about national emergencies. We won't get away with it much longer.'

Bernadette shrugged. 'We'll just have to deal with that when it happens. Now get on with your irregular verbs. Or whatever it is we're doing. I'm a bit lost myself.'

'Bern?'

'What?'

'Thanks.'

Bernadette sighed. 'Where would you be without me?'

At home, Dad hadn't phoned.

That night Mum cooked a roast dinner, a chicken with stuffing, roast potatoes, sprouts, carrots, gravy. She could cook well, when she stuck to simple things. She served wine for herself and Mort, lemonade for Laura.

The three of them sat around the small dinner table, Mort, Mum and Laura. Mort was in his uniform, with his jacket on and his tie done up. He'd made an effort. Mum was dolled up too, with bright make-up and her hair in a bun.

They ate in silence, except for the tapping of the cutlery on the plates, and the brisk crunching noise Mort made as he chewed. Under her fear of him, Laura had developed the kind of dislike for Mort that was so intense that everything he did, even the way he ate, irritated her.

Mort's big new rental telly was on in the background, in case of any more news about the emergency. A film called *Mrs Miniver* was being shown, made during the Second World War, a kind of propaganda thing about a woman being brave. Normal programmes had been scrapped, except for morale-boosting stuff like this, and the news, and even that was mostly government announcements.

'Great chow, Veronica,' Mort said at length, wiping his mouth. 'Traditional English fare, right? My compliments to the chef.'

Mum blushed. 'Well, we may as well eat everything up before it spoils. We won't have this on rations, you know.'

'Rations?' Laura asked. 'Who said anything about rations?'

'Oh, it's the first thing they'll bring back, you'll see. I wonder if they'll give us new cards.'

'Don't worry your pretty head, little missy,' said Mort, and he actually winked at Laura. 'I'll see you're OK.'

Laura glared at him. 'The way you saw Mum was "OK" in the war? I'll take my chances, thanks.'

Mort laughed. 'You'll come begging when you run out of candy bars.'

'Don't hold your breath.'

'Oh, Laura,' her mother said tiredly.

Mum served up rice pudding. Laura helped her with the dishes, taking care never to be left alone with Mort. The roast had been OK, but the pudding was both burned and cold. Laura would have thought that was against the laws of physics. But Mort ate up his portion as if he was a starving man, and his compliments made Mum blush again.

Laura helped clear up. By the time Mum served coffee, and Mort had lit up a fat cigar and loosened his tie, the film was ending in a surge of weepy music.

'There now follows a statement by the Prime Minister, the Right Honourable Harold Macmillan.'

'Good evening. I talk to you now at a time of grave international crisis. And yet I bring hope . . .'

'Oh, great,' Laura said. 'What's on the other side?'

'Macmillan,' Mort said.

'Hush, Laura,' Mum said.

The three of them sat down on the settee and armchair, facing the telly.

Macmillan's face was long and mournful, with sad bloodhound eyes and sagging pouched cheeks. He had been born during Queen Victoria's reign, and he looked it.

'I'm sure you're all aware, from President Kennedy's announcement and the news that has emerged during the day, of the continuing crisis over the Russian military adventure in Cuba. I have had repeated conversations with President Kennedy in the course of the day, and with other world leaders, as well as the Secretary General of the United Nations. Negotiations are intense and continuing, but though there are chinks of light in the clouds of despondency, I have to tell you that we have yet to make a breakthrough . . .'

Mort stabbed his cigar at the screen. 'I'll tell you where that old guy is right now,' he said. 'He's in a bunker, with his War Cabinet and his military chiefs. I went there once. Bleak kind of place in the Cotswolds. They call it "Turnstile".'

'*They're* all right then,' Laura said.

Mort said, 'It's not a place you'd want to be. They don't have their families down there with them, you know.'

'Why, look,' Mum said now. 'It's Mister Churchill!'

There was the familiar round, almost babyish face, the small serious mouth, the bulldog jowls. A caption read: 'The Rt. Hon. Sir Winston Churchill, MP.'

'My gosh,' said Mort, 'your wartime leader.'

'He's nearly ninety, I think,' Mum said.

Mum and Mort leaned closer. Their faces were lit up by the telly's silver-grey glow, and Laura imagined a million other homes, millions of other people, all staring at Churchill's comforting, moon-like face.

Churchill's voice was a bass rumble. 'The Prime Minister

has asked me to speak to you tonight, at this time of national crisis, as one who has seen it all before. How could I refuse? Even when he told me there would be no fee, I still couldn't refuse . . .'

Mum laughed, besotted, as if Churchill was a movie star. 'Always a bit of a one, old Winnie.'

'I once saw one of his scripts for a wartime speech,' Mort said. 'Pinned up inside a command bunker. It was set out like a poem, you know? It's no accident he speaks so well. He plans every word.'

Churchill's face dissolved to a map of Britain, and he talked about the new arrangements for the government during the State of National Emergency.

The central government would be working in its bunker, but there would be twelve 'Regional Commissioners', like local prime ministers, to run things in case communications broke down. The commissioners would be cabinet ministers. In the north-west, where Liverpool was, the Regional Commissioner would be Edward Heath, the government Chief Whip.

Under Heath there would be an Emergency Committee, including the Mayor of Liverpool, councillors, aldermen and town clerks. There would be an Army District Commander and a Regional Director of Civil Defence to run the military in the area. The committees would meet in bunkers and basements, and would stay there until the emergency was over.

There was a 'War Book', Churchill said, with instructions for what the committees and commissioners were supposed to do. Everything had been worked out in detail, he said.

Laura stared at the little captions. 'Regional Director of

Civil Defence'. That was who she was supposed to call about the Key, if the worst came to the worst. Maybe if she did call the number Dad had given her, she would be taken down into a bunker, like Mr Macmillan, until Dad could get to her.

She wasn't sure she had ever really taken Dad's dire instructions about the Key seriously. But seeing those words on the telly screen made everything seem real.

Churchill's face returned. 'Of course war has not yet been declared. But such is the lightning pace of modern technology that such a war as we must now contemplate may be over before it has time to be declared – or peace to be brokered.

'The French have a saying for times like this. *Déjà vu.* Well, we British don't say much. We just roll up our sleeves and get on with the job. On the accession of our gracious Queen Elizabeth, I said that she came to the throne at a time when mankind is poised between world catastrophe and a golden age. And so it is now. But when we have come through this crisis together, when we have built a better world for our children, future generations will speak of the courage we showed at a time of unparalleled danger. I wish you victory, and peace.' He held up his fingers in his familiar V-sign.

The picture faded to a Union Jack, rippling in the wind.

Another film started up. *The Dam Busters.* Wartime heroics.

'Oh, good,' Mum said. 'I always liked Richard Todd.'

Laura stood. 'I'm going to my room.'

Mort looked up at her. 'Laura. Listen to me. Everything will be OK, for you and your mother. There are places I can take you. I won't let anything bad happen to you.' He smiled, but his small eyes were blank. 'You're going to have to learn to trust me.'

Laura felt cold, deep inside. There was nowhere safe, she thought, nowhere in a dangerous world, not even in her home.

She walked out.

Mum called after her, 'Put the kettle on, would you, love?'

Chapter 16

Wednesday 24th October. 8 a.m.

I keep expecting Mort to just grab me, to drop the game-playing. He's still holding off. How much longer?

Dad called this morning.

'It's getting a lot harder to make these calls,' he said.

I could hear wind and birdsong. 'Where are you?'

'In a phone box. I tiptoed out of the base. I told them I needed a packet of fags.'

'You're giving up smoking.'

'They'll see through that, then. Not much of a spy, am I? It'll get better before it gets worse, Laura. The next few days are critical. In the crisis. Everything depends on how the Russians accept Kennedy's blockade of their ships. And –' Beep beep beep. 'Oh, damn –'

That was it.

Trust Dad not to have any coppers. No threepenny bit in his sock. He might win the Cold War but he's not very smart sometimes.

I still don't know what to tell him about Miss Wells, and Agatha. I haven't even spoken to him properly about Mort.

It's all about the Key. He gave it to me to make me feel

safe, but it's doing the opposite. A bit of me doesn't want to tell him about any of that, doesn't want to worry him.

Another bit wants to sit on his knee and curl up, as if I was five years old.

I wonder when I'll speak to him again.

'Morning, love!'

The wireless was on. Vera Lynn introducing wartime favourites. Mum was singing along as she set out breakfast dishes on the dinner table in the parlour. She looked happy as a bird. War was evidently good for her.

The newspaper was on the coffee table. But it wasn't the *Liverpool Echo* as usual. It was called *Britain Today: A Publication of the Central Office of Information.* It was only four pages. On the front was a photograph of the Queen and her children getting on a plane for Canada. 'Her Majesty's thoughts are with us!' Another photo showed London Zoo animals being led out of their cages, to somewhere safer. And in art galleries, precious paintings and sculptures were being boxed up and put in cellars.

There was an item on sport, which had all been cancelled, including Joel's precious football. The whole of the back page was given over to a big full-page feature called 'Dig for Victory'. It showed how you could dig up your back garden and grow your own vegetables and keep chickens, just like in the war.

It wasn't much of a newspaper. No entertainment news, no cartoons, not even a crossword. And there wasn't a shred of real news about what was happening on the other side of the world, in Cuba.

Mum said, 'Oh, look what came in the post.'

There was a stern-looking brown envelope on the coffee table. Mum drew out two bits of grey card, both stamped with serial numbers. One was from the Department of Pensions and National Insurance.

Mum said, 'It's your identity card, dear. Just like during the war.'

It had spaces for a small photo, a name, address, and a National Insurance number. Mum had stuck a photo in the space, and filled in Laura's details: MANN, L. There was her birth date, 6th September 1948.

Just as on Miss Wells's driving licence.

'I got the photo from your passport. And look at this.'

The other item was a little book from the Ministry of Agriculture, Fisheries and Food. *RATION BOOK: If Found Please Return to Any Food Office*. Laura's name and address had been filled in on the cover. Inside was a dreary list of allowances. Thirteen ounces of meat a week, six ounces of marge, two pints of milk.

Mum took that back. 'I'll go shopping later.' She went on with the breakfast, humming to Vera Lynn. She didn't seem at all bothered by the idea of having to queue for hours for bits of scrag end.

Laura tucked the identity card in her blazer breast pocket. It still smelled of gum where Mum had stuck on the photo. Then she grabbed a piece of toast and left the house, managing to avoid Mort again.

She didn't bother waiting for a bus. She just walked.

In fact she only saw two buses this Wednesday morning. One had soldiers in it. The other was full of little kids, who peered out of the windows sadly. She wondered where they were being taken.

Everything was different, even compared with the urgent mood yesterday.

There were queues at all the shops she passed, especially the food shops, the butcher's and baker's and grocer's, even the ones that weren't open yet. Laura supposed all the old stock would soon run out, as people grabbed what they could. Panic buying.

There were long queues at the petrol stations too. LAST PRE-RATION SUPPLIES, said a sign. FIRST COME FIRST SERVED. Another sign made her smile uneasily. It had read, LAST CHANCE TO FILL UP BEFORE THE A-ROAD. Some wag had crossed out ROAD and written in BOMB.

There seemed to be a lot of ambulances about. But they were calling at homes and *delivering* people, not collecting them. Sickly little kids with tubes in their noses, old people like shapeless grey lumps in wheelchairs. Nick was right. They were clearing the hospitals, for the war casualties to come.

There were road blocks on the main roads. Checkpoints. She saw one car being impounded, a fat salesman type complaining as two scuffers prepared to take it away.

And, nailed to telephone posts, there were signs directing you to bomb shelters, in pub cellars, and old air-raid shelters in the parks.

School looked as if it had been vandalised, with its windows clumsily splashed with whitewash.

She hung around by the gate. She wondered why she had come here at all. After all, Miss Wells lurked inside. But where else could she go? And at least in there she would be surrounded by a few relatively sane people, like Mrs Sweetman, and Joel, and Bernadette. She would be as safe in there as anywhere.

She walked into the school.

After assembly, Miss Wells told her form that the pupils were going to be taught more survival skills. A batch of seeds had been shipped in from the Ministry of Agriculture, and in the afternoon everyone was going to go out and dig up the playing field and plant cabbages and sprouts and other winter vegetables.

They started that morning with basic lessons about vegetables. They had to copy out pictures of carrots and cauliflowers into their jotters, from colourful little books. 'This is for those of you who think vegetables just come in plastic bags from the Co-op, ha ha,' said Miss Wells.

The books were meant for junior-school kids. In Laura's copy, some seven-year-old had scrawled SUPERCAR across a picture of a leek.

'I can't believe we're doing this,' she said.

Bernadette shuddered delicately. 'Ugh,' she whispered. 'Me. A farmer. With these nails?'

Joel had come to sit at the back with them. He was having trouble holding a pencil in his plastered fingers. He whispered, 'They're just keeping us busy. Distracted, while they crack down. They've already started. They've taken control of the food stocks, the petrol, the hospitals. Now they're making sure there's no way out of the country. They've grounded all the planes, BEA and BOAC. And stopped all the ferries. Roadblocks on the motorways. And they're rounding up "known subversives". Card-carrying Communists. Union leaders. There's a rumour they've arrested half the Labour Party front bench. And the telly folk. They've arrested David Frost! The excuse is, while we're getting ready for war, Soviet spies will start mucking about. Sabotage. Whipping up strikes. Spreading lies. That kind of thing.'

Laura asked, 'How do you know all this? It wasn't in the news.'

'Well, it wouldn't be,' Joel said. 'I've got contacts. Word of mouth.'

Bernadette said, 'They'll be coming for you, H-Bomb Girl. Nothing to stop them now.'

'So what should we do?'

Joel said, 'Stick with me. I've got a plan. At break, bring what you need. Not your satchels.'

Bernadette laughed at him. But she put her scarf around her neck.

And Laura slipped her diary into her blazer pocket.

Miss Wells glared at them, suspicious, cold, determined.

At break, the school gates were locked, and there were two scuffers standing on guard.

Nick was waiting for them outside the railings. He was hunched up in a heavy overcoat, thin and pale. His face was still swollen, his eyes hidden behind his sunglasses, though the day wasn't bright. 'Hello, losers.'

Bernadette sniffed. 'I'm not the old man hanging round a school fence.'

'Never mind that,' Joel said. 'Did you make the arrangements?'

'Yeah, yeah,' Nick said.

Laura didn't know what arrangements they meant. 'How's the head?'

'Like a red hot poker up the nose. Getting kicked in the head isn't like it is in the movies.'

'If you went back to the doctor, maybe –'

'Mind your own business.' That was a snarl.

'Somebody's coming,' Joel said.

The two scuffers opened the school gate. A green army van drove through, and squaddies started jumping out even before it had stopped. Two military officers, one in green and one in blue, got out and walked towards the school. The one in blue looked like Mort. And behind him rolled a man in a motorised chair. Miss Wells walked out to meet the officers.

Laura knew who that was. 'The Minuteman.'

'Who?' Nick asked.

'Nobody good.'

The Minuteman was here just for *her*, Laura thought. He was manipulating the British Army to come get her. His power was beyond scary.

'Time's up for you, Laura,' said Joel. 'Nothing to stop them now.'

Laura asked, 'How can we get out? There are scuffers on the gate.'

Bernadette grinned. 'That's the easy bit. We've done it before.' She took off her long black scarf and threw it up so it looped over the spike at the top of the railings. 'Give me a bunk up, Joel. And keep your hands off my bum.'

Even now, Laura hesitated before she followed.

Up to now, in all the strangeness and upset that had gone on, she had kept up the normal routines of life. Home, school, home, school, give or take a bit of burglary and hiding in cellars. If she ran off now she would be making a decisive break. And she couldn't imagine how her life would be after that.

A bit of her wondered if she should just give up. Surrender to the Minuteman and Miss Wells, and just hand over the Key. But she didn't know what they wanted to do with an ignition key for a Vulcan bomber. Nothing good, she imagined, given the way they'd behaved towards her.

And besides, Dad had given the Key to *her*. She was frightened, but she resented them trying to come between her and Dad.

Stuff them all, she thought angrily.

Miss Wells saw them and pointed.

Scuffers blew their whistles, and squaddies came running, rifles in their hands. As two puffing squaddies plodded by, one smart-alec kid shouted, 'I'll give you two to one on the fat bloke!'

Laura didn't wait any longer.

When they were all over the railings Nick stuck his fingers in his mouth and whistled. With a whine like huge buzzing wasps, two bright red scooters came belting out of the car park at the back of the pub over the road. Bert Muldoon was riding one, Mickey Poole the other.

'Woodbines to the rescue!' Nick shouted.

'Vespas,' Joel said. 'Cool.'

Bernadette was suspicious. 'How can you lot afford Vespas?'

Nick grinned. 'It's a National Emergency.'

Laura said, 'I'm impressed. You've planned all this.'

Nick eyed Laura. 'I still don't know what the deal is with you, darling. But we Woodbines don't fancy living in Heathograd any more than you do. Come 'ead, let's leg it before the scuffers get here.'

He insisted on driving one of the scooters. So Laura was jammed in between Nick and Bert, three of them on a scooter meant for two. Bernadette and Joel piled on behind Mickey Poole.

The Vespas roared away. Laura felt a deep surge in her stomach as the acceleration cut in, and the wind whipped back her hair. She wished she had a helmet.

'They're following!' Bert shouted.

Laura looked back. That green army truck had come barrelling out of the school gates, scattering kids as it went.

Nick grinned. 'Not for long!' He hauled the handlebars to the right.

Laura was wrenched sideways, and she nearly let go of Nick. They drove over somebody's front lawn, through an alleyway between two semis, over a back garden that was half dug up for vegetables, and then squirted through an open gate. It was terrifying. Nick didn't slow down for a second, even though both Laura and Bert yelled. Nick's mood had switched from miserable to manic in an instant.

But it worked. Mickey and the others were still following, but they had lost the army truck.

Chapter 17

At the Jive-O-Rama they piled off, breathing hard, exhilarated by the ride.

Bernadette fixed her hair with quick pushes from her fingers. Then she turned on Nick. 'Are you crazy? They must know we hang around here. They'll be down like a shot.'

'*With* a shot,' Bert Muldoon said gloomily. 'Did you see those rifles?'

Nick lit up a ciggie and began dragging on it furiously. He walked backwards and forwards, and every so often he lifted his hand to his head. He pointed at Joel. 'Don't blame me. His idea.'

'Come on,' Joel said. 'We got our skins saved here once before. By *her*.' He pointed to the doorway to the cellar.

Agatha's face loomed out of the darkness. Laura thought she saw her lips move, silently mouthing words. *Hello, Mum.*

Laura shivered. Agatha ducked out of sight.

'She's spooky but she helps us,' Joel said. 'And, anyway, anybody got a better plan?'

'All right,' Bernadette said. 'Let's just get inside. And hide these scooters.'

Bert and Mickey wheeled the scooters round the back of the house.

The others clattered through the open doorway. Joel ran his hand up and down the door frame. 'What happened to the door?' It was missing. The hinges had been unscrewed and ripped out of the paint.

At the bottom of the stairs, there was no Little Jimmy, and nobody in the cellar club. The cellar was cluttered with lumber, and mattresses were piled up against one wall. They waited, uncertain.

Bernadette called, 'Big Jimmy? You open?'

Big Jimmy appeared out from under the heap of mattresses. He wiped his hands on a rag and came over. He grinned, but it looked forced. 'How's my best customers today?'

Nobody replied.

'Like that, huh? Well, I don't think Mister Heath has impounded the last of my coffee yet. What is it, espressos all round? Agatha!'

'We haven't paid our door money,' Bernadette said. 'Where's Little Jimmy? Skiving off?'

Big Jimmy said, 'They took him away.' He kept smiling bravely.

'Who?'

'Mister Heath. Big green Corpy bus came by. Out of Service, it said. Full of kids. Out came a scuffer. Our Jimmy was on his list. Evacuated.'

'Where to?'

'Lake District. Had to pack him a suitcase. You should have seen him struggling with the great big thing.' His grin faltered.

Laura asked, 'Why didn't you go with him?'

'Scuffers wouldn't let me. Kids only. Mums can follow later. Of course Jimmy's mum's dead anyway. So he's on his own.'

'So we're about to go to war, and they break up families,' Bernadette said. 'Brilliant.'

'It's what they did last time,' Laura said, thinking of Mum.

Jimmy said, 'Ten million people they'll be moving, they told me.'

Laura wanted to hug him for comfort, but she knew it would be the wrong thing to do.

They sat at a table. Nick lit up another ciggie from the stub of the last one.

Agatha brought out coffees. She leant over Laura. She smelled of washing-up liquid, bleach and coffee. But there was another scent, something milky underneath, that somehow drew Laura to her.

'You did right,' Agatha said to Laura.

'What?'

'To come here. Have you got it?'

'Have I got what?'

'Your diary.'

Laura tried not to look down at the lump in her blazer, the diary in her inside pocket. 'How do you know about that?'

Agatha whispered, 'I knew you'd have it. It has to be there. To close the loop.'

'What loop?'

'The loop in time. The loop connecting future to past.' She turned and walked away.

Mickey said, 'That woman's scary.'

Bert said, 'You'd still give her one, though.'

They both laughed.

There was a warbling, like a bird. They all looked at each other.

Bernadette swore. She dug in her handbag and pulled out the 'phone'. It was flashing blue, and making that shrill sound.

'Nice fag case,' Bert said.

'It's not a fag case,' Nick said.

'Then what?'

'You don't want to know.'

Mickey and Bert shrugged.

Tentatively Bernadette opened the phone. The warbling stopped. Then she swivelled the phone around on the table-top so Laura could see. 'Guess who it's for.'

Laura peered into the tiny screen.

Text Message
FROM: Miss Wells
TO: Laura
MESSAGE: You can run but you can't hide. Old line but true. Any time you need help press the button with the little green phone.

Laura snapped shut the phone. It sat on the tabletop.

They all stared at it, as if it was an unexploded bomb.

'We ought to get rid of that thing,' Joel said. 'They might be able to track it. Find us that way.'

Bernadette said, 'Let's smash it up. Jimmy's got a hammer.'

'No.' Laura closed her hand over the phone and put it in her pocket. 'We ought to keep it.'

'Why?'

'You never know. I'll take the risk.'

Nick turned his ravaged face to her, his eyes masked. 'But if we stay together we all share the same risk. Don't you see that much, you stupid little bint?'

Laura was shocked.

Bert said, 'That kicking you got has done wonders for your charm, mate.'

Jimmy's hammering got louder.

'Oh, for chuff's sake.' Nick buried his head in his hands.

Laura wanted to get away from the atmosphere at the table. She got up and walked over to the heap of mattresses. 'Jimmy!'

He stuck his head out of the heap. 'What's up? Coffee cold?'

'What are you up to?'

'My patriotic duty. This is my Inner Refuge.'

'Your what?'

'Look.' He crawled out and lifted back the mattresses. They had been heaped up on doors, which had been taken off their hinges and leaned against the wall. Jimmy was proud of his workmanship. 'See, there's a bit of two-by-four nailed to the floor so you have something to prop up the doors. Then you pile up mattresses and stuff on top. The angle of the doors has to be exactly sixty degrees to the floor, for maximum protection.'

'Who says?' Bernadette asked.

'The government,' Joel said. 'He's getting all this from one of their leaflets.'

'Come inside.' Jimmy beckoned Laura, and she followed him under the doors.

Inside, it was like being in a little hut. Jimmy had spread sleeping bags over the floor. 'I have torches and a lamp. I'm supposed to collect fourteen days' worth of food and water. I made a start.' He showed her bottles, canteens, cans of beans and Spam. 'Even got a camping stove. Of course I'll need less, now that Little Jimmy won't be in here with me.'

'But what's it for?'

'To keep out the bombs,' Jimmy said. 'And the fall-out. Which is something to do with radiation. Fourteen days in here, you should be OK.'

'Where do you go to the toilet?'

He grinned. 'I'll have bottles. Empty cans. We got by, in the bomb shelters in the war. Or course we weren't down there for fourteen days at a time. Look here.' He found an old tin cigar box under a heap of cans.

'What's in there?'

'Our birth certificates. Mine, anyway. I had to give Little Jimmy his. My marriage licence, to Jimmy's mother, God rest her. Our ration cards and identity cards. Though I kept my old one from the war. Bank book, driving licence. All for when it's over, you see. The fourteen days. And things start to get organised.'

Laura looked at all this stuff. Here was Jimmy's whole life in a tin box.

Huddling fearfully under the doors, it was hard to remember this was the Jive-O-Rama. A place where you came to have fun. Now it was a place infected by fear and dread, like everywhere else.

'They're here,' Agatha said.

They scrambled out of the refuge. Laura heard engines rumbling outside, heavy vehicles rolling up.

Shadows crossed the stairs, and a torch flashed.

Laura heard a familiar growl. 'Is that little baggage down there? We done enough running around for one stupid kid.' The Minuteman, trapped at the top of the stairs.

Everybody was agitated but Agatha. She just stood there like a shadow.

'Agatha,' Laura said. 'Which way?'

'Like before. Come on.' She turned to lead the way out the back. Laura saw that the hardboard was already off the hole in the wall.

Bernadette said, 'They'll dig us out. This time they mean business.'

'We'll go on,' Agatha said.

'Where?'

Agatha wouldn't say.

Seconds left.

'Move it,' Big Jimmy said.

Joel grinned at him. 'I thought you trusted the government.'

'Not that much. Look, I take as I find. Agatha is a good women who needed somewhere to hide, and that's enough for me. And when the Army comes breaking down my door hunting for kids – well, I know which side I'm on.

'Enough chit-chat. You lot, get down the hole. You and you,' he said, pointing to Bert and Mickey, 'stay sat there. I'll get some more coffee. We'll hold them up.'

Bert and Mickey shrugged and sat down.

There was a clatter of boots on the stairs. A gruff male voice called, 'Hello? Anybody here?'

Jimmy's eyes were popping. 'Go, go!'

Agatha had already disappeared into the hole. Laura hurried after her. Bernadette, Nick and Joel scrambled behind.

Laura looked back. Just as Joel was putting the board back over the hole, she saw scuffers and squaddies coming cautiously down the stairs into the club. The soldiers had ugly looking rifles under their arms.

Jimmy walked forward, arms wide. 'Gents. What can I get you soldier boys? Jukebox, sixpence a throw. How about

Adam Faith, "When Johnny Comes Marching Home"?'

One of the soldiers lifted his rifle butt and hit Jimmy in the belly. Jimmy went down as if his bones had turned to water. Mickey and Bert lunged forward.

That was all Laura saw. Joel pushed her away. 'There's nothing we can do.'

She stumbled off into the dark. She heard angry shouts, and the thud of fists and rifle butts hitting flesh.

They huddled in the dark of next door's cellar. Agatha had a torch. Their faces floated in its light.

Bernadette said, 'So now what? They'll find that hole in the wall as soon as they finish with Jimmy and the boys.'

'We go on,' Agatha said. 'I told you.'

She led them to the back of the cellar, and pulled out a loose brick. Something small and furry jumped out of the hole, and went squeaking off. They flinched, all except Agatha, who seemed to be used to rats.

'What's through there?' Laura hissed.

'Another cellar. Next door.'

'And then what?' Joel asked. 'Another cellar, and another?'

'Yes,' Agatha said, matter-of-fact. 'We'll work our way west. Towards the city centre. There are other deep places there. More cellars. Storage places under warehouses.'

'Like the Cavern,' Nick said.

'Yes. And sewers.'

'Sewers. Oh, cracker,' Bernadette said.

'There have been traders coming into Liverpool since Roman days,' Agatha said. 'Smugglers too. There are all sorts of cellars, tunnels. Bunkers and air-raid shelters from the war. The place is a warren. Most big cities are, underground.'

Laura asked, 'And then what?'

'That's up to you,' Agatha said. 'At least you will have options.'

She led the way.

Laura followed her. 'Agatha. What about my mum? She'll be scared out of her wits. When can I go home?'

Agatha turned to her, her face silhouetted by her torch. 'Don't be stupid,' she said.

The phone in Laura's pocket, heavy and alien, began to ring again.

Chapter 18

Wednesday 24th October. 11 p.m.

Writing this by candlelight. Stub of pencil from my blazer pocket. Didn't think to bring a pen from school.

Haven't seen daylight since about three. We reached this last hole about six, I'd say.

Eight hours underground. About fifteen hours since I last spoke to Mum.

Joel thinks we're somewhere in the warehouse area, not far from the docks. Maybe near Mathew Street where the Cavern is. We've come miles, then.

It stinks in here, of rat poo and damp. I'm cold. My school blazer's not enough. I wish I had my overcoat.

No phone in this cellar. I wish I knew what was going on.

Three days to Black Saturday. The tension just keeps winding up and up. It's like waiting for Christmas (sarcasm).

We're frightened. But exhausted. I think I could sleep. We need to be sharp tomorrow, whatever happens.

Nick is handing out pills.

Agatha pulled back a filthy blanket to reveal a row of old lemonade bottles full of water. A rat scuttled away. 'The water's clean,' Agatha said.

Laura said, 'It must have taken you ages to get this lot together.'

Agatha looked at Laura, her eyes pits of blackness. 'I was born in a bunker. I grew up in tunnels, in the dark. Where I come from, everybody does. The rats aren't so bad. You can deal with that. I always knew I'd have to go back.'

'"Where I come from",' Bernadette said. 'And where's that, Agatha?'

Nick laughed, raucous. His mood had switched to manic. 'All you have to do is take your magic pills, and you can follow Alice-Agatha here down her rabbit holes. Look. I've got Prellies, and Black Bombers, and Purple Hearts, and French Blues. A regular chemist's shop in my pocket.'

'These are all amphetamines,' Joel said. 'Uppers. Pep pills.'

'Of course they are. This is what we used on stage in Hamburg, so we could keep playing "Besame Mucho" for German prozzies until the small hours.'

The others took the pills gingerly. Their faces were a circle of anxiety, lit up by a couple of candles.

They were alone in this cold damp place, with tunnels stretching off into the unknown dark all around them. And in the middle of all that, Laura thought, here they were stuck with a nutcase who was trying to make them take drugs.

Nick cried, 'Swallow! Swallow!' He took a mixed handful of pills and gulped them down with a mouthful of water.

The others passed the water bottle around. But they all palmed their pills, out of Nick's sight.

Agatha said to Nick, 'Your friends back there.'

'Mickey and Bert.'

'They stayed behind to keep the soldiers off us. It was a pretty brave thing to do.'

'Well, we Woodbines are brave,' Nick said. 'Although we're not too pretty.'

'And one of you's not too brave,' Bernadette said harshly.

'Ah, Billy Waddle. Billy Billy Billy.' Nick leaned his head back on the wall. 'I wonder how many other little Waddles are walking around Liverpool. Waddles waddling around, ha ha.'

'Billy's a scumbag.'

'Yes, he is. He's not even a very good drummer.'

Joel's face, shadowed in the flickering light, was a mask of hurt. He asked Bernadette, 'Why *him*? Stupid, shallow, cruel –'

'But good-looking,' Nick said with a sigh. 'Some of us are just drawn to the wrong sort, Joel.'

'This is nothing to do with you, Nick,' Joel snapped.

'Isn't it? Well, what's it got to do with *you*? No, don't answer. I think we all know. You wish that little bleeder in Bern's belly was a half-caste, don't you?'

Joel just launched himself at Nick. He only landed one punch, but Nick screamed from his old wounds. Bernadette and Laura jumped on them.

For ten seconds the cellar was full of struggling and muffled cries. Agatha just sat back, watching.

When the girls got them apart, Bernadette cradled Nick. 'He didn't mean it,' she said. 'That crack about half-castes.'

'He's a get,' Joel said.

Agatha said, 'But he's hurting too. Listen to what he said. "Some of us are drawn to the wrong sort."'

Nick put his shades back on, hiding his damaged eyes.

Laura remembered the way Nick had behaved on stage

and in the club when Billy Waddle had flirted with other girls. 'Bern was jealous,' she said. '*And so were you*, Nick. You fancied Billy too, didn't you? Wow.'

Bernadette's mouth dropped open. She stared at Nick. 'Is she right?'

Nick struggled to sit up. 'We really are crashing through the taboo barriers tonight, aren't we? Yes, all right. I was in love with Billy. Still am. Can't help it any more than you can, Bern. But I never did anything about it.'

Laura said, 'Does Billy know?'

'Oh, of course he knows. He torments me about it. That's what the likes of him do. I always fall in love with the wrong sort. Bits of rough like Billy Waddle. Straight, too.

'But he never wanted me, Bern.' There was a sort of desperation in his voice now. 'He wanted you. Or at least girls like you. He dumped you, but you had him for a while, didn't you? I'll never even have that much.'

Bernadette put her arm around his shoulders. Joel just sat watching them, stranded in his own misery.

Agatha tugged Laura's sleeve, and they moved away a little bit, into the dark.

'I've seen this before,' Agatha said. 'People stuck in situations like this. The pressure gets to them. They turn on each other. Say things they shouldn't say. Or maybe things they should have said a long time ago. Either way, it hurts.'

'Is it getting to me, then?'

'Yes. But you react differently. You soak it up. You don't look inside yourself the same way. You think about other people. You try to cope, to get everybody through. You have a certain strength. That's what I remember about you.'

'"Remember"?'

But Agatha didn't say any more.

'Agatha, listen to me. We'll have to go out tomorrow.'

'Yes. We need food. Better clothes. Candles.'

'There's something else.'

'What?'

'We have to get my mum.' This was a hard thing for her to say. She didn't want to be the adult, to make decisions for her mother. But she didn't see a choice. 'She isn't capable of looking after herself up there. Not without Dad around. She's better off with me, wherever I end up.'

She thought Agatha would say no, or call her stupid as she had before. But she just looked back gravely. 'Your friends won't like it.'

'I know.'

'And your home is the first place they'll be looking for you.'

'I know that too.' She was puzzled by Agatha's reaction. 'You're not trying to talk me out of it.'

'Oh, no. This is something you have to do. Your mother is family.' Agatha smiled thinly. 'I told you, you're strong. I couldn't stop you if I tried.'

She gave Laura the creeps. 'And is it getting to you? This pressure of being stuck down here?'

Agatha shrugged. The candlelight seemed to pick out the lines in her face. 'I'm used to it. And besides.'

'What?'

'I've got you back,' Agatha whispered.

Laura sat rigid.

Agatha leaned over, stiffly, and put her head in Laura's lap.

Laura stroked Agatha's hair. It was cut short, bristly, speckled with grey. And it was patchy, Laura saw. In places it seemed to have fallen out in clumps.

Agatha's shoulders shook, subtly. She was crying.

They were going to have to deal with this, Laura thought. Agatha and her. They would have to dig the truth out between them, and set it before them, and look at it honestly, whatever it was.

But not tonight. First they had to get themselves out of this mess.

She stroked Agatha's hair until the strange, skinny woman started to fall asleep.

She heard a soft thumping sound.

Nick, maddened by the pain of his headaches, was ramming the back of his skull against the brick wall. Bernadette was trying to soothe him.

Nick stopped at last, and lay in Bernadette's arms.

He whispered, 'Nuclear war is glamorous, you know. Those missiles they fire go all the way up into space, before coming down to earth. And the explosions are hotter than the sun. It's like space touching the earth.'

'Hush,' Bernadette said.

'*Suppose you had the power*, Bern. To push the button, like President Kennedy. The power to blow up the whole world. You'd be more powerful than Jesus. Wouldn't you be tempted to do it, just for the hell of it? Wouldn't you? Even if you would die yourself. All that *power . . .?*'

But the pain returned. He cried out, and went back to slamming his head against the wall.

Chapter 19

Laura was jolted awake by a blue flashing, a high-pitched beeping. Everybody was scared, save Agatha.

It was Laura's 'phone' – or rather, Miss Wells's. Agatha had taken it from Laura's pocket and set it up on a heap of rubble. The screen showed the time in big numerals. *7:00:02. 7:00:03. 7:00:04.*

'I thought we ought to make sure we woke up,' Agatha said.

Bernadette hissed, 'You might have set it off.'

Agatha frowned. 'Set it off?'

'You know. Told Miss Wells we're here.'

'It's just a mobile,' Agatha said.

'A mobile?'

She showed Laura what she had done to it to make it work like an alarm clock. 'See, you tab this key and scroll through the menu . . .' As she clicked the phone's keys with her thumb, words and numbers flickered across the little blue screen. 'It has a lot of functions. Calculator.'

'A what?'

'Like a slide rule. There are even a few games in here.' She smiled coldly. 'You can have a bit of fun, even where Miss Wells comes from.'

Laura had no real idea what she was doing. She took the phone and closed it up, so it went dark.

Joel said, '"Where Miss Wells comes from." You don't come from the same place.'

'Sort of. Not exactly. Actually we are from the same date. The year 2007. But we're not from the same timeline. I'm from a different history.'

Everybody just stared.

Joel said, 'Then how do you know how to muck about with a gadget like this?'

'We have similar stuff where I come from. Some things don't change. In fact we both come from 2007, because in both our timelines it took that long to develop the machines that brought us here.'

Laura said, 'We don't have time for this. We've got to get my mother.'

As Laura had known they would, they all argued. And just as Agatha had said she would, Laura held her ground.

Nick barely said a word. He slumped in a corner, eyes hidden, rubbing his face. He had come crashing down from his cocktail of drugs, but he was no better than yesterday.

Bernadette said, 'Whatever we do, I'm dying to drain my 'taters. Where's the bathroom, Agatha?'

'That's a point,' said Joel.

They all dispersed into the corners of the mouldy cellar.

It was Joel who produced something more substantial than just a piddle.

Nick hooted. 'Quite a log you left behind, brain-box. At least we won't have any trouble finding our way back here again.'

Joel hadn't done up his trousers. 'Shut up. We're in a survival situation. Umm, anybody got any un-scratchy paper?'

They moved back through Agatha's tunnel complex, away from the city centre.

They came up out of a dry old sewer, emerging in an empty workmen's hut. They were just outside Queen's Drive, the ring road that ran around the city centre, a short walk from Laura's home in West Derby.

By now it was gone 8 a.m. Even inside the hut the light seemed dazzlingly bright. They hung back for a moment, unwilling to go outside. But they had been sleeping rough in a hole in the ground, and a bit of finger-combing and spit wasn't going to make much difference.

They stumbled out. Nick staggered a bit in the daylight, and lifted his hand to his face. Bernadette took his arm.

It was a Thursday morning, Laura reminded herself. Thursday, 25th October. But it was nothing like a normal morning in Liverpool.

People hurried along the pavement, walking to work, looking anxious. Some clutched their identity cards, as if they expected to be challenged any moment. The shops were all closed up, with hand-lettered signs:

NO BREAD LEFT   NO MILK

RATION CARDS ONLY

There was hardly any traffic about. No buses. A few lorries, some carrying troops or police. One petrol tanker, with squaddies riding shotgun on the back. There were a few private cars on the roads, but they were all heading out of the city, crammed with families, with baggage and furniture piled up on their roof racks.

'If you've got any petrol left,' Joel said, 'you get out of the city.'

There was a phone box in the street, a red kiosk, standing empty. Laura stared at it. Joel said most private phones had probably been disconnected by now, but the public ones might still work.

She probably ought to make the call Dad had told her to make. To the Regional Director of Civil Defence, to tell him about the Key.

But were things bad enough yet? It would seem like giving up. She didn't want to distract her dad, who surely had enough on his plate this morning. And besides, she had Mum to think about. She couldn't just disappear down a hole and forget her.

'I can cope, Dad,' she said to the phone box.

Bernadette said, 'What?'

'Nothing.'

They heard shouting. Laura saw people marching past a block away, hundreds of them, a river of people heading for the city centre. They had banners and placards. They were flanked by police and soldiers. All the police seemed to have guns. The shouts and whistles of the crowd sounded like the cries of seagulls.

Bernadette pointed up. 'Look. A scally spotter.' A helicopter clattered overhead.

'Wouldn't like to be in the middle of that mob when it all kicks off,' Nick said.

Laura asked, 'What do you think it is?'

Joel shrugged. 'A strike? An anti-war demonstration? A rationing riot? There are plenty of people who just get angry when their lives are turned upside down.'

Laura tried to stay in the shadows, and she kept an eye on the soldiers for any signs of blue uniforms, any signs of Mort or the Minuteman.

Joel said, 'I wish we knew what was going on.' Even Joel,

stuck down a hole in the ground, was out of touch with his CND networks now.

'Soon fix that,' Nick muttered.

He led them to an electrical store. It was shut up, but it still had stock in the window, fridges and electric irons. He took off his coat and wrapped it around his hand.

Joel saw what he was going to do. 'Don't. They're probably shooting looters by now.'

Nick grinned. 'Got to catch me first.' He slammed his arm through the window. The plate glass shattered and flew everywhere. They all had to jump back out of the way.

Nick scraped away the glass, and grabbed a transistor radio. It was a brick-shaped Bush model. He switched it on and there was a hiss of static. 'Good,' he said, grinning. 'Haven't got to rob the batteries. Let's leg it.'

'No,' Joel said. 'Walk. Let's not look shifty.'

Bernadette mocked him. 'A real master criminal, you, aren't you?'

But they all followed his advice.

As they walked, Nick turned the radio's tuning knob. A glass panel was marked with the three BBC stations, the Light Service, Home Service and Third Programme. None of them had anything but a recorded message in a posh, plummy man's voice. 'This is a test of the Emergency Broadcasting System. In case of a civil emergency, this system will bring you news, advice and government instructions. This is a test of the Emergency Broadcasting System . . .'

Nick twisted the dial, flitting past bands of static and a few scratchy foreign voices, French and German. Then he came to an American-sounding voice.

'This is Radio Free Luxembourg. Here on Lucky Luxie

we're going to continue to bring you all the hits from the toppermost of the poppermost. But we're also bringing *you* all the news and views *they* don't want you to hear. I'm Tony Dixie. Here are the headlines at 8.30 a.m . . .'

'I know him,' Nick said. 'The DJ. Met him in Hamburg.'

'Shut up,' Joel said.

'That Yank accent is a total fake. Comes from a council estate in Rotherham.'

'Shut *up*,' Laura said.

Kennedy's 'quarantine' of Cuba had started yesterday, Wednesday 24th. Some Russian ships had turned back peacefully enough. Today the Americans were going to raise the crisis at the United Nations. Maybe there could be some more diplomacy there. Nobody had got shot yet. But the tension was still rising.

'They're talking with the ships,' Joel said. 'That's what they're really doing. Kennedy and Khrushchev. Testing each other out. The ships are like chips on a poker table.'

'I hope the soldiers and sailors understand that,' Nick said.

That was it for the news. The DJ said, 'Time for Tricky Dixie to spin another platter.' It was 'Wonderful Land' by the Shadows.

Nick threw the radio against the wall. It broke open and fell silent.

Joel was shocked. 'What did you do that for?'

Nick shrugged. 'I hate the Shadows.'

They neared Laura's home. Nobody could see any scuffers or squaddies about. That wasn't to say they weren't peering out of neighbours' windows.

'We can't just go in the front door,' Laura said. 'We might

be seen. And Mort might be sitting there waiting for me.'

'Can we get in that way?' Bernadette pointed. It was a narrow alley between Laura's house and the one next door. 'There's a window.'

'That's our kitchen window,' Laura said.

'Windows are there to be broken,' Nick said.

Bernadette said, 'If we sneak in we might make it without this Mort spotting us, even if he's there.'

They looked at each other. Joel shrugged. 'Worth a try.'

Nick had a tougher time than with the electrical store's plate glass, because this was a small window of thick frosted glass. When it was broken he pulled the jagged bits out of the wooden frame.

Then Joel wriggled through, followed by Laura. Bernadette came next, moving stiffly. When he tried to climb through, Nick was like a little old man, very fragile, and he complained in a whisper as they helped him through.

Agatha just slid through head first, pulled through her legs, and dropped to the kitchen floor. If she had grown up in tunnels and caves and cellars, Laura thought, she would be used to tight squeezes like that.

Laura led the way to the parlour.

Mum was sitting in an armchair, staring at the blank screen of a turned-off telly. She had her arms folded before her, and she was rocking backwards and forwards.

'Mum.'

'I know what you want.' Her voice was shrill. 'Looters. Mr Churchill warned us about you. Take what you want. Just get out.'

'Mum, it's me. Laura.'

Mum stood and whirled around. 'Laura? Oh, God.' She ran to Laura and grabbed her. 'Where have you been?'

'Is Mort here?'

Mum ran her fingers through Laura's hair. 'You're such a mess. I thought you were dead!'

'Mum – Mort –'

'He hasn't been home. I tried to phone the police but the phone is off. Then the police came anyway, and said you were breaking the curfew, and I'd be breaking the law too if I tried to protect you. I don't think they believed me when I said I didn't know where you were. And then –'

'Mum. It's OK.'

Mum looked at the others. Joel and Bernadette, two scruffy schoolkids. Nick, a battered wreck in a Teddy Boy jacket. Weird Agatha, hanging at the back. 'And who,' she snapped, 'are this lot?'

'They're friends, Mum.'

'Friends?'

'We came to get you. You'll be safer with us. You have to come, right now.'

'She's right.' Agatha came forward and stood beside Laura.

Mum stared at her, and at Laura, at their similar faces – two faces like her own.

Agatha swallowed. 'Come with us. Grandma.'

Mum gave a little cry. Then she collapsed into Laura's arms, in a dead faint. Agatha helped lower her to the floor.

Joel turned to Agatha. '*Grandma*?'

'Long story,' Agatha said. She grinned at him unexpectedly. 'But you're in it, Uncle Joel.'

He just stared.

'Let's get her out of here,' Agatha said. 'Laura, go pack her a bag. Bring sensible clothes. Slacks, shoes.'

Laura ran off to Mum's room. The others went to grab food from the kitchen.

Chapter 20

They returned to the hole in the ground. To Mum's credit, she didn't complain about the dirt or the damp or the cold.

They had stolen a little camping stove and were able to brew mugs of tea. Joel and Bernadette tended to Nick, who was having a headache so bad, he said, he couldn't even see.

Laura, Mum and Agatha sat together, blankets over their shoulders, cradling their mugs. Laura thought how strange they must look, the three of them, their similar faces in the candlelight.

'Dad phoned once since you left,' Mum said. 'Yesterday. He asked for you.'

'What did he say?'

'He's safe. He still hopes the crisis is going to end peacefully. Something about a deal they're cooking up. The Americans have got a missile base in Turkey, near Russia. If the Russians give up their missiles on Cuba, America will give up Turkey in return. But it's all hush hush.' She shrugged. 'Nothing we can do about it either way, I suppose.'

Laura said, 'Mum. I think we've got some talking to do.'

'All right,' Mum said.

'What's Mort doing in our home?'

'He's an old friend. I knew him in the war. I told you.'

'Yes. But, I mean, *how* did you know him, Mum?' She'd never had a conversation like this with Mum before.

Mum faced her. Her eyes were wide, her make-up bold and girlish, the lines around her mouth drawn tight. 'I'm not ashamed of it,' she said. 'Not even in front of you. Why should I be? It was wartime. We were adults. And we were in love.'

'Mum, you weren't an adult. You were, what, fourteen when you met him? My age!'

'But I looked older,' she said. 'I was always mature, you know. More than *you*. You had to be, in those days. There was a war on. You grew up fast.' Her eyes softened. 'He took me dancing. He didn't know how old I was, when we met. When he found out, he saw my identity card one day, he said he didn't mind, although we had to keep it hush hush. He called me his little bobbysoxer.' She giggled.

'Grandma and granddad never knew.'

'They were two hundred miles away.'

'You were living with Cousin Peggy –'

'Oh, that frumpy old bat. She tried to ground me in her flat, but she didn't have a clue . . . We danced away the whole war, it felt like. But then after VE Day he was assigned to a post back in the States. He said he'd send for me.'

'But he never did.'

Mum didn't try to deny that.

'And then you met Dad.'

Dad had flown Spitfires in the Battle of Britain. After the war he stayed in the air force, gradually working his way up the command ladder. In 1946 he was a hero, still young, and lonely. And, in London, just a year after the end of the war, he met Veronica Lynch.

'I was only seventeen, and gorgeous,' Mum said. 'He was terribly shy, but when he plucked up the courage to ask me to go dancing, we got on fine. Next thing you know, we'd fallen in love. A year later we got married, and a year after that –' She patted Laura's cheek. 'You! Nothing but trouble.'

'What about Mort?'

'We always kept in touch, Christmas cards, you know.'

'You forgave him for not sending for you to go to America.'

'Oh, yes. You've met him. You can't be mad at a man like that for long! Then, just a few weeks ago, he phoned and said he was to be stationed for a bit at Burtonwood, you know, the big RAF base on the road to Manchester. And when he heard I was coming back to Liverpool he asked to visit. Well, I said, why just visit? We would have room for him to stay. He said it would be a help; the barracks at Burtonwood are full.'

'Does Dad know about you and Mort? What you got up to in the war?'

'Oh, of course he does, he's not a fool.'

'And he doesn't mind Mort moving in?'

'It's nothing to do with him, is it? We're separated.'

Laura had another hard question. 'Mum – is Mort your lover now?'

'No!' That was another angry word. Then she said, more quietly, 'No. Oh, maybe in the back of my mind I wondered if, you know . . . But I don't think we ever will, not again. He doesn't want me, you see. He wants the little girl he met in the war. But she's gone. Might as well be dead.' She sounded as if she was going to cry. 'We did have some fun, though. Just like the old days. But it got worse after that awful man came.'

'What man?'

'You remember. In the wheelchair. The Minuteman. Some kind of senior officer with new orders for Mort. Well, Mort changed, I can tell you. Oh, he was attentive enough to me. But suddenly he was fascinated by *you*, after that. For something you have, I think. Or something you could tell him. *I* don't know. I didn't care, either.'

Laura said tensely, 'You're my mum. I felt threatened by Mort. You brought him into the home. You should have protected me.'

She gave a soggy smile. 'Oh, Laura, dear, look at me. When have I ever been able to protect anybody from anything?'

Suddenly Agatha put her arms around Mum. 'Don't worry. You're safe now. That's true, isn't it, Laura?'

Laura stared at her. Then she said, 'Yes, that's right.'

Mum seemed as surprised as Laura was to be embraced by Agatha. But she softened into Agatha's hug. It seemed to feel right, to her.

Later Mum tried to nap under her overcoat.

Laura faced Agatha, in the corner of the cellar. 'Now *we* need to talk.'

'I suppose so.'

'You called me "Mum". You called her "Grandma".'

'I know.'

'What's going on, Agatha? How can you be –' She could barely say the word. 'How can you be my *daughter*? You must be twice my age.'

'More. But it's true even so.'

'Where did you come from? How did you get here?' She frowned. 'Never mind that. What do you *want*?'

Agatha dug into the pocket of her ratty overcoat, and pulled out a diary. Laura's diary. Battered and scorched and stained.

Laura dug her own diary out of her blazer pocket. Except for the wear and tear, they were the same. Leather-bound, gold-edged pages. And she could see from the way the pages were dog-eared that Agatha's copy had been filled in, long past where she had got to.

This was a copy of her diary, from the future.

Agatha said, 'All the answers you want are in here.'

Laura looked up. 'There's something you want in return, isn't there?'

'Your Key.'

Laura felt oddly disappointed. 'You too? That's why you've been helping me, and Mum? Just to get your hands on my Key, just like Miss Wells?'

Agatha's cold face showed a flicker of shame. 'If I get the Key, if I use it properly, it will help everybody.'

'How do I know I can trust you?'

'I trust *you*,' Agatha said.

Laura thought it over. 'All right. Here's the deal. Give me the diary first. When I've read it, I'll decide about giving you the Key.'

Agatha hesitated. Then she nodded, and gave Laura the diary.

Laura held the two copies together, one on top of the other. They were a perfect match, one from her own bedroom, the other from some unimaginable future.

Bernadette called, 'You two. Giz a hand. I think he's having a fit.'

Laura could see Nick's long legs in their drainpipe trousers twitching and drumming on the floor. Laura and

Agatha hurried over to help.

It was only later, when things had calmed down and Nick had fallen into a post-drugged sleep, and Mum was dozing too, that Laura opened the diary again.

A smell of soot came off the pages as she turned them. Soot and ash.

Chapter 21

Saturday 27th October 1962.

9 a.m. So, Black Saturday.
Will it be as black as everybody's fearing?

It was utterly weird to see these words, in her own handwriting, but to have absolutely no memory of writing them.

And to see them written down under a date which was still two days in the future.

Noon. News on another transistor radio. Nicked by Nick, ha ha.

Radio Luxembourg says they've started fighting in Cuba. American ships blowing up Russian freighters, Russian subs blowing up the Americans. Then the Americans started dropping bombs on Cuba, and the Cubans and Russians started shooting down planes.

Maybe it won't go any further. But even on Luxembourg there isn't any news.

Have to speak to Dad.

'You aren't in this,' she said to Agatha.

'No. This is how things were, before.'

'Before what?'

'Before I came back. The first time you lived all this. I

wasn't here. There was just you and your mum and your friends, hiding in a cellar from the war . . .'

Saturday 1 p.m. We came up in Whitechapel, in the city centre. Boarded-up stores. Some of them burned out. Nobody about but scuffers and looters playing tick. Rivers of beer and pee flowing down the gutters.

Managed to call Dad from a phone box.

Dad said it was all an accident, in Cuba. Thousands of nervous Americans and Russians standing around with guns. All it took was one shot, to kick it all off. We'll probably never know who fired first.

But they're still fighting.

Dad says it's got worse during the morning. The Russian army has moved in Europe. They came over the Wall and took West Berlin in minutes. Now they are marching into West Germany. The Americans are trying to stop them with battlefield nuclear shells.

'The Davy Crockett,' Dad said. 'The M-388 nuclear bazooka. Six-inch nuclear shells. You'd have to be mad to fire the thing because you'd be inside the blast radius. But the soldiers are firing them even so. What do you think of that?'

So they're using nuclear weapons.

Even so maybe it won't go any further.

I was going to ask Dad about using the Key. But he was cut off.

When I came back to our cellar Mum had run off. Maybe she's gone back home. The others wouldn't let me follow.

I tried to help Mum. I hope she forgives me.

*

9 p.m. Cold and dark. Got to try to sleep.

Maybe it won't go any further.

*

Sunday 28th October. 9 a.m.

OK. OK. Write it down, Laura.

We heard a siren about 8 a.m. And the church bells started ringing.

We came up to see. Well, you had to.

People running everywhere, screaming, trying to get indoors.

We all looked west, towards the docks, where we thought the bomb would fall on Liverpool. Only Nick looked east. I think he was trying to be funny. His head was killing him. He even took his glasses off to see better.

Well, the flash came, not from the west, from the east, like a huge light bulb being switched on, and off. We all saw our shadows stretching in front of us.

'So much for the four minutes,' Joel said.

We all turned around. In the east, a huge black cloud was rising up, above the roofs of the houses. It wasn't like a mushroom, really. More like a huge hammer. The only noise was people screaming, and the sirens, and the church bells. No noise from the bomb.

'They've only gone and done it,' Bern said.

'That was Burtonwood,' Joel said. 'The air base. They're taking out military targets first.'

That meant Mort was almost certainly dead.

And Dad. Almost certainly dead. Already. That was what Dad had always said. Dead, as soon as the bombs start falling.

'Maybe it will stop there,' I said.

Then Bernadette screamed, 'Nick!'

I hadn't looked at him. He was just standing there. His

mouth was stretched wide open, but no noise came out. There was this stuff running down his face. He had looked into the blast. His eyes had melted.

Bernadette tried to grab him. But he punched her, and just ran off.

Joel held her back. 'We have to get back in the hole. The blast.'

I saw a sort of wall of smoke coming down the street. It was still far off. Shop windows were popping. I saw people being thrown up in the air. And a car, up in the air, tumbling.

We all scrambled back into the hole.

The noise came with the blast. It was like a huge wind that passed one way, then got sucked back the other.

Maybe it won't go any further.

Dad is dead.

It still isn't real when I write it down.

*

Sunday 10:30 a.m.

We're at the Jive-O-Rama now. But nobody's jiving.

When the blast had passed over, Joel said we had to get out of there. If a second wave of strikes came, against the cities, we would be too close to the 'epicentre'. We'd be baked alive. Jimmy's cellar, out in the suburbs and away from the city centre, would be a better bet.

All that CND stuff is paying off, for Joel. At least he knows what's going on.

So we came up and ran east, away from the city centre. That huge cloud from Burtonwood still hung over everything, directly ahead of us.

Nobody around. Everybody in hiding, I suppose. Every shop window was broken. Joel says probably every window in

Britain is already smashed.

Joel says it's no accident they struck when they did. It would have been about three in the morning in Washington. JFK asleep, everybody at their lowest.

I stopped at a few phones. I wanted to try phoning Dad, or maybe the Key numbers. None of them worked. Joel just hurried me along.

Now we're in Big Jimmy's Inner Refuge. Under the doors. Joel always said it would be useless, but it's the best we've got.

Big Jimmy is missing Little Jimmy.

*

Sunday 11:00 a.m. Waiting. Busting for a pee.

*

Sunday. 11:30 a.m. Siren. No no no.

*

Sunday. 2 p.m. OK. OK.

So they dropped the bomb on Liverpool.

The light first. Even in a cellar, even under the doors and mattresses, even through my closed eyelids, I could see it.

Then the blast. It was a great door slamming down. The whole place shook. There was a roaring. Then a whoosh like the sea over pebbles. That was the noise of Jimmy's house breaking up, all the bricks washing down on top of us.

The wind just went on and on.

Then it stopped. But it started to get hotter and hotter.

Bern was getting crazy. She wanted to go up to see what was happening. Joel tried to stop her, but he didn't have a chance.

I followed her. Joel too.

The house was flattened. We were lucky Jimmy's cellar

wasn't blocked in.

We looked west, towards the city centre. All the houses that way seemed to be burning. There was stuff whirling up in the air from them. Dust. Soot. Ashes. A black cloud gathering up over it all, with fire at its base. It was very hot up there.

'They hit the docks,' Joel said. 'They've taken out the military sites. Now they're going for economic, industrial, civilian targets.'

'Shut up,' Bern said.

'The Russians will have fired off all their missiles while they had the chance, before the Americans can knock out their bases –'

'Shut up!' Bern started hitting him, like it was his fault. I had to pull her off.

A great wind started blowing, towards the pillar of smoke and fire. And rain started to fall. Big dirty drops the size of marbles.

'We have to get back inside,' Joel said. 'That's the firestorm.'

'The what?'

'And the fall-out is going to come, in an hour or so. Radioactive muck.'

We went back, to where Jimmy was cowering in the dark.

*

Sunday 4th November.

Seven days since the bomb.

I've decided I should save paper.

It's dark and cold.

Jimmy's sick.

We're still in the shelter. Joel says we have to stay here for two weeks, until the fall-out is over. Jimmy agrees. The leaflet he used to build this Inner Refuge says two weeks as well. Good of him to let us in and share this. More than good. Saintly.

What the leaflet didn't say was how the four of us are all supposed to get on, under these stupid doors. We haven't killed each other yet. That's about all you can say.

Jimmy had planned the shelter just for him and Little Jimmy, for fourteen days. We ran out of food on Tuesday, water on Thursday.

On Thursday Jimmy went out to fetch some more food and water. Joel said he shouldn't go at all, but somebody had to, and Jimmy said it was going to be him as he was the oldest and had a duty to protect us. Especially Bern with her little one.

As I said. Saintly.

He brought back bottled water, and crisps and bread and stuff, from the Jive-O-Rama larder.

The power's off, he says. And the water. And the phone.

He peeked outside. He says it looks as if the city is still burning. But there's a vast black lid of cloud over the sky. All the dust from the burning cities I suppose. You can't tell if it's day or night. No wonder it's cold.

Since then Jimmy has got sick. He has a hot fever. His hair is falling out. He has diarrhoea. You can imagine what that's like to live with. Joel says it's the fall-out, and he shouldn't have gone outside.

Bern won't help us with Jimmy. Even though he took us in. She won't even touch him, in case she gets contaminated. She's hard inside. She's thinking ahead about her own survival. And the baby's.

*

Tuesday 13th November. Evening.

The two weeks are up.

Jimmy was bleeding from his gums. And he was sort of bleeding from his skin, even though he wasn't cut anywhere. He was asleep most of the time. But he was incontinent.

So today we decided to take Jimmy to Broad Green Hospital. It was our first big trip outside.

We had to walk Jimmy between us, me and Joel. Bern still won't touch him.

The sky is still black. OK, it's November, but it's so cold.

Half the houses around here are gone, burned or collapsed. Even the ones that stayed up are wrecks.

Bodies everywhere. Huddles in coats. Rats all over the place. We avoided them. Everybody alive is still hiding in holes in the ground I suppose.

All the food shops, if they're still standing, are smashed open, gutted.

We passed a Co-op. A big sign had been stuck over its doorway. REGIONAL COMMISSION. FOOD DISTRIBUTION CENTRE. There was a riot going on. A big mob faced a line of soldiers and scuffers standing in front of the store. That was the only time we saw a scuffer or a squaddie, guarding the food, not the people. I heard one shot fired. We went on.

The hospital was open. It even had lights. Joel said it probably had its own generator.

The crowd of people around it was just vast. Like the streets around a football stadium on a big match day. A noise like a football crowd too, a sort of murmured shout. Except people were limping, or being carried on backs or in wheelbarrows.

We just had to wait and join the crush.

Eventually we came to a scuffer. He took one look at Jimmy. He pinned a big amber star with a number 2 on Jimmy's jumper. Then he showed us which way to take him. Not a nurse or a doctor, a policeman, making medical decisions.

The scuffer looked very young, no older than Nick, say. He wore a cloth over his face. And he was dog tired, with black rings around his eyes. He told us they were calling the war the 'Sunday War'. Over and done in one day. Joel asked him who won. The scuffer just laughed.

We left Jimmy in the car park. Just on the tarmac, no beds or stretchers. There were hundreds like him, all with amber stars, lying there in rows.

Everybody sort of stumbles around. I don't seem to feel anything, about Jimmy or Nick or even Mum and Dad. I suppose we're all in shock.

*

Wednesday 21st November.

I've been working at the hospital.

I'm working with a porter called Fred. He's about fifty, I think. We lug people around, tend simple wounds, that kind of thing.

They need help. Fred says there are three hundred and fifty casualties for every doctor. No drugs left, no bandages, nothing. They used up everything on the first day.

I'm fit enough to do it. And I have a Brownie badge for First Aid. Which is more than most people have got. I had to lie about my age though.

Bern thinks I'm mad to work here. Joel too.

Well, it isn't 'Emergency Ward Ten'.

They call it triage. As soon as you 'present', as the doctors say, they take one look at you and put you in one of three categories. Green, amber, red, like the traffic lights.

In Category One, green, there's a chance you will live and they treat you.

In Category Two, amber, they leave you in a 'holding section', a bit of the car park. If you recover you get moved to Category One. Otherwise you die.

Jimmy died.

They take Category Three, red, to a corner of the car park, and the scuffers shoot you. The doctors say it's kinder that way. They're making a big heap of bodies there.

I've had to carry bodies to the heap. When we do things like that, Fred makes me look at his face, and he smiles, and makes jokes or sings hymns, so I don't have to look at what we're doing.

Fred is an Irish Christian Brother. As it happens he used to work at Saint Edward's, the school where the Woodbines played. Now the school's been taken over as an army base. Lots of them around now, army bases. Fred doesn't wear his dog collar. He says people sometimes attack priests or monks, as if it's all their fault, or God's.

People come walking out of the city centre, even now, looking for help. They'll hold their arms up, to ease the pain in their tight burned skin. Sometimes you see patterns, like shadows where clothes had been, bra straps or belts. You see women with shadows of flowers on them, patterns from their dresses burned into the skin.

Fred says that the people are like snapshots of the bomb. Wherever you happened to be sitting or standing or running at that moment, 11:32 a.m. on Sunday 28th October, is preserved in your body, your skin.

I'm no saint, to be working here. We get paid in food. Everybody's hungry. The only grub is in the government centres, and there's precious little of that. You can forget ration cards. They keep the fact that we get food secret, or everybody would want to be a nurse.

Also I'm hoping that Mum will turn up in the hospital. Where else could she go?

But she hasn't shown up.

One mad woman tried to tell me a horror story, about a little boy she saw lying on his back in Dale Street. His little fingers were burning like candles. Fred shut her up.

*

Monday 24th December.

Over eight weeks since the bomb.

We're burning the bodies. The doctors are getting worried about epidemics now. Typhoid, cholera. The priests make the Sign of the Cross over the big open graves. The scuffers have to stand around with guns to stop relatives trying to drag Mum or Dad or little Johnny back out again.

This greasy black smoke goes up from the pyres. You can smell it for miles.

Joel is working with one of the reconstruction squads. A hundred 'volunteers' under a fireman. It's awful work. Pulling down ruined buildings, by hand. Opening up cellars where people were baked under the firestorm. Flies buzzing. That sort of thing.

Joel hasn't got much choice. If you work, if you're strong enough, you get food. If you can't work, you don't get food. That's the way it is.

Some people are still dying of the radiation sickness. It works itself out in all sorts of ways. For instance, you might lose the lining of your stomach so you can't absorb liquids. You just dry out. You see all types in the hospital.

One doctor told me that a third of the population of Britain probably died when the bombs fell. Since then another third will have died from the radiation poisoning. And we, the last third, will have poison in the air and in the fields, in our blood and in our bones, for the rest of our lives.

Today, Fred and I drove into the city centre with an ambulance crew. One precious doctor. From Queens Drive we drove down Edge Lane. Army bulldozers had been down there before, to clear away the burned-out cars and rubble. We all wore masks and gloves. We carried buckets of paint to mark where the healthy people are, or where there are bodies, or where there is cholera or dysentery.

On the way in we saw a lot of people heading away from the city. All walking. Even if your car survived, there's no petrol. Some have suitcases, wheelbarrows, supermarket trolleys piled up. The men carry weapons, like cricket bats. Nobody much younger than me, nobody much older than Fred. The doctors say the radiation sickness and the epidemics and the hunger and the cold are taking the babies and the old people first.

A mile or so inside Queens Drive you can start to see the effects of the firestorm, where the big fires all joined up. Even so, bits survive. Houses here and there, almost untouched. Spared by chance.

In the heart of the city, some of the big classical buildings, like Saint George's Hall, are still standing. Roofs bashed in, columns fallen. They look like Roman ruins. In Whitechapel and Church Street the shops got shaken to pieces. Glass everywhere. Melted shop window dummies. NEMS is gutted, burned out, stacks of pop records turned to black sludge.

A lot of the telephone poles are still standing. They are all blackened on one side.

And the flash was hot enough to scorch brick and concrete. You can see shadows, outlines of cars or buses, caught in that second, burned into the walls. In one place I saw the shadow of a little boy with his leg outstretched, and you could see the football a yard in front of his toe. Of the boy and the ball, nothing is left.

The Pier Head is destroyed. The docks are rubble, miles of them. One Liver Building tower is still standing. The clock stopped at 11:34. It must have been a bit fast. Bern laughed at that when I told her.

I'm making a list, of people I haven't heard about yet, dead or alive.

Nick O'Teen.

Mickey Poole. Bert Muldoon. Paul Gillespie.

Billy Waddle. Bernadette cares about him. She has to.

My teachers.

Little Jimmy.

The Queen. Winston Churchill. Harold Macmillan.

Roger Hunt. Joel's hero. Plays for Liverpool.

Beatle John.

Mum.

Dad.

Tuesday 25th December 1962.

Christmas Day.

A priest tried to hold a Mass in the hospital car park. Hardly anybody went. No one's got the heart. Half the priest's face was burned away, and he could hardly say the prayers.

Fred gave me a bit of cake. Who knows where he got it from.

I shared the cake with Bernadette and Joel.

Joel is thinking of joining the army. Well, they're recruiting.

You can never have too many soldiers nowadays. That's where the food is going to be, he says. That's where the power will be, in the future. Joel has a brain. He might do well.

'Now we are all "hibakusha",' he says. That's what they called the survivors of the bombs the Americans dropped on Japan at the end of the war. He isn't much like the CND-badge kid he was a couple of months ago.

Bern has had a miscarriage.

There's a lot of that about. My periods have been funny too. Something to do with losing red blood cells because of the radiation.

'The bomb got my baby,' Bern says.

It was a week ago. She kept it to herself. Her face is hard as stone.

Now she's leaving the city. 'We're all just starving to death. Maybe I can find something to eat out in the country. I'll skin a sheep.'

Joel laughed. 'And then what? Become a farmer? With those nails?'

She's going, no matter what we say. She always was the hardest of us in some ways, the strongest. She faces things the way they are, then deals with them.

It will be hard, though. It's been cold since the bomb.

We kissed Bern goodbye. She said that if I ever ran into Billy Waddle I should give him a message. I can't write it down here. I don't even know if I can spell it.

The three of us are still in our school uniforms, or what's left of them.

Many of the entries that came after that were fragmentary. Laura's future self was worried about using up the paper in her diary. And her life became so unfamiliar to Laura that it was hard to work out what was going on.

There was a longer entry from 1966. Laura would have been eighteen.

Saturday 30th July, 1966.

OK. OK.

Two things to write about today.

Another day in the potato fields.

I'm a Land Girl now, working on North-West Protectorate Collective Farm Number Twenty-Seven, otherwise known as Sefton Park. Back-breaking. Sun like a hot iron over your head. You sweat like a wet rag.

There's no petrol for the combine harvesters, which is why I'm digging in spuds by hand. There's talk they are doing up a steam-powered tractor, an old Victorian relic out of one of the museums. I'll believe that when I see it.

The bomb has messed up the weather.

Sometimes I remember how cold it was, that first winter and spring after the bomb. All that smoke and ash in the air. That all cleared in the end. Now there's hardly a cloud in the sky from April to October, hardly any rain. The sun burns your skin, and it's doing in everybody's eyes. Some people are living underground to escape it, in old cellars and basements. All you can do is cover up, even though it's so hot.

On my day off yesterday Corporal Wesley marched a bunch of us into Liverpool, and back out again, to look for stuff.

We went into the ruins of the old stores, and actually found a cellar full of stock that had only been gone through a few times. C&A Mode. I'm sure I remember this place. Seems so long ago. I found a coat and men's trousers and a decent pair of leather boots, even if they are pink.

The whole city is like a huge rubbish tip, with people picking over it like gulls. That's all that's left of the old world. Just garbage. I mean, if the fashions hadn't stopped we wouldn't be wearing pink leather boots now. It's as if time stopped in 1962, and everything turned to junk.

Corporal Wesley gave me a big floppy straw hat.

I've hated Corporal Wesley since I was put under him, after the National Reorganisation of 1964 when the army took over. He's about fifty. Got through the Sunday War in a command bunker in the country. Now he's based in the big Protectorate compound in the crypt of the cathedral. All mod cons down there, they say.

He's fat, when we're all half-starved and working to death.

And he likes having power over us workers.

He has this way of looking at you.

Of course he's in a position to get what he wants. I've seen him take girls into the officers' tent.

Last night the squaddies were in a good mood. They brought back a crate of whiskey from Liverpool. They let Joel bring a gramophone into our hut, and an old car battery to run it. Joel had some records. One of them was 'Love Me Do' by the Beatles. 'The only proper record they ever made,' Joel said to me.

It was strange to hear music again. We all danced. We had our heavy clothes on and our boots. The mothers with babies dandled them on their knees. 'We looked like Russian peasants,' Joel said. Although if there are any peasants left in Russia these days they might as well be on the Moon, for all we hear about them.

Today, at the lunch break, I thought of the Beatles again.

As we queued up for our bread and blind scouse, the loudspeaker over the serving table blared out the news from Radio

Free Britain.

'Headlines for today, Saturday July 30th, 1966. President for Life General William de Vere, who is touring the South-East Protectorate, announced that the General Survey of Britain he ordered on taking power from the corrupt government of Prime Minister Edward Heath is nearly complete.

'The population of the British Republic is about five million citizens. This compares to fifty million before the Sunday War. This is about the population of Britain in the Middle Ages. President de Vere said this is probably the post-War minimum, and our numbers should rise from here on.

'But he warned that mothers who hide any radiation-damaged infants from Protectorate inspectors could expect a severe penalty.

'In London, the execution was carried out today of a thousand dissidents. The executions were held at the Wembley Stadium Special Provisions Detention Camp. Among those eliminated were the notorious "underground" leader, musician John Winston Lennon . . .'

Poor old Beatle John. Just when I'd heard his record for the first time in years.

And there was something funny about today's date too. Something from before the war.

Joel said today would have been the date of the football World Cup Final. 'It was all scheduled, before the bomb. Roger Hunt might have been playing for England in the Final, in front of the Queen. Instead they're using Wembley to shoot pop singers.'

He couldn't say much more. He is in the army himself, after all.

In the evening, when I lined up for chow again, Wesley called me over. He had my food, bread and a bit of cheese and a scrag-end of meat. My mouth watered just looking at it.

I knew what he wanted. I've seen him do it before. I had to go into the officers' tent with him. If I did I'd get the food. If I didn't, I'd go hungry, and I'd get no food tomorrow night either. Until I gave in, or dropped.

I went with him. What else could I do?

He lay on top of me, and grunted and sweated like a pig. I was a virgin. I think that got him more excited. At least it hurried him up.

He'll do it again tomorrow. But I hope he'll get bored with me quickly. That's why I gave in fast. To get it over.

The worst thing about the bomb is that it took way all the things that are supposed to protect you. The vote. The law. Parents.

Those days before the bomb seem like a dream now. My memories seem to be dissolving. Baked-hard ground to scrape, a sky like an oven, mouldy potatoes that never grow right, hunger all the time. That's the world. That's reality. All there will ever be for me, I suppose.

All that and Corporal Wesley.

Laura flicked forward. The next long entry was from the following spring.

Monday 15th May 1967.

In People's Hospital Number Seven. A cellar in Huyton. They keep us mums-to-be underground to shield the babies from the sun, and the radiation.

Baby due any time.

The food's good in here. Beds clean. They look after mothers.

General Gresson, the American who kicked out General de Vere, is keen on mothers. One day, he says, we will build an army again, and cross the Channel, march through what's left of Europe, and dish it to the Russkies once and for all. He needs mothers to produce all those soldiers.

During the Sunday War, they kept on until they'd fired off everything they could, shot off every missile, dropped every bomb. I suppose they'll keep on now until they're down to killing each other with rocks and bare fists.

But my baby isn't going to be a boy. The doctor told me. I think I'll call her Agatha.

Laura looked at Agatha, who was watching her read. Forty years old, scrawny, her hair patchy, her eyes were bright.

Joel visited. He's Lance-Corporal Joel, now.

He's getting into technical projects. He always was bright. He says he's having a chance to complete the education that was cut short by the bomb.

He says a group of officers have got a secret plan.

When the bomb fell there were military bunkers all over the place. In Britain there were tiny little bunkers, for two or three men each, where men of the Royal Observer Corps holed up with their chemical toilets and their stacks of baked beans, while the Third World War raged over their heads, and made notes.

Some of the bunkers that survived, especially in the States, had advanced technology. Computers, lasers, all that. They were the best the military could buy. And after the bomb, while the rest of us were scratching away on the farms, in the bunkers and citadels, all that technology kicked off new research.

Joel says his officer buddies are talking about a time machine.

The Sunday War was a huge mistake. Probably even

General Gresson, our new American emperor, would agree to that. So, suppose you could go back to 1962 and fix it? Stop the Cuba crisis blowing out of control the way it did? Wouldn't that be worth doing? 'You could save forty-five million lives in Britain alone,' Joel said. 'At a stroke.'

'What would have happened instead?'

'I don't know.'

'Then how do you know things would have been better?'

'They could hardly be worse, could they?'

Anyhow it's all a dream. We can't even grow enough potatoes, and he wants to build a time machine.

He always did like conspiracies, Joel. All his whispering buddies in CND before the bomb. Of course CND turned out to be right.

Also, Joel brought Little Jimmy to see me. Not that he's so little now. Eleven years old, he grew up on a farm in the Lake District, and he's as strong as an ox.

Jimmy was a bit wary. Maybe he didn't remember me. But when he came into the ward I held out my hand. 'Shillin'.' Then he grinned.

The three of us got weepy, talking about old times.

I admitted to Joel what Corporal Wesley had done to me.

After that, somebody beat Corporal Wesley to a pulp.

Laura looked up. Her eyes were tired from trying to read by candlelight. And she was tired inside too.

Agatha just watched her.

Laura flicked through the diary, until she came to the last entry of all. The handwriting was big, like a child's, and it wandered over the page.

Saturday 18th April, 1970.

I can barely see to write. Stupid cataracts.

Joel came to see me, in the ward. He bounced Agatha on his knee. She's always loved her Uncle Joel.

Joel looked clean, well-fed, healthy. The army lads always do. Not that I can see much of his face but a blur.

He says the Timeline Rectification Project is going well, but it might take another thirty or forty years to complete.

Too late for me. I said he should be looking for a cure for cancer. Like the cancer that's going to take me away from Agatha before her third birthday. The bomb got me in the end. It gets all of us, said Joel.

We talked about old times. And we talked about what might have happened if not for the bomb.

I'm twenty-two. Might have gone to college, might have kids, might have a job. Joel says men would have walked on the Moon by now. England would be getting ready to defend the World Cup they would have won in 1966 (in his dreams). The Beatles would have retired, rich and famous.

And Joel might have married Bernadette. That really is a dream, I said.

The nurse is coming to give me my bed bath. Joel is paying for her. You only get nurses if you pay for them. The National Health, another thing the bomb put an end to.

Joel has taken Agatha for a walk. I'm glad. She's spent most of her life in holes in the ground, poor kid.

The sun is bright outside. Not harsh like it was a few years ago. There's a bit of green in the fields, and I can hear a bird singing. When Agatha comes back I'll tell her how mu

The last entry finished there, an unfinished sentence, an incomplete word.

Agatha was watching.

Laura didn't know what to say. 'I'm sorry I left you.'

Agatha looked away.

Joel came out of the dark. 'Nick's still sleeping. So's Bern.'

Laura passed him the diary. He read bits of it, quickly. Then he passed it back.

'I get to wear a uniform,' he said.

'Looks like it. Joel, will it really be like that?'

'Oh, yes. If the war comes it will be a catastrophe that they will talk about for a thousand years. The way we learn about the Black Death in school. This is what they don't want you to know.'

'Then we can't let this happen,' Laura said. She glanced at Agatha. She couldn't let this happen to her daughter.

Joel laughed, hollow. 'Good luck.'

Laura asked Agatha, 'Are you part of this "Timeline Rectification Project"?'

'Yes. They sent me because they thought there would be a bond between us.'

'And you want my Key,' Laura said.

'Yes.'

'Why? To stop this awful war from happening?'

'Oh, no,' Agatha said. 'Not that. Don't you see? We have to fight it even harder. This time we have to win.'

Chapter 22

The next time Laura wrote in her own copy of the diary, she felt oddly self-conscious, as if a crowd of possible future Lauras might be watching her.

Friday 26th October. 7 a.m.

It's only forty-eight hours until the Sunday War bombs are supposed to start falling.

Still in this hole in the ground.

We've all woken up thirsty and cold. Bern says she could eat a scabby donkey.

Mum has put herself in charge of keeping us fed. She used the little camping stove to make us breakfast, tinned rice and beans. And hot tea. We've got no milk and we drank it black. Mum is being a mum, this morning. Well, she is the only adult, if you don't count Agatha.

Nick is in a bad state. He woke up in a panic because he couldn't see again. Then he slumped back, out cold. There's nothing we can do for him. If nuclear war wasn't breaking out he'd be in a hospital for sure.

Bern is down too. She's seen some of the diary. Well, that's enough to get anybody down. Joel is fretting about her. She lashes out at him for fun.

I'm worried about Bern. I'm worried about us all.

Joel and I have decided to go outside. Even though we're risking being found by the Minuteman or Miss Wells or one of their squaddies. We need to know what's going on.

I need to decide what to do with the Key. I haven't decided whether to give it to Agatha. I still don't know what she wants to do with it.

Or I could use it the way Dad told me, calling the authorities. After reading Agatha's diary, I'm starting to think I shouldn't do that. Everything's very tense. I don't want to disturb things.

Does that make sense? I mean, it is the key for a nuclear bomber. One bomb dropped could kick it all off.

I want to try to call Dad, though.

Mum asked me to fetch back some milk. Fresh bread, if there is any. She gave me a bit of money.

'Yes, Mum,' I said. She still doesn't get it.

The streets were deserted. No traffic. A smell of burning rubber. They could hear shouting, off in the distance, a crash of glass, and a wail of police sirens. Smoke drifted across the sky.

It was about nine in the morning. Liverpool was waking up to a bad day.

They crept along the pavement, keeping to the shadows. They passed burned-out cars, and there was broken glass all over the road. And yet there were milk bottles set out on the pavement. People trying to continue normal lives.

They came to a parade of shops. The food shops were gutted. Certainly no bread or milk. 'Not even any conny onny,' Joel said. Condensed milk.

A hardware store next door to a torched baker's had

been looted. Its big plate-glass window was smashed, and little price tags showed where vacuum cleaners and steam irons had been stolen. Joel rummaged around in the broken glass, but there were no radios.

'No news today.'

'I need to phone my dad,' Laura said.

There was a phone in the shop. It was disconnected.

In the street, they came to a row of three red phone kiosks. Only one was working. A recorded voice repeated, 'This telephone is for essential public use only. Make your call brief. You will be cut off in one minute. Normal charge rates apply. Please have your coins ready. This phone is for essential public use only . . .'

Joel grinned as he fished coppers out of his pocket. 'You'd think the Post Office would give us free calls in the circumstances. I think those scallies are getting closer. We'd better get a shift on.'

Laura called the last number Dad had given her. To her huge relief he picked up the phone immediately.

'Laura? Where the hell are you? I had somebody call at the house. You and Mum –'

'We're in hiding. We both are.'

Dad snapped, 'What? Hiding? Who from?'

'From a teacher at school. You remember Miss Wells?'

'That's ridiculous.'

'Not ridiculous. Complicated. She's working with Mort.'

He was silent.

'Dad, are you there?'

'What do they want?'

'The Key. Dad, you do believe me?'

'Of course I believe you.'

'I want you to come and get us.' She tried not to sound

like a helpless kid. But she couldn't think of where else to turn. 'We're in a cellar, under –'

Dad said sharply, 'No. Don't say it. If you're right this phone call might be monitored. I'll find you.'

'How?'

'Never mind that. And I'll find out what Mort is really up to. I'll try, Laura, I promise I'll try. But *use the Key*, if you need to.'

But she was starting to think she couldn't use the Key, no matter what.

She tried to be brave. 'Maybe all this will still blow over.'

'Well, they're arguing in the United Nations. The Russians still haven't tried to crash through the Q-line, with their ships and their subs. But on the other hand they haven't started dismantling their missiles on Cuba yet.

'And they're panicking in Washington. They're frightened Khrushchev might have been deposed by his generals. But Khrushchev might think the same about Kennedy.

'It's all this rotten communication.' He sighed. 'I don't believe anybody really wants to go to war. But the next twenty-four hours will be critical.'

Black Saturday, Laura thought. 'Dad –'

But the phone started beeping in her ear, and though she tried to cram in more money, she got no more time.

Laura held on to the handset, even when it fell silent. She didn't want to face Joel. Hearing Dad's voice for the first time in days affected her more than she expected. After all, last night she'd read about how he was due to die, when the first wave of Russian missiles landed on the military targets on Sunday morning, less than forty-eight hours from now. And she hadn't even been able to tell him goodbye.

Joel said, 'Hey, look.'

Something glinted in the sky. It was a milk bottle, filled with some brownish fluid, with a bit of burning cotton wool stuck in the neck. Spinning over the roof of a house, it looked quite beautiful.

The bottle landed, and fire splashed over the road.

'A Molotov cocktail,' Joel said. 'You wonder where they got the petrol.'

A mob erupted from an alleyway only fifty yards from the phone kiosks. They threw rocks and bricks, and waved crowbars and wrenches, and hurled more petrol-bombs. As they ran into the road a force of police came the other way. In their helmets and black uniforms the scuffers ran in formation, with bits of wood held in front of them, improvised shields.

The rioters were mostly men, young and angry, but there were some older men, a few women, and even kids, ten or eleven or twelve. All hungry, Laura supposed, all frightened.

Joel said, 'Those scuffers haven't got their numbers on their coats. That's against the law.'

The two forces clashed in the middle of the road. Rioters fell under blows from truncheons, but the police were being battered as well. One scuffer went down, his uniform on fire. The fires from the petrol bombs started to gather together into a major blaze.

A shell whistled up into the air from the police lines. It landed among the rioters and white gas splashed.

'Tear gas,' Laura said. She took a handkerchief from her blazer pocket and stuck it over her mouth, and pulled Joel away.

As they ran back to their hole in the ground, she heard the muffled pops of gunfire.

Lunch was more tinned rice, tinned beans, black tea.

Joel sat alone, eating his lunch in the shadows. Bern cradled Nick, who was sleeping again, his hands clamped around his head. Bern had barely said a word all day.

Laura sat with Mum and Agatha. 'We've got family business to sort out. And you need to know who we're hiding from, Mum.'

At last, she tried to explain the whole truth to Mum.

'So let me get this straight,' Mum said. 'Miss Wells, your teacher, is actually yourself, from the future. The year two thousand and something.'

'2007,' said Agatha.

'I think so.'

'And you,' Mum turned to Agatha, 'are Laura's daughter. My granddaughter. And, you say, you're older than *me*. But you won't even be born until 1967. Five years from now.'

Agatha just looked back steadily.

'And you grew up after an atomic war.' Mum, on impulse, cupped Agatha's cheek. 'You poor thing. You've had a rotten life, haven't you? That's why you're so – joyless.'

Agatha closed her eyes and leaned into Mum's hand.

Laura stared. 'You're taking this very calmly, Mum.'

She shot back, 'You don't think much of your mother, do you, Laura? I'm not some sort of imbecile. This business of time travel. I did watch *Quatermass*, you know. And a couple of years ago there was that rather good film with Rod Taylor. What was it called?'

'*The Time Machine*,' Nick said. His voice was muffled by his hands.

Laura turned. 'I didn't know you were awake.'

'I'm not,' Nick said. 'I just fancied Rod Taylor.'

Mum said, 'As for all this business of meeting a granddaughter who's older than me, if you're brought up a Catholic you get used to believing two impossible things before breakfast. Compared to the Mystery of the Holy Trinity, a time-travel paradox is a piece of cake!' She actually laughed. 'But there are some things I don't understand.'

Laura nodded. 'Like what?'

'You said Miss Wells is your future self.' She turned to Agatha. 'That would make Miss Wells your mother, wouldn't it? And,' she said to Laura, 'the diary says you, well, darling, you *die*, in 1970. You'd only be about twenty-two. So how could you live to be sixty-something to become Miss Wells, and come back here in a time machine?'

Laura opened her mouth, and closed it. 'I hadn't thought of that.' She hadn't put all these things together, the presence of Miss Wells, Agatha, her own death in the diary. 'I suppose I'm not used to thinking this way.'

'There's no paradox,' Agatha said. 'Miss Wells *is* your future self. But she's not the future self who became my mother.'

Mum asked, 'How can that be? You're both from the future.'

'But from different futures.'

'Woah,' Nick called weakly. 'I think we just crashed through another conceptual barrier.'

Laura tried to get her head around this. 'OK. OK. Agatha, you came back from your atom-war future.'

'We say, the "Sunday War timeline",' Agatha said.

'But Miss Wells isn't from that timeline,' Joel called over. 'She's from a *different* timeline. Is that right? What kind of future is that?'

'You'd have to ask Miss Wells.'

Mum said, 'If you're all from these different timelines, how can you all be coming back to the same place? Liverpool 1962?'

'Because this is where they all branch off from,' Agatha said. 'All the histories.'

Laura thought she understood. The timelines were like roads leading off from a roundabout: Agatha's Sunday War, Miss Wells's unknown future, maybe other possibilities. There was a different version of herself in each of the futures, each marching down her own road. And 1962 was the roundabout, the place all the different histories met.

'I suppose it all depends on the way the Cuba crisis works out. Peace, or nuclear war.' This was the crucial point in human history, the moment so dramatic that it would shape all history to follow.

Agatha said, 'I knew you'd understand, Mum.'

'Don't call me that.'

'So that's why they've come here, to this pivot of history,' Joel said. 'Two futures, fighting to be real. And 1962 is their battleground.'

Nick, lying on his back, cackled. 'You should write for the comics, our kid. Dan Dare, maybe.'

'He's right,' Agatha said. 'This is a fight for the future. And here's how I'm going to win.'

Agatha said the military planners, working in their citadels in the post-nuclear ruins of Britain in the year 2007, had 'war-gamed' how America and its allies could have *won* a nuclear war in 1962.

By 'winning', they meant surviving more or less intact, while destroying the Russians. In the Sunday War the whole world had been bombed flat. The plan now was that it should be just Russia that got bombed flat, while the west survived.

It all depended on Laura's Key.

'That's the trigger,' Agatha said. 'That Key can be used to launch one Vulcan, one British nuclear bomber plane.'

'Aha,' Joel said. 'And given how the whole world is on a knife-edge over Cuba, that could be enough to change things.'

In the Sunday War, the first nuclear bombs would fall on Sunday 28th October. But Agatha intended to change history – to use the V-bomber controlled by Laura's Key to drop the first bomb twenty-four hours *before* that, in the small hours of Saturday 27th.

Joel said quietly, 'Tonight.'

The British bomber, striking without warning, would take out one Soviet city.

The Russians wouldn't believe the British had acted alone. They would retaliate by striking at the Americans. The fastest way to do it would be to fire off their Cuban missiles, while they had the chance, at mainland America.

'And almost certainly,' Agatha said, 'one of the Cuban missiles would hit Washington. That was what they were designed to do. Kennedy and all the American decision-makers – all dead.'

After that the American military machine, decapitated, would immediately lunge into total war.

'It would all be automatic,' Agatha said. 'They call it the Single Integrated Operations Plan. It's what's supposed to happen if all the leaders are killed. First the big intercontinental missiles would fly, the Atlases, the Jupiters, the Thors, the Titans. The nuclear bombers would follow, the B-52s, the supersonic B-58s. And the submarines around the coast, and all the missiles from places like Turkey.'

If Kennedy had survived, he might have pulled back. As it was, the machine would take over. That was the whole idea. To trigger America's war machine to destroy Russia, unthinking.

'The Russians couldn't strike back,' Joel said. 'Not with anything like the same firepower. And they couldn't defend themselves against the missiles, the bombers. So their cities, industries, military bases –'

'All destroyed before dawn in Moscow,' Agatha said. 'Nine hundred and fifty atomic weapons landing on Russia in the first wave. And it wouldn't end there. Later in the day the Americans would launch their second wave.'

Laura asked, 'What would be left to attack?'

'The trees.'

It was called the *taiga*, a vast belt of fir-tree forest that stretched across the north of the Soviet Union, halfway around the North Pole. After three hundred and seventy more nuclear strikes, Russia would become one vast firestorm.

'With all that smoke in the air blocking out the sun, not a blade of grass will grow in Russia for a whole year. The Nuclear Spring, they will call it.'

By Christmas 1963 perhaps a tenth of the Russian population would be left alive.

'While America will lose a few million,' Agatha said. 'Tops.'

'And that's what you call a victory,' Laura said.

'Yes! Don't you see? In a nuclear war, the only way the Russians can hurt us is if they have time to fire off their weapons. That's what happened in my timeline, the Sunday War. But if you attack them first, if you just hit them really hard with all you've got, you can wipe them out before they can respond.'

'And,' Laura said, 'the one V-bomber controlled by my Key –'

'That starts it all off.'

Joel stared at her. 'You're talking about starting a nuclear war deliberately. The deliberate genocide of two hundred million people. Maybe a tenth of everybody alive on the planet. What kind of monster are you?'

She looked hurt. 'You haven't lived the life I've lived, Uncle Joel. Don't call me a monster. You don't *know*.' She turned to Laura. 'Now you know it all. Will you help me, Mum? Will you give me the Key?'

Laura stared back. 'I need to think.'

'We don't have long,' whispered Agatha, and the candlelight made her face look deeply lined.

Chapter 23

Friday 26th October. 8 p.m.

We're running out of time.

Four hours left to Black Saturday. Which will get even blacker if Agatha has her way.

We keep hearing shouts. Screams. Cracks that might be gunfire. Maybe it's the police against the rioters. Or maybe the police have just withdrawn and left them to it.

Either way they are getting closer to us.

If we're going to do something it has to be soon. But what?

Joel was talking about time travel with Agatha.

'What about time paradoxes?' he said. 'I've read Ray Bradbury and Robert Heinlein.'

'Go on.'

'Suppose Laura gave you the Key, and your Nuclear Spring future came about. Then *you* would never have been born. Would you just –' he waved a hand in the air '– fade out of existence?'

'No. It turns out it doesn't work like that. I would continue to exist, to live and breathe. But I'd be stranded here. The last relic of a future that will never happen.' She touched her diary. 'Everything written down in here wouldn't happen. Everything I remember would never happen. But I would remember it even so.'

'That's a paradox.'

'So is disappearing . . .'

Laura called a council of war. Everybody except Agatha, who she asked to sit out so they could talk things over.

And except for Bernadette. She wouldn't play. She skulked off to a dark corner, complaining of a headache.

Joel said, 'Come on, Bern. We need you. You're the only sensible one here.'

'Bog off.' Her voice was slurred.

Laura was suspicious. 'Bern, what's up? Are you drunk? You're not supposed to drink when you're pregnant, are you?' She leaned closer, hoping to smell Bernadette's breath.

But Bernadette pushed her away and curled up. 'I said bog off.'

Laura gave up and rejoined the others.

They sat in a circle around a candle, Laura, Joel, Mum, Nick. Their faces floated in the dim light.

Nick still had his sunglasses on. '"When shall we three meet again, in thunder, lightning, or in rain?"'

'There are four of us,' Joel said.

'"When the hurly-burly's done. When the battle's lost and won." *Macbeth*. Did it for O-level.'

'Is this helping?' Mum asked sensibly.

'Sorry, Missus Mann.'

Mum turned to Laura. 'So what do we do?'

Laura blurted, 'You're my mum. You should be telling me.'

Mum smiled, a bit sadly. 'Dad gave you the Key, not me. It was probably a wise choice.'

Joel said, 'What are the options?' He counted them on his fingers. 'One. You could give the Key to Agatha, as she asks. So she can kick off her Single Integrated Operations Plan and kill all the Russians.'

Nick said, 'You'd be swapping tens of millions of deaths in the Sunday War, for hundreds of millions in the Nuclear Spring.'

'I don't want to be responsible for *one* death, let alone a million.'

Joel shrugged. 'Fair enough. So the Nuclear Spring timeline bites the dust. Who's going to tell Agatha?'

'Option two,' Mum interrupted. 'You could use the Key the way Dad told you to. You have the code, the phone number. You could call this Regional Who's-it Controller of Whatchamacallit.'

'I've got a threepenny bit,' Nick said, mocking. 'You can pay me back after the nuclear holocaust.'

'Then we'll all be taken into safety in some government bunker. And drink tea and eat choccy biscuits until it's all over.'

'No,' said Laura. She was making her mind up as she spoke. 'The Key. *I can't use it.*'

Joel said, 'What? Why not?'

She'd been thinking this over ever since reading Agatha's diary. 'The Key controls a nuclear bomber. Megatons. Agatha wants to use it to set off a global nuclear war deliberately. Well, maybe if I try to use it at all, I'll set off a war *by accident.*

'You know what the diary says about Agatha's timeline. How the Sunday War starts tomorrow. Something triggers it, some small incident somewhere. What if the Key is the trigger?'

Nick said, 'It might be nothing to do with your Key. It's probably some divvy on either side in Berlin, or Cuba –'

'But it *might* be the Key.' She patted her chest. 'And I know that if I keep the thing tucked away in here it can't do any harm. I don't want there to be a nuclear war,' she said fervently. 'Any war. Because, for one thing, as soon as any bomb falls, anywhere, Dad will be killed.'

Mum looked away.

Joel nodded. 'Right. And that's why you tried to get your dad to come and get you out of here, when you rang him this morning. Because you can't risk using the Key.'

'H-Bomb Girl,' Nick said, 'listen to yourself. You are a fourteen-year-old girl, stuck in a hole in the ground, in Liverpool. How can you talk about causing wars or not? How can you talk about *choosing* futures? Who do you think you are, the Virgin Mary or Supergirl?'

But she was at the pivot, Laura thought. Because of the Key. She was at the place the futures were fighting over, to become real. She didn't ask for it to be that way, but that's how it was. Maybe everybody thinks they're the centre of the world. But, Laura thought now, maybe whole futures, whole worlds, billions of lives and deaths, really did depend on the decisions she made in the next few hours.

She looked around at them, her mum, Agatha, battered Nick, troubled Joel, curled-over, pregnant Bernadette. 'I've made my mind up,' she said.

Agatha asked, 'To do what?'

'For a start, not to give you my Key. There's not going to be a Nuclear Spring.'

Agatha dropped her head.

Joel asked her curiously, 'Are you angry?'

'I don't know. I might be angry later. Here and now I'm

with you, Mum,' she said to Laura. 'That will have to be enough.'

Nick said, 'So what *are* you going to do, H-Bomb Girl?'

'I'm not going to start a nuclear war. Any sort of one. And I'm going to save everybody.'

Nick laughed. 'And how will you manage that?'

'I don't know yet.'

'Well, we can't rely on your dad,' Joel said gravely. 'We might have to look after ourselves. We need a Plan B.'

In fact Laura had a Plan B, in her head. But she didn't want to tell anybody about it, not yet.

Bernadette screamed.

They all rushed over. Agatha brought a torch and held it up.

Bernadette was lying on the hard brick floor, with dark sticky stuff pooling between her legs. She was crying, her face twisted in agony, and her mascara was all over the place.

Mum took charge. 'Move back. Let me see what's what.' Her motherly tone got through to them, Joel in distress, Nick in near-hysteria. Mum pulled up Bernadette's skirt and began to examine her.

Laura leaned close to Bernadette and smelled her breath. 'Gin. I *thought* you were drunk. You had a bottle of gin in your school satchel, didn't you?'

'Doesn't everybody?' Bern croaked. She opened her smudged eyes. 'Nicked it from my mum. I tried all the usual stuff. Gin. Castor oil. Made me throw up. The baby just did the backstroke in it.'

'Oh,' Joel said, 'you're trying for an abortion.'

'And then she used this,' Mum said. She lifted something up, dripping with blood. It was a knitting needle.

'I hid it in the lining of my blazer,' Bern said.

Laura looked at it with horror. 'Bern. How could you?'

'What choice have I got? I don't want my baby growing up like *her*.' She pointed at Agatha. 'If the bomb falls it's better off dead. So am I. We all are.' She broke down, and Joel cradled her head, rocking.

'No,' Mum said. She pulled up Bernadette's blouse, and put her hand on her exposed belly. 'You've made a right mess of yourself, missy. You need a doctor. But the baby's still alive. I'm no expert, but I can feel it move. In the end you couldn't hurt your baby, could you?'

Bernadette covered her face with her arm. 'I'm useless.'

'Joel,' Mum said now. 'Find my handbag. I've got a bottle of TCP and some tissues. Let's get this lot cleaned up.'

Joel went for the bag.

Then Nick cried out, and slumped against a wall, limp as a doll. He had blacked out again.

And a crash on the ceiling brought dust and plaster sifting down on them all. Some of the candles blew out.

'The rioters are getting closer,' Agatha said to Laura. 'We're running out of time. If they break in here –'

'I know, I know,' Laura said.

She looked around helplessly, at Nick, sprawled and unconscious, Bernadette bleeding from a dozen self-inflicted wounds, Joel lost in his concern, Mum bearing up but brittle. Laura had the sense of everything falling apart.

'Time for Plan B,' she said.

She dragged the 'phone' they had stolen from Miss Wells from her blazer pocket, and opened it up. She pressed the green button with the phone symbol. Then, uncertainly, she held the phone beside her ear.

Miss Wells replied instantly. 'Laura. I've been expecting

your call,' she said dryly.

'Help,' said Laura simply.

'Just don't touch any buttons. We'll track the phone and come and get you.'

Agatha stared. 'And this is your plan? To ask *her* for help?'

'She said she'd help. She must have doctors. And we can't stay here. Do you have any better ideas?'

'But when Miss Wells gets hold of you –'

'I'll think of something,' Laura said, trying to sound more confident than she felt.

It took half an hour.

Then the wall exploded, the bricks bursting inwards.

A huge steel screw, shining silver, came pushing through, whirring. It was like the bit of an immense drill, on the end of a cylinder maybe four feet across.

On the cylinder's flank was a symbol, a green Earth in an iron fist, and a slogan written underneath: PEACE THROUGH WAR. Laura had seen it before, on Mort's computer, and Miss Wells's phone.

When about ten feet was sticking into the cellar, the bit stopped whirring. The sudden silence seemed loud. The cap of the drill hinged down, and blue light shone out.

Laura walked up to the open cylinder and peered in.

Miss Wells was crouching awkwardly in the cylinder. She was wearing a featureless grey coverall.

Laura stared at her. 'You took your time.'

'And you're pushing your luck. I knew you'd call, in the end.'

The hammering on the roof got worse.

Laura said, 'You're the lesser of two evils. It was you, or

wait for the looters to get here.'

'That's not very nice. After all, *I'm you*. You've worked that out. If you can't trust yourself, who can you trust?'

Behind Miss Wells, inside the cylinder, Laura glimpsed a wheelchair, a stocky man sitting in it. It was the Minuteman.

'What's he doing here?'

'He's my boss,' said Miss Wells.

'He wanted to be here, Laura. When we found you.' That was a man's voice. Mort stood up behind the Minuteman, and put a hand on his shoulder. 'We both did. But you'd expect that, given the circumstances.'

Looking at them together like that, Laura suddenly saw it.

They were the same man, separated by forty years and a dreadful injury.

Miss Wells held out her hand. 'Get in.'

Chapter 24

Saturday 27th October.

Black Saturday.

Time unknown. They took away our watches, when they brought us into this place.

Miss Wells calls her machine the Burrower. It just squirms its way through the ground, leaving a tunnel behind it. It's like an underground spaceship. If I was a boy I'd probably think it was pretty neat.

The crew came out into the cellar and loaded up Bern and Nick on stretchers, and shepherded the rest of us walking wounded aboard the Burrower. Nick was out cold. Bern was crying from the pain, where she'd stabbed herself.

Joel got away. 'I'm off.'

'Why? Joel, come with us. It's not safe here.'

He sniffed. 'I don't see too many black faces inside those grey suits. You get an instinct for that sort of thing. Take care of yourself. And look after Bern.'

And I looked away, and he was gone.

Inside, the Burrower is like a military helicopter Dad gave me a ride in once, with canvas bucket seats and webbing. It backed up into the tunnel it had made. It was a noisy ride, like a bumpy underground train. Mum held my hand.

So we came to Miss Wells's underground lair. Very James Bond. At first we didn't see much of it.

Bern and Nick were taken off on stretchers.

Mum, Agatha and I were put through a shower room. All steel walls and fluorescent lights. We had to strip off, and our clothes were taken away. I knew what was going on. We were being scrubbed clean of any contamination by radiation. It was the same in 'Doctor No'.

So I've learned that people from Miss Wells's future live in bunkers, and are terrified of radiation.

Without her clothes on, Agatha is thin. Half-starved. I pitied her. But she seemed to enjoy the hot shower.

We were given clean underwear, and shapeless grey coveralls, like Miss Wells's. 'Ugh,' Mum said. 'First chance I get, I'm accessorising.'

Miss Wells led us to a tiny bedroom, with four bunk beds, and its own little toilet. 'En suite,' said my mother. 'Very nice.' There was a jug of water, some fruit. Some of our belongings are here, Mum's handbag, this diary. Not our watches, though.

They let me keep the Key, incidentally. But then Miss Wells knows the Key is useless without the code numbers in my head.

None of us could resist the soft beds. We hadn't slept much for days. Agatha sighed as she lay down.

I don't know how long I slept. Maybe the water was drugged.

The others are still sleeping. I'm writing this with a make-up pencil from Mum's handbag. Waiting for the strangeness to kick off again.

When this is all over, I wonder if I'll get back my school uniform from Miss Wells. Or if we'll have to buy a new one.

Miss Wells called for them.

She led them through corridors to a narrow balcony that overlooked a larger chamber. On the balcony, a metal table and chairs had been set up under a screen, like a small cinema screen.

They sat down uneasily, Mum, Laura, Agatha, Miss Wells. Like Laura and the others, Miss Wells wore a steel-grey coverall that zipped up the front. But Miss Wells had epaulettes and shoulder flashes, like Flash Gordon.

Bernadette was led out by a nurse in a white uniform.

Laura ran to embrace her. Bernadette, still sore and a bit woozy from anaesthetics, was stiff. 'No fuss,' she said. But she hugged Laura back.

There was no sign of Nick.

The balcony overlooked the heart of Miss Wells's complex. 'We call it the Hub,' she said proudly. 'A little bit of 2007, built under Liverpool, 1962.'

The Hub was a mess of cramped tunnels, probably cellars and sewers and drains. But they had plated some kind of silvery cloth over the walls, and there were bright strip-lights everywhere, so it was all flooded with light. It was like a cross between a hospital and a milk bar, Laura thought.

In the big central chamber under the balcony, computers hummed away, big boxes the size of wardrobes, with tape reels, flashing lights, and chattering teletypes. There was a smell of electrical gear, sharp like seaside air.

There was also an odd sort of doorway that seemed to lead nowhere, just a frame filled with a milky light.

And there was a pool, that glowed blue.

Technicians crawled all over the place, working the computer consoles, taking the temperature of the pool. The technicians wore all-over suits of clear plastic, with sealed helmets. Miss Wells said they were NBC suits, for protection from nuclear, biological and chemical contamination.

In the middle of the floor they had actually put up a flagpole, with a black flag held out with a bit of wire. The flag had that Earth-and-fist symbol. Above the planet was one word in spiky silver letters: HEGEMONY. And below it the slogan: PEACE THROUGH WAR.

It was incredible that all this was stuck down a hole, somewhere under Liverpool.

They all carried guns.

At the table they sat and looked at each other. Laura. Mum, Laura's mother. Agatha, Laura's daughter, from one timeline. Miss Wells, Laura's older self, from another.

'What a freak show,' Bernadette said, and she laughed.

'Well, we've a lot to talk about,' Miss Wells said briskly.

'First things first,' Bernadette said. 'How's Nick?'

'Recovering,' Miss Wells said. 'No thanks to whoever kicked him in the head.' She reached under the table and pulled out a tray, on which sat a keyboard, like a typewriter's. She tapped at this, and the big screen above their heads lit up with an X-ray image. It showed a man's skull.

'We have other scanning techniques, actually, in 2007,' she said. 'We brought some gear back. I don't suppose you know what a CAT scan is, do you? Or MRI? Never mind. The X-ray will do. Look here.' A small arrow appeared on the image and pointed to the curve of the skull. 'See the indentation in the skull? The pressure on the brain was causing bleeding of the right ventricle. He should have gone to hospital.'

'Try telling Nick that,' Bernadette said.

Laura asked, 'But Nick will be OK?'

'Our doctor operated. Non-invasively. He ought to recover. As for you,' Miss Wells said to Bernadette, 'you've needed a few stitches. But the internal exam showed you haven't done any lasting harm to yourself, or your baby. You were desperate. But you weren't very determined, were you?'

Mum said, 'Leave her alone.'

Bernadette's face was twisted. 'You don't know what was going on in my head,' she said to Miss Wells. 'You don't *know* what it felt like.'

'No. I don't. And I'm glad, frankly.'

'You're a cold woman,' Agatha said, unexpectedly. She stared at Miss Wells, with a complicated mixture of longing and loathing. 'You're *cold*. You don't care about Bernadette, or that boy who might have died. All you care about is using them to get to Mum – Laura. That's true, isn't it?'

'So in another timeline,' Miss Wells said, 'in which I spent my life scratching in the dirt of some dismal farm, I spawned you. And here you are, scrawny, skinny, self-pitying. How repulsive you are.'

'I'm your daughter.'

'Not *my* daughter. I have no children. You're a time-travel accident. You shouldn't even exist.'

Laura said, 'I can't believe I will ever become you.'

'Now, now, ladies,' Bernadette said. She looked at Agatha and Miss Wells. 'You both want this stuff out of Laura, the Key and the codes in her head. Why didn't you just pounce on her? You've been sniffing around for days.'

Agatha shook her head. 'It doesn't work like that. As soon as you go back in time, you start to change things. History unravels a different way.'

'We had to be careful,' Miss Wells agreed. 'Remember,

we're both trying to make history come out the way we want. If we were too drastic, we might have made changes we didn't intend.' She glared at Agatha. 'We're on opposite sides. But we share that much.

'Just by being here we changed things. You'd think I'd be able to find you, Laura, because I'd *remember* what you did, when I was you. But things have changed just enough to make that impossible.

'And anyhow,' she said, smiling at Laura, 'isn't it better this way? I don't want to *take* the Key from you, Laura. I want you to give it to me of your own accord. I've spent my whole life working to avoid war. That's why I'm here. I'd have thought you'd be impressed by that. And, after all, we're the same person, you and I. If we can't work together, who can?'

'Go on then,' said Bernadette. 'Tell us your master plan for taking over the world.'

Miss Wells looked at her in disgust. 'I can't believe that in any past life I was ever drawn to you, O'Brien.' She tapped another button on her keyboard, and the screen over their heads filled up with images of planes, ships, submarines, missiles. 'This is what's happening right now.'

'Cuba,' Laura said.

'You all slept a long time. It's now six in the evening. Around one in the afternoon, in Cuba.'

'But it's still Black Saturday,' Laura said.

'Oh, yes. And things are tense on the Q-line.'

Some shooting was going on. The Russians and Cubans had shot down some American warplanes, and a U-2 spy plane. In the water, American Navy ships were using depth charges on a Russian submarine. Behind the scenes Kennedy was talking to Khrushchev about his deal, how if

Khrushchev got rid of the missiles on Cuba Kennedy would dismantle his base in Turkey.

'Let me tell you what's about to happen, in *my* timeline,' Miss Wells said. 'Which we call the "Phoney War".'

Just as in Agatha's old timeline, the Sunday War, the serious shooting would soon start in Cuba, by accident. An American warship would be sunk by a Russian sub. In retaliation the Americans would launch air strikes against the Russian missile bases. Panicking, the Russians would fire off some of their Cuban missiles at the American mainland. In retaliation again, the Americans would launch nukes from their bases in Turkey at southern Russian cities. Millions dead, within hours.

'So it begins,' Bernadette whispered to Laura.

But in this timeline the Soviets held back at that point. The Americans held their fire too. It was just chance, Miss Wells said. A line of communication got through between Washington and Moscow.

The bombing stopped. The political leaders on both sides, not yet dead, frantically negotiated.

'The whole world held its breath,' Miss Wells said. 'And the combatants backed off. No more bombs.'

So this was a third way for the war to turn out, Laura saw. Or you could have the Sunday War, global bombing, which Agatha had lived through. You could have America annihilating Russia – the Nuclear Spring Agatha had hoped to set up. Or there was this more limited version, Miss Wells's 'Phoney War'.

'No wonder you're frightened of radiation,' Bernadette said.

'And this outcome,' Laura said, 'is what you've come back here to muck about with.'

Miss Wells smiled. 'Come and see what we've built. I

think you'll be impressed.'

She led them down a narrow staircase to the floor of the chamber. Bernadette was stiff and a bit dizzy, and Laura helped her.

The chamber floor vibrated, as if huge energies were stirring all around them. And the computers hummed and whirred. Tape reels spun, paper tape and punched cards chattered, lights flashed and needles flickered.

'Data is pouring into this place, the Hub, from capitals and military bases across the planet,' Miss Wells said proudly. 'In October 1962 we have recruits, like Mort, embedded in every major nation's capital.'

'You have been busy,' Bernadette sneered.

Laura wasn't all that impressed. 'If you're from 2007, why do your computers look like they're from 1962?'

Miss Wells sighed. 'Because they are from 1962. Look, time travel is very energy-hungry. In fact we've only got one shot at this; if we fail to change things as we wish, we won't be able to try again – well, we can't fail, that's all.

'And we haven't been able to carry much with us, into the past. Small things, like the mobile phone you swiped from my locker at school.

'Otherwise we've had to work with what's here. Most of what you see around you is from 1962. And you can't make a 2007 computer from 1962 components. Why, you still use valves! I know you have transistors, but you've never heard of a chip, a microprocessor, have you? There are whole industries that haven't been invented yet.'

Bernadette walked up to the pool. It glowed with pulsing blue light. 'I should have brought my water wings.'

'I wouldn't go dipping in here,' Miss Wells said. 'That's our power source. A small fission reactor.'

'Nuclear,' Laura said.

'Yes. The water is for cooling, and for protection from the radiation. That blue glow is Cerenkov radiation. Electrons from the pile.'

'What do you need a nuclear reactor for?'

'To heat up all the valves in these ridiculous Bakelite computers. To run the Burrower. And to keep open the Time Portal.'

This was the odd doorframe that stood in the middle of the room, filled with a sheet of misty light.

'I suppose it looks like an airport metal detector,' Miss Wells said. 'Ah, but you don't have those yet, do you? It's actually a wormhole mouth. But you don't know about spacetime wormholes either. It's a tunnel that connects two points.'

'Like the Mersey Tunnel,' Bernadette said.

'Yes. But this tunnel connects two points in time, not in space. You can walk through that doorway and pass straight from 1962 to 2007, without having to live through all the boring years in between.'

Laura asked Agatha, 'Is that how you got here? A Time Portal?'

Agatha shrugged. 'Our technology's more basic. My time machine's a bit like a car.'

Miss Wells looked down her nose. 'Your timeline does sound a bit scruffy, I must say.'

'We lived through a global nuclear war,' Agatha said.

'Which is exactly what the Hegemony avoids.'

Laura said, 'I think you'd better tell us what you're doing here in 1962.'

'I'm here to save mankind from itself,' Miss Wells said. She smiled.

Chapter 25

The nuclear pool cast blue light on the faces of the big computer boxes. Laura saw that the pool's water bubbled quietly, slowly boiling, and there was an acrid stink of acid.

'I don't even know what "Hegemony" means,' Laura said.

'The word means a power complex,' Miss Wells said.

'Why does that surprise me?' Bernadette asked.

In Miss Wells's timeline, even though some atomic bombs had fallen, Kennedy and Khrushchev pulled back from the brink. The United Nations called a truce, hasty peace negotiations began, and each country, America and Russia, sent aid to the other.

But in the deep shadows behind the public actions, some big players weren't happy.

Miss Wells said, 'They call it the "military-industrial complex". The generals in the big military power centres, like Whitehall in Britain, the Pentagon. The industrialists who grew rich selling bombs and planes and tanks to both sides. The scientists who came up with new types of weapon.

'Even before 1962 they all knew each other, across the world. A five-star general in Washington understood a field marshal of the Soviet Union far better than he understood President Kennedy.'

The military-industrial complex was horrified by the fitful Phoney War of Sunday 28th October. If you had a peace it had to be secure, so you could make money out of selling weapons. If you went to war you had to push it to a conclusion, to win, so you could make money out of rebuilding the loser and rearming the winner. This wishy-washy excuse for a war was no use at all.

'But of course you wouldn't want total annihilation either,' Miss Wells said. 'Like the Sunday War. That went too far. The purpose of war is the resolution of conflict. If everybody ends up dead, what's the point? You can see that the whole global situation needed managing competently.'

'I can see you need your bumps felt,' Bernadette said.

The big, secretive players began to talk to each other, American to Russian, British to Chinese, in the lull on Sunday 28th.

'In those first few hours,' Miss Wells said, 'the Hegemony was born.'

If the politicians were too stupid to run things, the military and industrialists would do it for them. The Hegemony, led by soldiers and businessmen from across the world, became a secret government that ran the planet. But it was all behind the scenes.

'Nobody wanted to alarm the public,' Miss Wells said. 'Or to have anyone bleating about *democracy* or *human rights*. The work was too important for that.

'And I was in it from the start,' she told Laura. '*You* were. After Dad was arrested, I was put in a sort of military college. The Hegemony knew it would need bright young people to run things in the future, and I was one of them.'

All Laura could think about was Dad. Arrested? Why?

'So I was there, Laura. I was there in 1964 when the new Labour government was brought down. Anthony Wedgwood Benn? Too socialist by half.

'I was there in 1969, aged twenty-one, working on the American technical team that landed men on the Moon. We started testing nuclear weapons up there on the Moon in 1970.

'I was there in 1973 to help President Nixon hush up the Watergate scandal.

'I was there to help Thatcher and Reagan get elected in 1979 and 1980. Our sort of people, *they* were.

'I was there in 1989, when the New French Revolution, two hundred years after the first, put our lot in control in France. They were always an awkward bunch, the French. Not any more.

'And I was there in 1990 to help throw Nelson Mandela back into jail, and prop up apartheid South Africa.'

'Joel was right to leg it, then,' Bernadette whispered.

'I've been there all my life. Working to make sure the Hegemony's grip is absolute. You could say I grew up with it. I was involved in the Fire Power movement in 1967, and the Live Hate concert at Wembley in 1985 . . .'

'And thanks to you,' Bernadette said, 'the Cold War just goes on and on and on.'

'Yes. All over the world, in Berlin and Cuba, across the North Pole and in the depths of the Pacific, American and Russian forces face each other, bristling with nukes. We're in a state of unending war.

'*But nobody gets hurt.* That's the point. Peace has reigned since 1962. And it always will. Peace Through War!'

'The real point of your Hegemony,' Bernadette said, 'is that you get to boss everybody about.'

'You rule them by fear,' Laura said. 'Fear that more bombs will drop.'

'But it's for their own good,' said Miss Wells.

'The lady's right.' There was a whir.

The Minuteman was approaching in his motorised chair, with Mort at his side. Now they were side by side their similarity was obvious. Mort and the Minuteman, like Laura and Miss Wells: two editions of the same person, plucked from different times. The Minuteman's chest was half-covered by a big band of campaign ribbons and medals, and his epaulettes had tassles.

'The Minuteman,' said Miss Wells reverently, 'is on the Hegemony's Inner Council.'

Bernadette scoffed. 'He looks like a cinema usher. Hey, mate. Got any choc ices?'

Laura giggled.

'Silence,' Mort barked.

Mum seemed on the verge of tears. 'Mort. You betrayed us. How could you?'

'Veronica. Babe. It's not like that. It's a question of higher loyalties. I was recruited *by my own older self.* Who comes from a future where he – I – have been working for the elimination of war for forty years. How could I refuse a commission like that?'

Laura said, 'You lied to us. You hid equipment in our house. You came sniffing around my school, trying to get at my Key. How noble was that?'

'What do you know?' Mort sneered. 'In the future, I'll be a hero.'

The Minuteman barked, 'This is the nature of peace and

war, when atomic devastation is hanging over all our heads by a thread. In an age like this, you need soldiers in charge. Because only soldiers understand war. That is the principle of the Hegemony and always will be.'

'So,' Bernadette asked insolently, 'what happened to you? Fall out of a bomb bay?'

'I'll have you know I gave up my health in the Phoney War. I was stationed on a B-52 that flew out of Mildenhall Air Base. Came down over Soviet territory. Never walked again. Did my job, though. Did my duty. And that's the point. And this man here,' he said, glancing at Mort, 'is going to face the call in a couple of hours' time. If it comes he will do his duty just as I did. Won't you, Mort?'

Bernadette said, disbelieving, 'So you'll fly your plane even though you *know* you'll be crippled?'

'Yes, ma'am! This man is my future,' Mort said, and he put a hand on the Minuteman's shoulder. 'I can think of no higher calling than to become *him*.'

'Heck, boy, don't make me cry,' groused the old man. 'The tears short out the chair.'

Bernadette said, 'So everybody thinks they're at war. Even though American and Russian soldiers haven't fired a shot in anger for forty years. Doesn't anybody ever rumble you?'

'Of course,' Miss Wells said. 'Every ten years or so you have a new crop of teenagers who can't see anything to be afraid of. Who get suspicious. Who want to be free, to live their own lives.'

'And you can't have that,' Laura whispered.

'Every ten years or so, they have to be reminded.'

'By what?'

'A bomb in the heart of Russia. A missile hitting America.

Rogue strikes by either side. The devastation, the fear, the suspicion, the paranoia – that's what prods the public back into their sheep pens.'

Laura said, 'People die, because of what you do.'

'Isn't it better that a few thousand are sacrificed in a burning tower block, than that the whole world burns up in nuclear fire?' She glared at Laura. 'You're judging me, aren't you? Mort admires his future self. Why can't you be like that? I've worked for peace for forty years. You don't know how hard it's been. Living in steel caves in the ground, the endless competition, knowing that if you make one slip you'll be chucked out to live among the drones on the surface. It made me hard. It will make *you* hard. Will it really be so bad, for you to be me?'

Laura looked at her wrinkled face, pale from a lifetime underground. Her hair grey as a gun, pulled back severely from her forehead. Her eyes, so like Laura's own, but wet, rheumy, old. Laura pitied her.

She asked, 'What happens to Dad?'

'Dad?'

'In your timeline. You said he was arrested.'

'He was a refusenik,' the Minuteman snapped.

'A what?'

Miss Wells sighed. 'In the lull, after the nuclear strikes while the negotiations went on, your dad and other officers waited in their airbases and missile silos. There was a mistake. An order to launch the V-bombers came. Dad didn't believe it. He prevented a squadron from taking off.'

'How?'

Miss Wells smiled. 'He always was handy with his fists.'

'He was tried,' the Minuteman barked. 'By a Hegemony court. Found guilty of not following orders in a time of war.'

'But the order was a mistake!'

'What's that got to do with it?' the Minuteman said. 'He was shot. Along with all the other refuseniks.'

Laura's heart broke a little bit. 'Isn't there a higher duty? To common sense? To the ordinary people who would have got blown up for nothing?'

'Oh, no,' Miss Wells said. 'Orders are orders, and that's all there is to it.'

Laura looked at Miss Wells, at her own face. No matter what kind of life she had to lead, could *she* ever care so little about what became of Dad?

She recognised something of herself in Miss Wells. Laura was bright, she knew that. She was strong too, dogged. She could survive in the Hegemony's world if she had to. But Miss Wells had no compassion. A frozen heart. Miss Wells, this grown-up copy of her, after a lifetime of bad choices, was like a projection of bits of Laura, but not *all* of her.

Miss Wells was Laura. But she was less than Laura. This was like a nightmare of growing up.

Mum gripped her hand hard. 'Never forget who you are,' she whispered.

'I won't,' Laura said.

Bernadette said to Miss Wells, 'So what do you want in 1962? Why are you chasing after Laura's Key? Your Hegemony already owns the world, according to you. You own the whole future.'

'But the future is not enough,' Miss Wells said. '*We want the past too* . . . Come. Let me show you.'

Chapter 26

Laura and her companions huddled together in the middle of the huge main chamber.

Banks of screens, like tellies fixed to the walls, started to light up around the room. The images were military, of bomber bases and missile silos, bunkers and war rooms and citadels.

And a vast map of the world lit up on the floor, under their feet, the capital cities glowing green.

There was a whir and a squeal. The Minuteman came rolling across the world map towards them, with Mort striding at his side.

'Watch out,' Bernadette called. 'You're leaving skid marks on China.'

'Shut her up,' the Minuteman said.

Mort bunched his fist and marched towards Bernadette.

Mum stepped before him. 'She's a child. She's *pregnant*. You'll have to get through me first, Mort.'

Mort glared, but backed off.

He marched around, pointing at screens. 'I'm not the only recruit. These are military centres around the world. Holy Loch in Scotland. The US Air Force command centre in Montana. Canada. Australia. India. China. Africa. All the major countries of western Europe, including West Germany. And the east – Poland. Hungary. Czechoslovakia. More than thirty bases inside the Soviet Union itself.

'These are all men and women of 1962, like me. All soldiers. All of us willing to do whatever it takes to bring about the shining future of peace and order the Minuteman has described for us.'

'All traitors to the countries you swore to serve,' Laura said.

Mort flinched at that.

Bernadette said, 'In 2007 you already run the world. What more do you want?'

'But our hold is fragile,' Miss Wells said. 'Here's Agatha, interfering with this turning point in history – with the founding of the Hegemony itself. We must eliminate the chance of that happening again; we must guard against an invasion from some other future.'

Laura said, 'I don't understand. How can you control the past?'

Mort said, 'By conquering it. By taking over 1962, as the Hegemony has taken over 2007.' He waved a hand at the banks of screens. 'Here is the plan. As soon as I have your Key, Laura, I'll be taking up that Vulcan nuclear bomber. And I'll be flying it –'

'Where?'

'London.' He pointed at the floor map.

The green spot that was London turned black.

'You can't be serious.'

The Minuteman said, 'The news will flash around the planet. There'll be panic, riots, the usual civilian guff. But it won't matter a red cent.' He chuckled, a noise like an echo in a graveyard.

'The destruction of London will be like a beacon, lit on a hill,' Mort said. 'A signal to all those like me, waiting in the bunkers and citadels around the planet. And they will act.'

All over the map of the world, the lights of more capitals flickered out, one by one, green to black. Paris. Rome. Pretoria. Canberra. Washington. Moscow.

'They'll turn on their own cities,' Bernadette said, horrified.

'Think of it,' the Minuteman whispered. 'The civilian leadership of the whole planet, amputated. Sloughed off, as a snake sheds its skin. And the Hegemony will rise up. A new world order established at a stroke.'

Laura was horrified. 'You're talking about destroying major cities with nuclear weapons. Millions will die.'

'Millions more will live in peace,' Miss Wells said.

'The peace of sheep in their fields,' Laura said. 'Of cattle in their pens. With no choice, no freedom, no hope.'

The Minuteman started rolling backwards and forwards across the map of the world. When he spoke his spittle flecked the floor. 'We don't have to stop here,' he ranted. 'In 1962. Once we've established our control of this era, we can go further back. 1940, for instance.'

'Yes,' Miss Wells said. 'We could deal with Hitler before he has a chance to wreck Europe.'

'Oh, no,' the Minuteman said. 'Recruit him! Those Nazis were a bunch of thugs, but there's a lot about them to admire. Order. Efficiency. Control.

'And further back still.' He grinned at Mort. 'Our surname is Mortinelli. We've been Romans from way back. Shall we go back to the Caesars? A Roman Empire with nuclear weapons! Do you think we have the blood of emperors in our veins, boy?'

Even Mort looked a bit uneasy now.

'We have the technology to make it happen. We have the vision. We have the will! We have – ulp.' There was a pop, and a smell of burning insulation, and the wheelchair came to a dead stop in the middle of the Atlantic. The Minuteman rocked his head back and forth, frustrated. 'Oh, to heck with this thing. Get me off of here, boy!'

Mort hurried forward and pushed him off the map.

Laura turned to Miss Wells. 'But if you change history you won't be able to go home again, will you? Back to *your* 2007. Because everything will be different.'

'Oh, no,' Miss Wells said. She was smiling, but it was forced. 'We will be stranded, the only survivors of our future. Just as Agatha is the only survivor of *her* timeline. But that doesn't matter. My place would be here, to finish what we've started. To make the future perfect.'

Bernadette said, 'You're unhappy, so you smash everything up. Is that what it's all about, Miss Wells?'

Miss Wells turned on her. 'You won't understand me if you live for a century.'

'Time's up,' the Minuteman said. 'It's now nineteen hundred local. Seven p.m. By twenty-one hundred I want Mort at angels thirty, thirty thousand feet, on his way to London.' He glared at Laura. 'Decision time, missy.'

Laura pulled the Key on its chain out of the throat of her coverall, and lifted it off her neck. It was a beautiful object, she thought, finely tooled, exquisitely made for its job. Just like the war machines stacked up around the planet, all waiting to be launched.

'I think I wish Dad had never given this to me,' she said.

'But he did,' Miss Wells said.

The huge room went quiet, save for the chattering of the

computers. Laura had the sense that everybody was watching her, even in the other war rooms and bunkers around the world. Everybody waiting for her choice.

'But it's not much of a choice,' she said. 'Between a nuclear desert, Agatha's world. And a planet that's a huge prison, Miss Wells's world. Either way my dad dies in the next few hours, doesn't he? Well, no bombs have fallen yet. I want to keep it that way.'

She boldly walked over to the nuclear pool and held the Key out over the water.

There was a soft clicking all around the chamber, as weapons were made ready to fire.

'Don't do it,' Miss Wells said. 'It's only the Key that is keeping you alive, Laura.'

'And you're out of time, missy,' the Minuteman said.

'Oh, shut your gob.'

It was Nick. He was pointing a revolver at the Minuteman.

Nick had been hiding behind a computer stack. He wore a technician's NBC suit, which was how he had sneaked around the complex without getting caught. Now he had the hood pulled back, to reveal a bandage wrapped around his forehead. He was deathly pale.

He grinned. 'Glad to see me, girls?'

Bernadette said, 'You look dog rough. You sure you know what you're doing with that gun?'

'What gun? . . . I'm joking! You do fuss, Bern. Well, now, isn't this nice? What shall we do? I know. I Spy With My Little Eye, something beginning with N.'

'Nutters,' said Bernadette immediately.

'Yeah. Too easy. Your go.'

The Minuteman's face was twisted with fury. He seemed to be straining to get out of his chair. Mort put a hand on his shoulder. The Minuteman said, 'This changes nothing, you little faggot.'

Nick said, 'You don't scare me, Pinky and Perky. Of course that could be the drugs talking.'

The Minuteman yelled at Laura, 'Girly, thirty more seconds and I'm going to prise that Key out of your dead fingers. Twenty-nine. Twenty-eight.'

For all Nick's bravado, Laura knew she was running out of bluff. In seconds, they could all be dead, and a nuclear war inevitable.

She reached for Mum's hand, and grasped it.

Then there was a crashing noise.

Everybody looked around.

It sounded like electric guitars, echoing from beyond the walls.

Chapter 27

That Saturday evening, Joel had broken the teenagers' curfew.

There had been no posters, no announcements on Radio Luxembourg, no new editions of *Mersey Beat*. But even in a city under military law, word of mouth still worked. If parents and teachers couldn't put a stop to it, half-trained scuffers and squaddies certainly wouldn't.

And Joel had heard whispers of one last concert.

So, with thousands of others, he crept through streets strewn with broken glass and bullet casings to the Cavern.

He had been alone since Miss Wells and her tunnelling machine had swept in to 'save' Laura and the others, and he had managed to slip away in the confusion. He had stayed in the shadows, lingering in holes in the ground, drinking from broken water pipes, eating whatever he could scavenge. For fear of being swept up by soldiers or scuffers, he hadn't even dared go home. He was still trying to think of a way to tell his family he was safe.

It wasn't exactly fun. But he was getting good at it, he thought, this life as a human rat.

But now there was this concert. One last huge gesture of defiance. And he decided he wasn't about to miss that, curfew or no curfew, no matter who was after him.

When he got to Mathew Street there were no queues of shop girls and schoolkids. The night was silent save for an occasional police siren, and, far off, angry shouts and cries. But there was the Cavern entrance, a deep dark mouth, waiting.

When he thought there was nobody about, Joel took his chance and legged it over the road.

He made his way down the steep, worn steps, slick with old sweat, so familiar from the hundred or more concerts he'd been to down here.

No bouncers on the door. Nobody collecting any money, no Cilla collecting coats. It wasn't like the Cavern's owners to miss out on a bit of profit, but there you were.

Inside, the Cavern's gloomy arches were lit only by candles and what looked like oil lanterns. No power on. The vaulted ceiling made the place look like an old, run-down monastery. But the walls were still coated with tatty posters for Rory Storm and the Hurricanes and Gerry and the Pacemakers.

And there were teenagers crowded in here. There must have been hundreds of them, shoved up against each other in the dark, hard to see in the dim light. They didn't make much noise. Everybody spoke in whispers, if at all. Nobody mucked about or threw water bombs or wrestled. The faces, glowing in the candlelight, looked pinched, hungry, some a bit grubby.

But they had all come in their finery, Joel saw, the girls in their beehives and stilettos and slacks, the Teds in their frock coats, the Mods in their parkas. While the adult world went mad above ground, everybody had come down here to celebrate what they had, one last time.

'Hello, Joel.'

Joel swung around.

'Hey, take it easy. It's just us.'

Joel found himself facing the Woodbines: Mickey Poole, Paul Gillespie, Bert Muldoon. Even Billy Waddle, skulking at the back.

Mickey said, 'What are you doing breaking the curfew? Don't you know there's a war on?'

Bert Muldoon, in his filthy sheepskin coat, looked as out of it as ever. 'What war?'

Billy Waddle, father of Bernadette's baby, just looked shifty. He wouldn't look Joel in the eye.

'Where have you lot been?'

'At home with my mum,' Mickey said. 'What about you?'

'Hiding. Long story.'

'Where's our lead singer?'

Bert said, 'What lead singer?'

'Another long story. He took a good kicking that night, Mickey. Head injury, I think.'

'Nothing serious then,' Mickey said, but the black humour was forced. 'Do you know where he is?'

'Sort of.'

Mickey looked at him. 'You on your own? Well, you stick with us. You'll be all right.'

Suddenly there was a crashing electric guitar chord, a howl of feedback. Electric light flooded, and Joel was dazzled. There must be a generator, then.

Everybody turned to the stage.

A thin, sardonic young man in a collarless jacket stood at the front of the stage, a rhythm guitar slung around his neck. Behind him, a big-eyed bass player patiently tuned his left-handed instrument. A young-looking lead guitarist winked at the girls in the crowd. A big-nosed drummer played cheesy riffs on his snare drum. They were silhouetted by the lights, wreathed in ciggie smoke. Clean, sharp, intelligent, they looked like gods, Joel thought.

The sardonic one with the rhythm guitar grabbed a mike. 'Sergeant Lennon here and you're all under arrest. Well, you lot sound happy, considering you're all about to die . . .' That drew an ironic cheer, and there was a clatter of feet as everybody rushed to the stage.

Joel was swept up by the excitement. But he'd learned caution, these last few hours of hiding. In the light from the stage he took a good look around the club for the first time.

At the back there were some older men, half a dozen of them, big, beefy men in overcoats. Alarm bells rang in Joel's head. They stood near another older man Joel had seen before. He was thin, posh-looking, maybe thirty, with a neat suit and an old-fashioned haircut. A word came into Joel's head: *dapper*. Joel thought he was something to do with the group, their manager maybe.

One of the heavies produced a lighter. The dapper man leaned, elegantly, to light his cigarette. The heavy's coat fell open. Underneath was a camouflage jacket.

Joel turned and ran.

And he collided with a pillar of a man in a blue air-force uniform. Joel bounced off his chest and went flying back. He knocked down a couple of girls. One of them belted him with her handbag. 'Oi! You with the head! Watch what you're doing!'

He ignored the girls' squeals, and got to his feet.

Two massive hands caught his arms. He struggled, but he was held, as if by iron bars.

'Joel. It is Joel, isn't it? Take it easy.'

'Hey.' Mickey Poole challenged the man. 'Get off him, Douglas Bader.'

The big man didn't take his eyes off Joel. 'I'm not going to hurt you.' His face was grave, strong. 'I've been looking for you. My name is Harry Mann. I'm an officer in the RAF.'

'You're Laura's dad.'

'Yes. And I need your help. Come on.'

Harry led Joel to the back of the Cavern.

The Woodbines followed, still suspicious.

At the back of the hall, Harry nodded to his men, and shook the hand of the dapper man. 'Thank you, Brian.' He said to Joel, 'I had a feeling I'd find at least one of you here, when I heard about the concert. This gentleman was kind enough to point you out.'

'What's going on, Mister Mann?'

'Tonight I'm Harry. Got that? And these chaps here are military policemen. We've got more troops outside. A few hundred actually.'

'I didn't see them,' Joe said ruefully.

'Well, that's their job.' His accent was almost comically Spitfire-pilot, like Terry Thomas or David Niven. He was immensely reassuring to Joel, now he was here, and in command.

'You've come for Laura, haven't you?'

'I certainly have, and about ruddy time. She has a Key.'

'I know about that.'

'Yes, more than you should, I dare say. The point is that it has a little radio gadget buried inside the plastic. It gives off a tiny signal – not much, but enough to pick up if you know what you're looking for.'

'You tracked the Key.'

'Precisely. And as it happens, the Key, I presume still in Laura's possession –'

'Yes.'

'– is *just the other side of that wall.*'

'You're kidding.'

'Not at all. There aren't that many tunnels under Liverpool, for heaven's sake. And in a few minutes we're going to go busting through the brickwork and then we'll see what's what. Eh?

'Now, look here, Joel. We know we're dealing with some rum coves here. I've been finding out about them since Laura told me she was having trouble with Mort. We know they are calling themselves the "Hegemony". Warmongers – there's always a few of those bally fools about. There've been rumours of some kind of conspiracy that might even cross the Iron Curtain. Now they've been whipping everybody up, forcing through evacuation and martial law, making the authorities overreact to the whole Cuba mess. There's really been no need for all this, and now we're going to sort it out. What I need to know from you is what we're going to come up against on the other side of that wall.'

'I don't know for sure,' Joel said. He couldn't tell Harry that Miss Wells and the Minuteman were from the future. Laura's dad or not, he just wouldn't believe it, and they would all waste time. 'They're soldiers. A military organisation. I don't know what they'll have. But they're armed.'

'Well, so are we,' Harry said grimly. 'Private Cooper here is carrying what can only be described as a bazooka. Don't ask where he's hiding it. One reason for your pinched expression, eh, Hen-coop?'

'If you say so, sir.'

'We're just waiting for this beat combination to start up their racket. They're sure to be heard from the other side of this bally wall. That might distract our opponents while we blow in the brickwork, just for a second or two. Surprise, you see, Joel. A second can make all the difference.'

'The difference between life and death?' Joel asked.

Harry looked at him. 'You know, you shouldn't be here. Chaps like you are supposed to be protected from this sort of thing by chaps like me. You stick with me when the balloon goes up.'

Mickey Poole stepped forward. 'What do you want us to do?'

Harry looked at him dubiously. 'Thanks for the offer. Leave it to the professionals.'

'They've got our pals in there.' He glanced at Joel. 'And our lead singer?'

Joel nodded.

Private Cooper murmured, 'Extra bodies wouldn't hurt, sir, if it comes to hand to hand. And besides, when we blow the walls in half this crowd of capering kids is going to fall through with us.'

Bert Muldoon growled, 'Hand to hand? Fist to goolie more like.'

Mickey Poole grinned. 'Woodbines to the rescue. They'll make a film out of this.'

Joel saw that Billy Waddle was trying to back off. 'What about you, Billy? Bern's in there. With your kid inside her.'

'It wasn't my fault. It's up to the bird not to get up the duff.'

The other Woodbines glared at him.

Joel said, 'You've run out on her once before. You going to run again?'

'All right, all right,' Billy said. 'Count me in.'

Harry looked at the group on stage, who were still fixing their instruments, messing with their amps, mucking about with the crowd. 'Take their time, don't they?'

'That's musicians for you,' Joel said.

'If you can call them that. Not my cup of tea, I'm afraid.' Harry grinned at the dapper man. 'Do you think your boys will make enough noise to cover us?'

'Oh, I think so. That's the one thing they're good at, above all else.'

'Thanks for all your help, Mr Epstein.'

That sardonic voice sounded from the stage again, now hugely amplified. 'Well, we're in tune. Or as much as we ever are. Thanks very much for coming. Or if you didn't come, thanks for nothing, but you're not here, so what do I care. The four minute warning's just sounded, but George has been taking his slimming pills so we should be able to pack in a full set . . .'

The crowd roared, and surged forward again. On stage, smoke curling around them, the dazzling light caught the musicians' hair and profiles. Before the stage, under the Cavern's brick arches, shining young faces swayed like flowers.

'Our first number's called "I Saw Her Standing There". One two three *four*!'

A guitar lick crashed down from the brick roof, and the group just launched themselves into the music. The song was a driving rocker, and the words, blunt and direct, were about sex and lust and joy. Everybody screamed, and the noise and the energy in the Cavern rose and rose.

Joel stopped thinking. He gave himself up to the music, and jumped and yelled with everybody else. Just for a few seconds he forgot everything in his complicated life except the primal force of the song. Just for a few seconds, he was at home.

The group crashed into a howling middle eight, and everybody screamed louder.

And it was back to business.

'This is it,' Harry yelled over the din. 'Joel, you stay behind me. *Behind* me, got that? Cooper, you others, you know what to do.'

'Yes, sir.'

'OK. Tally ho.'

Cooper raised his bazooka.

Chapter 28

The wall blew in, showering old bricks and bits of silver panelling over the computer banks.

And a horde of Liverpool teenagers burst through the hole in the wall, like rats from a broken sewer. Girls with pencil skirts or slacks and towering beehives, and Teds with quiffs and drainpipes, ran screaming across the floor of the computer pit. Surrounded by the silver walls and fluorescent lights and flashing computer panels, they were laughing and yelling, full of youth and energy. All this to a drive of rock music, belting in from the dark spaces beyond the broken wall.

Laura's group just stood and stared, amazed.

Then the fighting started. Two Teds caught one of the Hegemony technicians and ripped off the hood of his NBC suit. Some of the girls took off their stilettos and began smashing at monitors, and they ripped reels and paper tapes out of the computers. Telly screens flickered and went blank.

Among the youngsters there were soldiers, Laura saw now. Big men taking off overcoats to reveal camouflage uniforms with 'MP' arm bands. They had guns.

But so did the Hegemony people. Mort produced a pistol and began firing in the air, trying to scare the crowd. The teenagers screamed and scattered. But they kept fighting, and hacking at the equipment.

Laura looked around. With Bernadette, Mum, Agatha and Nick, she was still backed up against the nuclear pool. There was nowhere for them to run.

The Minuteman had got his chair moving. His face was a mask of pure hatred. 'I'll beat you yet, you little witch!' He drove his chair straight at Laura.

Laura held out the Key on its chain. 'Is this what you want? Then get it!' She threw the Key back over her head, high in the air.

'No! It's mine!' The Minuteman barrelled forward, eyes raised, trying to get under the Key's flight.

But it was falling just where Laura had thrown it – straight into the nuclear pool. It hit the surface making barely a ripple, and then sank into the fizzing blue waters.

And the Minuteman was moving too fast to stop. His chair tipped off the edge, and chair and man descended into the water with an immense splash. The water boiled around him.

He came up once, screaming. His flesh was peeling from his face. Laura looked away.

When the chair thudded into the bottom of the pool, the lights flickered.

Joel came running up. Laura was amazed to see Billy Waddle at his side. They were breathing hard, and Laura saw that Billy's knuckles were bleeding.

'Bern!' Joel yelled. 'Are you all right?'

Bernadette said, 'You two took your time.'

Billy panted, 'I'm sorry.'

Bernadette smiled at him. She reached up and stroked Joel's cheek.

And Mort was standing before Laura. His face was flushed, his tie half ripped off. He had his pistol pointed squarely at Laura's face.

'The Minuteman was right,' he said. 'You are a witch. You've ruined everything. My life. My plans. The whole future.'

Mum came running. 'Mort, no!'

But Mort just held up the flat of his hand and pushed her away. The pistol never wavered.

Laura stared back at Mort, determined not to show weakness.

Mort said, 'Now I'm going to put an end to you, once and for all, in this and any other future –'

There was a tap on his shoulder. 'I beg to differ, old chap.'

Mort turned. And Dad's right fist slammed into his jaw. Mort went spinning back and clattered to the ground.

Dad picked up his pistol. 'Right, safety on. And I think we've had enough of *you*. Cooper, arrest this American buffoon. Now then, where were we?' He grinned. 'Hello, chicken.'

'Dad!' Laura hurled herself at him, and let his strong arms wrap around her.

Mum was here too, and Dad spared an arm for her.

'Dad, you came. I knew you would.'

'Well, better late than never. But I can see you've coped pretty well without me. You've kept everybody alive, *and* avoided starting a nuclear war. Not a bad day's work.'

There were greetings all round now. The Woodbines gathered around Nick, belting him on the back. 'Mind the bonce,' he protested.

Laura looked around for Agatha. In the confusion, she'd vanished.

The lights flickered again, and there was a drop in the tone of the air-conditioning fans.

'Look!' Bernadette yelled. 'They're legging it.'

The gunfight was still going on. But the Hegemony staff were running towards the time portal. As each of the technicians ran into the portal, he or she just disappeared.

Joel said, 'They're trying to get back to 2007 before the portal shuts down. But *which* 2007 . . .?'

The portal was flickering, like the lights.

'It's the power,' Bernadette said. 'You've just shorted out a nuclear reactor, Laura.'

'On any other day,' Nick said dryly, 'that would be quite a stunt.'

Miss Wells reached the portal. She looked back once at Laura. She shouted, 'You little fool. You don't know what you've done.'

Laura yelled back, 'I know I'll never be you. That's enough for now.'

Miss Wells looked wistful, just for a moment. As if she wished she could swap places with Laura, in her dad's arms. Start her life all over again.

And then she walked into the portal, and disappeared.

'Let me get this straight,' Nick said. 'That's a doorway to the future, right?'

'So we're told,' Bernadette said.

Joel said, 'But we don't know which future. If there's not going to be a Hegemony everything's changed –'

Nick grinned. 'I'll take my chance. I never did fit in round here.' He grabbed Billy Waddle by the ears and gave him a kiss, full on the lips.

Billy stepped back, gasping.

'That's what you're missing, Billy Waddle. Remember

me!' Nick called. And before anybody could stop him, he ran across the chamber, and disappeared through the portal.

The power finally gave out, and everything went black.

Chapter 29

Monday 10th June 1963. 7:45 a.m.

Another Monday morning, yuck.

School's back to normal. I've got to think about my O-levels next year. Et cetera. You'd think Miss Wells had never even existed.

Miss Wells. We had the worst winter for years. Snow on the ground until March, packed down to ice. The milk froze in the bottles on the doorstep every night. Miss Wells didn't like the cold. She would have hated the winter. Ha ha.

Mondays are the worst days for Joel.

Bern was taken out of school at Easter, when her bump started to show. We don't know where she went. Joel has had to follow her progress in his head. 'Now they'll have put her in one of those mother and baby homes with the nuns. Now she'll be in hospital, a public ward where the nurses look down their noses at you.' On and on.

And he reads me horror stories from the 'News of the World' about back-street abortions. 'Irish takeaways', he calls them. That's why Mondays are so grim for Joel, because he reads awful stuff in the Sunday papers.

The thing is, Bern should have had her baby by now. Or

got rid of it. I think it's driving Joel crazy not knowing, one way or the other.

I'll take Joel down the Jive-O-Rama this afternoon.

No call from Dad today.

'Shillin'.' Little Jimmy's grin was wide.

Joel ruffled his hair. Laura paid up, and added a three-penny bit as a tip.

Little Jimmy being brought back from his evacuation and reunited with his dad had been one of the happiest moments of the unravelling of the war panic. Little Jimmy just lapped it up. And he was making good money out of all the tips.

The Jive-O-Rama was back to normal, crowded with teenagers, noise belting out of the jukebox. But Jimmy had kept the nuclear fall-out shelter he'd built out of doors and mattresses. It was a feature now. It was painted in crazy colours, and there were floor cushions and lamps underneath the doors, where you could have a quiet ciggie. But he'd had to buy new doors to fill all the empty doorframes in his house.

Everybody dressed a bit differently now. The lads wore their hair brushed forward with a straight fringe, 'Beatle haircuts', and collarless jackets and Cuban-heeled boots, just like the 'Fab Four'. It had all taken off for the Beatles since Christmas. Right now 'From Me To You' was hammering out of the jukebox, their *second* number one. But the Beatles only rarely played the Cavern these days.

There was a buzz in the air, Laura thought. They'd been spared the war, and the sixties were going to be an exciting time.

They bought espressos. The girl who served them, with a

small, pinched face under a towering beehive, wasn't Agatha, who nobody had seen since October, though Laura looked for her every time she came here.

And here, sitting around a table, they found three Woodbines: Bert Muldoon the rhythm guitarist, Paul Gillespie the lead guitarist, and Mickey Poole the bass player.

'Well, well.' Mickey Poole grinned as he pulled up chairs. 'We haven't seen you two since we all got shot at in that underground lair.'

'We got shot at?' Bert Muldoon was still buried on his huge sheepskin jacket. 'What underground lair?'

Paul, as ever, didn't say a word.

Laura felt unreasonably glad to find them. 'I never thought we'd see you lot again. You went off to London.'

'Everybody did,' Mickey Poole said. 'All the record companies wanted groups from Liverpool.'

'And Cilla,' Bert said.

'Who?'

'You know, that girl who took the coats in the Cavern. She can sing. Good luck to her.'

'But,' Joel said carefully, 'not you lot.'

Mickey sighed. 'We had two problems.'

'Our lead singer is lost in time,' said Paul.

'And our drummer's gone back to be a joiner in the bottle factory in Bootle,' Mickey said.

Bert snorted. '"Joiner." That's what he says. Billy's just a can-lad.'

Mickey said, 'We tried out others. Never the same. The Woodbines are going to be nothing but a glorious memory, I think.'

Laura asked, 'So what will you do?'

Paul shrugged. 'Look for a job.'

'Have a bath,' said Bert.

'Go into engineering,' Mickey said unexpectedly.

'Really?' Joel asked.

Mickey shrugged. 'It's a family tradition, with the Pooles. Always fancied it, even though I'd never admit it to my parents. I'm a year behind now, but I can do my A-levels at college next year. I'm going to stay with my brother Jack in Manchester.'

Bert sneered. 'Once a Manc, always a Manc.'

'Better than the bottle factory,' Mickey said.

'Good luck,' said Laura.

'We all miss Nick though,' Mickey said.

Joel said, 'I'm going to put a quid in a bank account for him. By the time he gets to 2007, thanks to compound interest it will be worth a fortune.'

'I wonder what 2007 will be like,' Mickey said. 'Flying cars? Robots to do the hoovering?'

Bert said, 'I'll be happy if they've just filled in the bomb sites in Liverpool.'

Laura wondered what would happen to Nick. A 1963 teenager, lost in 2007! Maybe she'd find out when she got to the future herself, the long way around, one day at a time.

A car horn sounded, just audible over the music.

Big Jimmy came to find them. 'Laura, your mum's outside.'

'Mum?'

'Come to pick you up. Something to do with Saint Bernadette.'

Joel and Laura looked at each other, eyes wide.

'They found her,' Joel said.

'Mum doesn't drive,' Laura said.

They said their goodbyes to the Woodbines, and raced out of the cellar.

At the top of the stairs, Mum and Dad were waiting.

Laura hadn't seen Dad since November. He hadn't even been home for Christmas. She just threw herself at him.

Mum said simply, 'We found your friend.'

Chapter 30

They all piled into Dad's car. It was his precious new Ford Cortina. Joel and Laura sat in the back. The car smelled of Mum's perfume and hairspray, Dad's aftershave, the sweet stuffy smell of their cigarettes.

Dad drove off towards the city centre. It was about five, rush hour, and the traffic was heavy.

Laura stared at the back of Dad's neck, shaved down to the usual crisp stubble. She could hardly believe he was here, that they were all in the car together like this.

Joel was full of curiosity about Bernadette. But he tried to be polite. 'Nice car, Mister Mann.'

'Thanks,' Dad said.

Laura said, 'I thought you were going to sell it.'

It was a consequence of the Separation. Dad wouldn't have needed a family car any more.

'No need.' Dad flashed her a grin, then turned his eyes back to the road.

Laura didn't want to get her hopes up. 'What are you doing here?'

'I've been busy,' Dad said. 'All that fuss about Cuba took some sorting out even after the crisis was over. Well, the Russians have packed up their missiles and subs and planes and gone home. And the Americans have come out of Turkey. I have a feeling Kennedy and Khrushchev might handle their next problem a bit more sensibly. And then there was all that other funny business to sort out.'

'The invasion from the future,' Joel said.

'If that's what it was.' Dad had always been sceptical. 'All we actually found, when the dust settled, was a global conspiracy within the military. People plotting to topple governments and take over the world.'

'People like Mort,' Laura said.

'Yes. The usual idiots. Well, it took us some time to root them all out, but we've got them all now, the whole shower.' He said with satisfaction, 'We've seen the last of Lieutenant-Colonel Giuseppe Mortinelli the Third. Got him for treason, among other things. Banged up for forty-four years, and good riddance.'

Laura did the sums in her head. 1963 plus forty-four years came to 2007. The year Miss Wells claimed to have come from. She felt a flicker of unease. But it was just a coincidence of dates. She put aside her worry.

'Time travel's perfectly sensible,' Joel said. 'The BBC are making a show about it, that will be on telly in the autumn.' Joel always knew about that kind of thing. 'Called *Dr Who*. There will be this old man and his granddaughter, and a time machine.'

Dad cut him off. 'I'm not interested in all that nonsense. Never was, never will be.'

Which was why, Laura thought, nobody was ever going to be told the full story of what had happened, during those few days in October. Because officially it had never happened at all.

Laura had helped save the world, but nobody was ever

going to know about it. She grinned. She quite liked the idea.

'Anyway,' Dad said, 'now all that ruddy business is done and dusted, I can think about what to do next.'

'Dad, your career is in the air force.'

'Yes, but look here, I've fought in one world war and helped put a stop to another one. I rather think I've done my duty, don't you? Quite enough nights away from home for one lifetime. Now I'm planning to buy my way out.'

Joel asked, 'So what will you do?'

'Well, old chap, I rather fancy getting back in the air again. Those shiny new VC-10 airliners won't fly themselves, you know.'

Laura said carefully, 'So you're staying in Liverpool.'

'Looks like it.'

'Will you move in with us?'

Dad glanced at Mum. Mum just sat silently. Dad said, 'That's the current plan. Now look here, chicken, you're old enough to understand how, umm –'

'Complicated,' Mum said.

'Complicated, yes, that's the word. How bally complicated these things are. Compared with sorting out a marriage, debunking a global conspiracy is a piece of cake, believe me! But we're going to give it a go. Aren't we, Veronica? That's the plan.'

'That's the plan,' Mum said.

Laura left it there. You could never *fix* a family, at best it just sort of limped along like an old banger. At least there was a chance.

Joel, silent, was grinning at her.

The car pulled up. They were outside a big old building with bleak, grimy stone walls. There were bars over the narrow windows, and high railings around the grounds.

'Ugh,' Laura said. 'It's like a prison.'

Dad switched off the engine and turned to face them. 'Now, listen to me, you two. We know how attached you were to Bernadette O'Brien. So we did a little digging at the school. After Miss Wells and all that nonsense, they owed me a few favours. I spoke to your Mrs Sweetman. Nice woman. She said Bernadette had been sent here. Couldn't cope at home, it seems. We thought you'd like to see her before –'

'Before what?'

'Well, before the baby gets taken away for adoption.'

Joel's face went slack.

'It's for the best,' Mum said. 'I know it's hard. But a girl of fifteen with a baby! Bernadette's whole life would be ruined before it even started. And what about looking after the kiddie? With no support, how would she pay the bills? They find good homes, you know. People who'll love the baby.'

'But it won't be with its mother,' Joel said.

Dad said, 'Go on, you two. Half an hour. That's all you've got, I'm afraid. We'll wait for you.'

They got out of the car.

The baby was a boy.

He was called Patrick, after Bernadette's granddad. He was wrapped up in a blanket that smelled of carbolic soap.

'He looks like Winston Churchill,' Laura said.

'Better than looking like Billy Waddle,' Joel said.

'Don't knock Billy,' Bernadette said. 'He actually showed up, once. The nuns made him say a confession. He said he'd send me money.'

Joel snorted. 'Do you believe him?'

'He's had the stuffing knocked out of him, has Billy. We're not getting married. We're not even stepping out. But he'll help, I think.'

Joel stared at the baby with longing.

Bernadette handed him the baby. 'Here. You're worse than my aunties.'

A grin spread over Joel's face, like the sun coming up.

They were in a sort of lounge, with a cold wooden floor, high walls, and narrow windows that barely let in the light. There was no telly, but there was a huge crucifix on the wall from which hung a very realistic dead Jesus. In one corner a Catholic nun in a long black habit brushed the floor.

'The whole place is like this,' Bernadette whispered. 'Worse than a church. Mass every morning at seven. Confession twice a week. The nuns have you washing the floors.'

'I bet you fit in well,' Joel said dryly.

'On my first day I chucked a cup of tea over the Mother Superior. Had to clean the floor with a toothbrush. Seven months gone, I was.' She grinned. 'It was worth it.'

Bernadette, without a trace of make-up, looked as if she had been scrubbed with carbolic herself. But she didn't take her eyes off the baby.

'When I went into labour they took me to Broad Green Hospital. I was put into this big ward with a load of other women. Half of them had their babies already, and they sat there grinning with their kiddies. The rest of us couldn't even have visitors. All we had was the nurses glaring at us because we were all bad girls.

'In the end they wheeled me off to the delivery room. They gave me gas and air. I had one last big push, and out came Patrick. They cleaned me up, wheeled me back to the ward, and put him in my arms.' Bernadette smiled at her baby. 'He had this tiny little face, all squashed up and red. He smelled of soap, even then.

'Then the Mother Superior came and said I had to give him up for adoption. She said it was better to take him off me right then, before we got used to each other.'

Joel asked, 'What did you do?'

'Punched her in the gob.'

Laura said, 'So they brought you back here.'

'More floors to clean.'

'But they'll take him away eventually,' Joel said dismally, still cradling Patrick. 'They're too strong. The nuns, the social services, the whole lot of them. They'll even call the police. Take him off you by force. It would be horrible. It's what they do.'

'No,' Laura said impulsively. 'We can't let that happen. There must be another way.'

'I knew you wouldn't give up, Laura. Not you.'

The new voice was the nun who had been sweeping the floor. She was standing over them, her face masked, her brush in her hand.

Bernadette snatched her baby back from Joel and held him close.

'It's all right,' said the nun. And she pushed back her wimple.

It was Agatha.

Laura stood up and faced her. 'What are you doing here?'

Agatha's thin face was strained, and she looked vaguely frightened. 'Are you glad to see me?'

Laura said honestly, 'I don't know. It's complicated.' Agatha was a figure out of a kind of nightmare. And yet

Laura was tied to her. This was her daughter. Or would have been – or something. 'I thought you'd go back to your own time machine.'

'I smashed it up.'

Laura frowned. 'Why?'

'I came here to change the future, remember. I failed. And *my* future doesn't exist; it never will, because there was no Sunday War. I can't go home.'

Laura wondered if Agatha was telling the truth about destroying her machine. Agatha was an instinctive survivor. Even if she decided to stay here, she might have wanted to keep her options open. A time machine, hidden in 1963. What if it still worked? What if somebody found it?

'What will you do here?'

'I don't know. Get a job. Make a few friends.' Her pale face was pinched. 'Believe me, even if I end up sleeping in the streets, I'm better off than where I came from. And in the meantime I've come to help you,' she said to Bernadette.

'Help me do what?'

'Get out of here. With your baby. That's what you want, isn't it? Give it five minutes. The Mother Superior does her rounds, regular as clockwork. We have to wait until there's a gap. Then we'll get out the back.'

Joel grinned. 'Ace. It's like breaking out of Colditz. But what about your mum and dad? Aren't they waiting out the front?'

'I'll phone them,' Laura said. 'They'll understand.'

Bernadette looked bemused. 'But what then?'

Joel looked Bernadette in the eyes. 'Bern – look – there's something I never told you. The way I feel about you. I mean –'

Bernadette touched his hand. 'Poor old Joel. I always knew.'

He seemed amazed. 'You did?'

'Of course. Everybody could tell. You're no actor, you silly sod.'

'You chose Billy Waddle over me. I understand that. But now Patrick's here I want to be with you. I want to help you raise him.'

'Oh, Joel. You're just a kid.'

'I'm older than you,' he said. 'A bit. And I want to help you. Even if, you know.'

'What? Spit it out.'

'Even if we're never *together*. I'll help you even so.'

'But,' Laura said awkwardly, 'it's not just that you aren't Patrick's dad. You aren't the same colour.'

Joel said, 'So people will give us stick for that. So what?'

Bern looked him straight in the eye. '*People* can all bog off. You're on, soft lad. Tell you what, though. From now on, I'm on the pill.'

'Then it's settled,' Laura said. 'We'll all help. I'll twist Dad's arm, to help get rid of the nuns and the social. Bern, I bet your mum will take you in if we can help support you. There's that bit of money from Billy Waddle for a start. We'll work it out somehow. All we have to do is get out of here.' She looked at Agatha. 'But why are you doing this?'

'For you. She's your friend.'

Laura nodded. 'All right. But you look, well, frightened.'

Agatha forced a smile. 'Not of the Mother Superior. I've been frightened every day since I decided to stay here.'

'Why?'

'Because,' Agatha said slowly, 'history has changed under me. The world I came from will never exist. *I shouldn't have been born*. I'm a sort of mistake in time. All this Catholicism is worrying me. What about my soul? Will I go to heaven or hell? If my timeline has gone, do I still have a soul at all?' Her eyes were hollow.

Bernadette was astonished. 'Don't tell me you were brought up a Catholic.'

Joel said, 'Well, I'm still in CND. We got through the Cuban crisis but the bombs still exist. That's what *I'm* worried about.'

'None of us knows how long we have,' Bernadette said.

Laura said, 'No. And Dad says there will always be something to be frightened about, always some hideous threat of the end of the world, just around the corner. You just have to be sensible and keep on muddling through. And make the most of now.'

'She means,' Bernadette said, 'never miss a chance to shop.'

Agatha smiled, pale. Then she glanced at a clock. 'It's time.'

Bernadette clutched the baby in her arms. 'I'm packed.'

The way out the back was through a laundry room, where giant steel cylinders swallowed up heaps of towels. As they seemed to be in the charge of Sister Agatha, nobody stopped them.

The door at the rear of the building wasn't locked. They burst out into the open air.

The evening sunlight was bright over Liverpool, reflecting from the windows of the terraced houses, and making the roof tiles shine pink. They ran off into the maze of terraced streets, laughing and talking, the four of them with the baby, until they were sure nobody could catch them.

Afterword

The Cuban Missile Crisis really happened. In October 1962, the Cold War almost got very hot indeed.

In 1962 the Soviet Union, Russia, was losing the arms race with the west. The US had 5000 nuclear weapons it could have used to destroy Soviet targets. The Russians only had 300.

The Soviet Union was a poor country, compared with America. But Premier Khrushchev saw a cheap way to even up the balance of power. He decided to plant bases for short-range missiles close to America on the island of Cuba, where there was a friendly Communist government. President Kennedy's America had earlier mounted a failed invasion of Cuba.

During the summer of 1962 the Russians sent cargo ships to Cuba laden with missiles and warheads, and 40,000 soldiers and technicians. All this was kept secret. Khrushchev planned to reveal the missile bases to a stunned world when they were ready.

But in October 1962 American spy planes spotted the missiles and their launch pads, still under construction. President Kennedy could have ordered air strikes, or invaded Cuba. But he feared triggering a third world war.

So Kennedy ordered a 'quarantine'. US Navy ships were ordered to turn back any more Russian vessels. Kennedy was trying to show firmness without provoking a fight.

Behind the scenes there were frantic negotiations with the Russians. But things could have gone horribly wrong. Communications were poor, and soldiers on the ground might have started shooting on their own initiative.

The emergency preparations for nuclear war shown in this book, with children being evacuated from the cities and everybody urged to build fall-out shelters, are based on plans the British government actually made at the time. They weren't put into place during the Cuban Crisis; the events in this novel didn't come to pass. But the Vulcan bomber fleets really were put on stand-by, and there were protests against nuclear war in many large towns and cities.

Saturday 27th October, 'Black Saturday', was the most dangerous time of all. An American spy plane was shot down by the Cubans, and the US Navy forced a Russian submarine to the surface. Black Saturday was perhaps the closest we ever came to an all-out nuclear war, and the systems used, such as the 'Single Integrated Operations Plan' shown in the story, really were hair-trigger.

If the war had come about, it would have been every bit as terrible as depicted in this story. In 1956 Harold Macmillan, who would be prime minister in 1962, said, 'We cannot hope to emerge from a global war except in ruins.'

But the Russians and Americans calmed down. Missiles on Cuba just weren't worth risking war over.

On Sunday 28th, the Russians agreed to a secret deal. They dismantled their bases on Cuba, and in return the Americans got rid of missiles in Turkey. Kennedy and Khrushchev ordered a 'hot-line' telephone link, so they could talk directly to each other if there was another emergency. President Kennedy won great praise for his calmness and firmness in the crisis. It was a great shock when, just over a year later, he was assassinated in Dallas, Texas.

A recent book on the Cuban Missile Crisis is *High Noon in the Cold War* by Max Frankel (Ballantine Books, 2004). A movie about it, called *Thirteen Days* and starring Kevin Costner, was released in 2001.

Nobody has built a time machine, and nobody knows what would happen if you went back in time and tried to change history. Some scientists like Stephen Hawking think it would be impossible. Others think you wouldn't really change history but create a whole *new* future, starting from the point where you made your change. So you could end up with lots of 'parallel' futures, in which people's lives work out differently. That's the idea used in this book.

And, like Agatha in the novel, if you did go back to change the past, you might find yourself stranded in the new future you created, watching your own life working out differently than you remember. If you're interested, try *How to Build a Time Machine* by Paul Davies (Penguin, 2002).

'Merseybeat' groups really did play in my old school, Saint Edward's College in West Derby. Even the Beatles played there, in October 1961. Apparently the highlight was Paul McCartney singing 'Besame Mucho'.

Any errors or omissions are my sole responsibility.

Stephen Baxter